The Coin
and
the Crown

MEGAN D. HARDING

authorHOUSE®

AuthorHouse™
1663 Liberty Drive
Bloomington, IN 47403
www.authorhouse.com
Phone: 1 (800) 839-8640

Published by AuthorHouse 07/18/2018

ISBN: 978-1-5462-5200-9 (sc)
ISBN: 978-1-5462-5194-1 (hc)
ISBN: 978-1-5462-5195-8 (e)

Library of Congress Control Number: 2018908466

Print information available on the last page.

This book is printed on acid-free paper.

"PERHAPS YOU WERE CHOSEN FOR SUCH A TIME AS THIS." ESTER 4:14

ACKNOWLEDGMENTS

First of all, I would like to thank God. With Him all things are possible. Secondly, I would like to thank my husband, Aaron, for all of the encouragement and support. Also, for watching the kids so I could write. My children, Bella, Noah, and Emma are my world. Thank you Cassandra Wengewicz (@Bibliophagist90) for all of your help and support. Not only with editing, but with your continued encouragement in writing and parenthood. Lastly, thank you to Laura Prevost for creating my lovely book cover and bringing my vision alive. We have had some fun times. In all of my work I pay remembrance to my mom, Stacy Jo Roberts, my brother Justin Keith Parrish, and my grandfather, Joseph Edwin Roberts. You are missed.

CHAPTER ONE

Night Games

Amira

Night winds howled, muffled only by the roaring cheers of men. The room appeared dark, lit merely by lanterns that swung from the wall casting shadows throughout the dim tavern. Overcrowded with the familiar and lingering smell of musk and beer, only miscreants were out at this time of night but that hasn't stopped me yet. One man towered over the rest. Rugged, torn clothes hugged his body a little too tightly and his scruffy beard gave off a foul smell. He laid his cards down on the table so roughly the mugs of house brew shook. Words weren't necessary, the smirk that crept upon his face said plenty. Scars covered his arms, intimidating most that crossed his path. The mark on his arm suggested he was a hunter.

So, the rumors were true. The Queen had begun to brand the citizens. The coins were not enough anymore, too easily stolen I suppose.

All eyes darted to the old wooden table. On the far side lay three Jacks and two Queens. Full house. He had a right to smirk.

Three other men lay their cards face down.

Cowards.

Only one hand remained.

Time to play the hand that I was dealt.

Ten. Jack. Queen. King. Ace. A royal flush.

Men roared and a pair of strong hands slammed the table scattering cards and drinks to the floor. "Cheater!" The grizzly loser yelled.

"Now, now...just because you lost to a girl doesn't mean that I cheated." I smirked as I gathered the coins from the table into my coin purse hidden in a satchel under my robes. I had made sure the coin around my neck remained visible, not that everyone here didn't know who I was. I was anything but a stranger to these parts. "Now, if you will excuse me, it's awfully late for a lady to be outside the castle. Wouldn't you agree?" Keeping my eyes firmly locked on Cyrus, the man who clearly had a problem losing to a lady. He held out his arm cornering me against a wall. The potent smell of fish and body odor burned my nostrils. "That's no way to treat a lady, right gentlemen?" I stood my ground.

The room had gone quiet. The remaining men, bartenders, and even the 'working women' stopped to see what would happen. "Perhaps you should let her go. Best not to quarrel with a lady of the court." A man's voice sprung from the dark.

"You, Amira, are no lady!" Cyrus grunted while withdrawing his arm back to his side. "Get out, but I had better not see you in here again." His voice was loud enough for everyone in the tavern to hear.

I never lost my calm. Instead, I smiled sweetly at Cyrus and narrowed my eyes. "That wouldn't be any fun, now would it?" Cyrus bit his tongue and made his way to the bar ordering a pint to soothe his ego.

He was right, it was late. A lady shouldn't be outside the castle at midnight. Let alone outside the castle without company. I had other people to play cards with but Lorin had thought it child's play and I couldn't take money from Aryn. I hid my satchel as best I could. Robbers would frequent the streets under the dim light of the moon. I was practiced with a blade and kept a dagger easily accessible at my side, but I was small and the blade in need of sharpening. A group of men could easily take advantage of a woman my size.

The air was crisp and the few street lanterns lit a path around the city. The nights were becoming longer, the trees slowly shedding their leaves. I pulled my cloak in closer, the soft fabric gently caressing my chilled cheeks. Although the days were hot, the night was filled with winds from the North. The seasons were changing. The stars were enough when the lanterns became too few. Still, I kept to the shadows. Best not to be seen. I was good at not being seen. Although I was a lady of the court, shown off as prized merchandise, I spent my days as a maid just as the rest of the young ladies at court. 'Jewels of the court' we were called, but we had to earn our keep none the less. With many years slipping around the palace fulfilling my chores, I easily learned to go unnoticed when I wanted.

Even if I ran into guards, I could easily play the role of a silly lost girl. It would be all too easy to explain away some menial task, even for the night. The Royals were anything but patient people, most of them. The guards knew not to question the maidens or give them too much attention. The Queen allowed little interaction with her property. That is unless they were prepared to pay the price.

The halls were silent as I crept to my quarters. If that's what you wanted to call it. It had everything but room. A nice bed, a large vanity, and stacks of dresses. A lady must be kept well presented for suitors at all times. Paid for by the work they did and the dowry money that came when they were 'chosen' for a suitor.

I had weaseled my way out of all the suitors that had come my way, and early on there were many. Not so many now that rumor had spread of my 'uneasiness' to claim.

I loosened my robes and emptied my coin purse on my bed. Five gold coins, better than most nights, but not as much as I had hoped. The castle had been stricter on guard duty lately, making it nearly impossible to slip in and out. Luckily, I knew my way around very well.

I slipped under the small of my vanity. I hadn't any need for a lamp, my fingers knew the grooves well. With a small knife I carved a stone from the wall and took out a small box. I placed my earnings from the night inside and replaced the box, leaving no trace of its existence. Not much longer, I hoped.

After changing to my night-gown, I slipped into my lumpy bed, closed my eyes, and slowly drifted into an uneasy slumber.

CHAPTER TWO

Morning Light

Aryn

Shadows filled the grand hall, falling along the pillars. I crouched low, steadying my breath. The nearly empty room echoed and mocked even the slightest sound. I was being hunted. The sound of a rolling pebble caught my ear. Shifting my weight slightly, a loose strand of hair fell in my eyes. I silently cursed myself. I knew better than to fall for a distraction. Especially that of a small pebble. Fortunately, I stayed in a position that gave no hint of my whereabouts, yet I had to move soon. Sitting prey was easy prey.

I closed my eyes, I knew this room well. Even down to the smell. A faint whiff of musty smoke burned my nostrils. He was close.

Gripping my sword tighter, I lunged out at my attacker. The steal of my sword caught my opponent's. Our eyes locked, the flame from the lanterns ignited the face opposite of mine. His expression stern and unchanged. I leapt back and lunged toward the swordsman again. We were both fit and strong, but where he was muscular I was lean. My advantage would be my quick feet and stamina. If I could continue to strike as a viper, I could catch him off guard.

Slipping in for another charge, I felt my feet being swept from beneath me. Tipping forward I took an elbow to the chest, knocking the wind from me, causing me to fall on my back coughing for air. My sword hand been knocked out of my hand but laid only inches from my reach. I stretched my aching fingers to find my weapon while my eyes adjusted to the dark corner I crawled toward. A heavy boot stepped on my arm shooting a pain up to my shoulder. At last, a sharp sensation tickled at my throat. A sword.

"Say it." The man demanded.

"Never!" As I swallowed, the sharp blade scraped against my Adam's apple.

The sword dug deeper into my throat, a single drop of blood slowly dripping down my neck.

"Fine! Uncle." I yelled, slapping the floor by his feet.

The familiar arm reached down and I grabbed it. Lorin, my opponent, grinned in victory. It was short-lived and a scowl soon crossed his face. What now?

"You're not a quick as you think you are. Your weakness is confidence. How many times have I told you to slow down and know your opponent?" Lorin began to light more lanterns. "Also, your grip is too tight. Treat her like a beautiful woman."

I rolled my eyes and wiped my neck, finding just a light scratch left by a sharp blade. It wouldn't be too hard to hide. I threw my hand up to straighten my hair, trying to hide the disheveled emotions coursing through my body. "Just distracted is all." I averted my eyes, looking at the ground in an attempt to hide my disappointment in myself. Although, Lorin knew me too well. I was hiding nothing from him and I knew it. Swordsmanship was one of the many things I had to master. The desire for perfection drove me yet held me back.

"I could imagine," Lorin said as he began dusting me off. "Speaking of which, you had better run or you'll be late for the festivities."

I nodded and patted my friend on the back before returning to my chambers. It was early morning and the sun was soon to rise.

The end of the week marked the beginning of the Choosing Festival. All the preparations were in motion. Everyone was thrilled. The Kingdom rang with excitement. Everyone but me, it seemed. As I paced my dark study, I placed my hand on all of the ridiculous fabrics, lacing them between my fingers, tracing the pattern of my family's crest. The Royal Crest. The same crest that was inscribed on my coin that I held so tightly it left an imprint on my skin. I lifted the hulking coin, the size of my palm, and its chain over my head to rest around my neck. It felt heavier today.

The sun peeked behind the curtains allowing a dusty glow to ignite the room.

Dawn. The only time I was allowed any peace.

Even that would be taken from me soon.

I stretched out my arm and ran my hand through the blond mess upon my head. My mother always hated how young my hair made me look. With scruffy blond curls encircling my ears and deep blue eyes, I was too pretty. The women didn't mind, but I heard whispers and snickers from the men surrounding me.

I made my way to the mirror. Using my fingers to comb my shaggy hair away from my face and straightening my broad shoulders, I compared myself to my father. Surely, I wasn't ready for this.

I inhaled the silence, letting it resonate within me.

Just then, Amira glided into the room bringing me back to reality. She skipped right past me and brushed open the enormous curtain that hung from the top of the twenty-foot room, allowing the sunlight to sting my eyes.

"Was that necessary?" I scolded my housemaid and wondered how she was able to slip in so easily. That had never seemed to be a problem for her, especially with Tauren, my personal bodyguard.

Tauren hadn't come by all morning. Perhaps my bodyguard had a more important task than guarding the Prince, the sole heir to the throne. More likely, he was too busy celebrating with the rest of the kingdom. It didn't matter. There was plenty of security throughout the castle, more so than usual.

"No, but I do enjoy tormenting you so." Amira replied, cutting off my trail of thought. "Besides, what are you still doing in your room? I've been up working for hours and you're, what, combing those pretty blond curls of yours? If your mother-"

"The Queen you mean?" My eyebrows arched as I stared into her mischievous eyes.

"Yeah, her. The Queen would have your head for lollygagging during the week of the stupid ceremony."

"Why do you insist on calling it stupid? And I would be careful if I were you. She seems to have even less patience than normal with you these days."

Amira just smiled and bowed, waving her arms in an exaggerated motion while backing toward the door. Just before she exited the room, she peeked her head back in and stuck her tongue out at me.

Anyone else would have been severely punished for such an act, or for even talking to me as she had. But that wasn't the case with her.

The Choosing Festival could not have been set at a better moment. Times have been hard on everyone and with King Ezra being sick, there was a rumor of uprising.

Now I was approaching my seventieth name day. My parents weren't old, but with my father being sick, plans had to be made. To keep peace in the kingdom, hope must be kept alive. At least, maintained, according to Queen Beatrice.

The festival would bring people from all over the kingdom. Every family wanted to enter their daughter's coin in hopes that destiny would allow her to be chosen, granting their daughter the role of future queen. This would not only raise her status, but also that of her family.

I knew the myth behind the coins, as did everyone else. The coins governed the people. I wanted to believe that the right girl would be chosen, but I remained apprehensive. Most people had the freedom to choose who they would wed. My bride would be picked from a bucket of coins…by chance. A part of me trusted the system. Only young eligible women would be allowed to enter. I also knew that young girls who didn't meet certain criteria were…discouraged from entering.

It was still hard to believe that by the end of the week some random woman would walk into my life and be by my side until 'death do us part'.

I couldn't hide in my study any longer. The whole room, larger than most farmhouses in the kingdom, was filled with books and records from floor to ceiling. Collections of events, military records, battles, and stories from all of the kingdoms. I have always been bright. It was the General who noticed my passion for learning. A lump formed in my throat thinking about him. I looked up to the General and because of that, I had all but memorized every book in my study. I spent more time in there than I had in my own bedchambers. In fact, I often slept in the old velvet lounge chair by the door connecting the study and my quarters. I took a deep breath and straightened my shoulders.

Time to be the Prince.

CHAPTER THREE

Queen B

Aryn

"Prince Aryn…" A timid house maid panted as she bowed awkwardly. She was new around the palace, one of the extra hands taken on for all of the upcoming festivities. I could tell from the coin that hung from her neck, just above the coarsest lining of her dress, in the style of the house maids.

I quickly picked up on her apprehension. Working in the palace was a privilege and looked good to employers. Even if she wouldn't stick around. Most house maids who were not born into service of the palace, or at least come with an extensive recommendation, tend not to last long here. Whether let go or matched with a gentleman, only time would tell.

"You're… The Queen needs to see you. In the royal chambers… That is." Her eyes wide with caution. She stumbled into another curtsy and waited to be dismissed.

I nodded and began to make my way to the royal chambers. And yet…I couldn't help but think there was something sweet about that girl's smile. "Thank you." I turned and said, nodding my head slightly.

She exhaled and relaxed her shoulders. Her pale skin turned a bright, silky pink as she suppressed a smile.

I nodded once more, in assurance. "You're doing just fine. The palace is lucky to have you."

Her green eyes lit up in her pale-blushed face.

She must have been lucky to have worked indoors all of her life. She was a young girl, perhaps sixteen. She had curly, light red hair that was kept tight behind her back, but a few frizzy strays managed to escape. Her skin

8

was ivory with freckles that danced upon her nose. I was close enough that her scent of fresh mint and grass tickled my nose. She wasn't exceedingly beautiful, but innocence and hope filled her face. I found her refreshing amongst the tired crew I was used to.

For a moment, I felt good. It was frowned upon to converse with the help, especially anything encouraging. They were meant to be kept in their place. It never felt natural to me to put others down. Yet, I knew that everyone had their place and that was what kept the kingdom at peace.

My pace quickened as I headed to meet Queen Beatrice. Though the halls were busy, buzzing with people and decorations, I kept my pace. Weaving through the traffic, I was careful to avoid running into anyone or tumbling into any expensive statues or decorations.

Every inch of the palace seemed filled to the brim. New decorations were arriving by the hour. Statues of ivory and stone, carved in remembrance of past royalty, coated with specks of gold or gems. Others just fine art to show off expensive taste. Queen Beatrice always expressed that the show of wealth was a show of power, and from the looks of things she wanted to appear powerful.

Or, at least, I was to appear powerful.

Every room was filled with different fragrances. I deeply desired to stop and see what was causing each delicious smell. My imagination ran wild envisioning the imported chocolates, sweets, spices, and meats. My taste buds began to water, causing my stomach to growl. With all the work that had to be done, I barely had a chance to sit and eat.

The palace was filled with so many servants, chefs, and decorators that it made getting to the royal chambers an exhausting task. I could walk these halls backward and blindfolded but today it was difficult. It was my home, but it often felt like my prison.

The King and Queen were expected to produce many children. An "heir and a spare" at the minimum. After the loss of their eldest son, my brother, Isaac, they tried to conceive again. Yet after years of trying they were left with only one royal baby...me. Which was enough, but it left me extra guarded. I was the last of the line. No doubt the King had a few bastards floating around, but the Queen made sure that they remained unheard from. I would be the one to assume the throne and the time would soon come.

I wasn't allowed to leave the palace often. Although I could roam the castle freely, when I left its safety, I was heavily guarded. I knew every notch and groove in every corner and every hole. If it hadn't been for my childhood friend Amira, I wouldn't have seen the outside of the castle until I was sixteen. Unless you count parades and business meetings. I had only been beyond the kingdom once, during a diplomatic meeting between Astrean and Picis.

The kingdom of Astean was the wealthiest, most beautiful, and best protected of all seven kingdoms. With enormous mountains scaling the borders of the lands and water surrounding the kingdom, it was nearly impossible to invade. Especially since the Royal Navy was more than ten times the size of any other, the ships built with far better durability and speed than any seen before. It was the Promised Land. At least, that was how the legend went.

I finally rounded the corner leading to the massive grand hall that gave way to the royal chambers which held my Mother and Father, the King and Queen. I smiled at the door keepers, then took a deep breath, straightening my shoulders and brushing down my outfit to perfection. Finally, I nodded to the door keeper and braced myself for entry.

A labored smile spread across my face, straining my cheeks, as I made my way close to the King's desk. I didn't feel comfortable in the large chamber, but I had often sat close to my father silently accomplishing my schooling. That was when the king allowed me to be near. It was Isaac who had been born to take the throne, but his death passed the crown to me. From that moment I was to be trained to take the King's place.

Just as the halls, ballrooms, and kitchen were crawling with helpers, so were the royal chambers. It felt more crowded than usual and I wondered if my presence went unnoticed in all of the chaos. My eyes scanned the room taking in every action, every presence. King Ezra stood near his bed with fabrics and jewels draped upon him for fittings. His robust frame was beginning to appear frail, something no one would dare mention, but easily covered by the fine clothing. His grand crown was laid out upon his bed, shined and polished. It glimmered in the night, especially his coin that was embedded in the center for the world to see.

I had never been particularly close with my father. Mostly, I grew up listening to the King rant on and on about how entitled the position of being king is, how it was chosen for him. This led him to believe he was nearly a God. And that was the way he lived, answering to no one. Although the position of the king held many responsibilities- King Ezra lived primarily for fun and pleasure.

Queen Beatrice was the true backbone. She wore a long regal dress- black and gold- with a v- neckline that trailed off of her shoulders coming to a distinct point. It gave off the impression of power and did a fine job of showing her coin which was placed on a ribbon tied so tightly to her neck that I found it astounding she could breathe. The more visible the coin was, the more status one held.

The Queen paced the lounge area near the fireplace with ladies' maids and decorators following, trying to keep up while listening to every precise detail she demanded. The Queen was rarely in the Royal chambers. The massive bed that could fit both King and Queen was merely for show. It was common knowledge that the queen did not reside there, but rather had her own quarters attached with a passage way. This was to create an illusion of a strong marriage. Although whispers carry fast among the workers.

"Aryn, you're here. Finally." The queen spoke out. I perked up and filled my face with a tight smile, as I neared my mother.

Her perfume overpowered my senses. She was tall and thin with high cheek bones, accented even more by vibrant makeup. Everything about her, from the way she stood to the dresses she wore, to the pointed high crown upon her head seemed to convey power.

I knew very little of my mother's life before meeting my father. I had heard stories that she was from a family of high standing who had lost almost all of their fortune. Her family was well educated but fell into the business of menders and seamstresses' over time. She was a young striking beauty with many suitors. Her family had fallen into great debt and nearly took to begging, she denied all suitors that came her way, even if they would have helped her and her family. She felt she was destined for more. Fate smiled upon her and her house when she entered into the Choosing Festival and her coin had been picked.

From that moment on, everything changed. Her family coin was remade to display royalty. Each member of her family received a new coin that signified high status, education, and politics. They were all given education and important political rolls around the palace. Even her sisters' statuses rose, leading to many proposals in which the new queen made arrangements for marriage. I had never met any of my aunts, they were sent away upon marrying.

Even looking at the queen now, she radiated power and nobility as if she were born for the role. That was the idea anyway. The enchanted coins decided fate, so it must have been true that she was destined for the power handed to her.

The tales had been told for generations. No one knew for certain if they were true or made up. The tales gave way to tradition and tradition turned to law.

"Do I need to remind you of the importance of this? You should be honored and thrilled. And if not, you had better act like it. You know how important this is. You will be the focus of all of this. You...and the girls that is."

"I am honored and excited." I threw on the largest grin I could manage. By now my cheeks were in pain and this was only the beginning.

After a side dismissal from my mother, I turned my heels toward my father's desk and snatched up the stack of papers I knew was meant for me. Papers which had already been approved for me to look at. If I were to be King soon, I would need to be trusted as more than a child. That was how the King and Queen saw me... How everyone saw me. Even though I was approaching my seventeenth birthday at the end of the week, being crowned king the very next day, I knew I was to be treated as my mother's puppet.

Even long after my father passed, it would be my mother who was truly in charge. I was merely the handsome young face. No doubt Queen Beatrice had also arranged for advisors to stick around beyond her passing as well, in which case, I would never be more than a puppet...- like my father.

I yearned for so much more.

I remembered the anxiety I felt on my thirteenth name day ceremony. They had held a separate ceremony specifically for me, in the palace. It was a royal affair with lightly kept traditions. I had dressed up in coats and furs so heavy I feared I might fall. Embarrassing myself wasn't an option.

As I walked the entire Great Hall all eyes were on me, especially those of my mother. Music played so loudly I could feel the vibrations up my legs with each step. Everything sounded muffled, turning almost to silence the further I walked. The only reminder of noise was felt through the tingling of my feet as they hit the floor. Fear crept through my body, taking every ounce of concentration to keep from trembling.

I approached the steps that led to the thrones. Three of them. The largest for the King, a smaller, more regal one for the queen, and the smallest of the three at the right hand of the King. It was meant for the crowned prince. The one who would be the next to rule. I had not been allowed to officially sit upon the throne- chair is really what it was- but it was so much more than that. It was power, it was meant for me. That was the day it was to be made official.

At least, that was the expectation.

It was rare that a prince born of royal blood would not be selected to be the kingdom's next ruler. In fact, it hasn't happened in several generations. I hated to think of what it would mean if I were to receive a different destiny.

In truth, I hadn't always expected it. Isaac was the one born to rule. I was only meant to follow, to guide. But things don't always go according to plan.

I had held my breath that day as I handed over my coin to the Dator, the old man who was appointed as the giver of destiny. Essentially, the old guy who passed out coins once a year or on special occasions.

My coin was then placed on a royal receiver- a fluffy red pillow with too many ruffles- and brought to an altar. Since the ceremony was not taking place where it would normally, water was brought from the fountain and poured over the coin and followed by a reciting of words which to this day, I can still not remember. I think it was some prayer to the ancient Source.

Finally, the Dator faced me, asking me to flip the coin and receive my destiny.

I looked to my mother who nodded with assurance, which was probably the first and last time I had felt a warmth from her.

In front of the entire kingdom, I held my coin and revealed it to the People.

All of the loud sounds, the abundance of people, and foreign languages overwhelmed my senses. I desired to retreat and be alone, but as the prince, I was never alone. Although, I knew of one place that would surely be empty, if I could just have five minutes alone to breathe. After all, I was only days away from assuming the throne to the best kingdom in the world and marrying a complete stranger. Surely, I deserved that much.

I weaved through the hallways smiling and waving at all of the noble passersby, stopping to quickly commune with those I was expected to. Luckily, I had learned how to speak briefly and rush past people quickly while looking to be on an important mission, rather than appearing rude.

I found my way to the small corner with a passageway that opened to a small dark nook that could hold no more than five people. There were secret rooms throughout the palace for hiding during attacks. But since attacks were rare, they were mostly used for storage. That or for secrets. This was one of the smallest rooms, cold, dark, and forgotten about, unlike the others which were decorated with furniture, art, and often mistresses. This was more like a hole in the wall, but that was exactly where I wanted to be. In a hole in the wall.

Once I found the entrance I closed the door, took a deep breath and leaned back letting every inch of myself relax. It was as if the statue I had made myself into began to melt away. There was a slit in the wall for a window. It was maybe three inches wide and six inches long, letting in the smallest amount of air and light, but everything was still dark and would take a minute for my eyes to adjust.

"Fancy meeting you here," a mischievous voice rang out, causing me to jump and reach for my sword.

CHAPTER FOUR

Close Quarters

Aryn

The hair on my neck rose and my body stiffened as I reached for a sword that was not there. I cursed myself for leaving it with the weapons master for sharpening. I heard a giggle and my eyes began to adjust. I let out a deep breath and kicked at the floor like a child throwing a tantrum. Of course, it was her. Who else would it have been?

"What are you doing here?" I said sharply.

"Same as you, I suppose." Amira replied in a warm voice.

"You shouldn't be here. If you got caught skipping out on duties-"

"Me? What about you? I just need a few minutes to breathe. That's the same reason you're here. And besides…I wanted to know how you were holding up."

"What like you knew I would come here?"

"Like I don't know you better than anyone else in the world? Come on, best friends forever, right?" She said as she eased her way closer to me with concern in her eyes.

"That was a long time ago." I nearly whispered.

So much had changed since we were young. At times I felt sorry for Amira, for all that she had lost. Mostly, I envied her. She lived life with so much tenacity. There was no one there to watch her every move. Although, yes…she was watched closely as a house maid. She had responsibilities and had to perform every task perfectly. Although everyone around her told her what to do, no one told her how to think. And honestly, no one would ever be able to.

"Okay then, well happy birthday to you too." She hissed and began to storm off.

I reached out and gently grabbed her arm. She stopped but refused to face me. "Amira. I'm sorry. It's been…crazy here. I didn't forget." I stood there quietly for a moment but knew she wouldn't be the first to speak. "Of course, I remembered your birthday. You're three days older than me. How could I ever forget, you remind me every chance you get."

She turned toward me with one hand on her hip. Her other hand playfully slapped my chest with a dirty cloth, leaving a smudge on my coat. If she had been anyone else, she would be in serious trouble. But it was Amira. She only smirked.

"Any plans for the big night?" I asked.

"Actually…" Amira began. Her eyes light up with mischief. Something that both pushed me away and drew me in at the same time. She always had an effect on me.

"I should have guessed you were up to no good."

"We both need to get to our duties. If you're brave enough, meet me at the gate at twilight." She walked away as if not waiting for my response.

"Brave enough? You mean stupid enough?" I called out behind her as she shut the door. Amira always had a way of making me relax and forget about the stresses of the kingdom. She had a carefree spirit, which felt warm and inviting.

I took another deep breath and leaned against the wall once more closing my eyes, trying to refocus myself before exiting the hiding place. I seemed to be outside in the hallway only a minute before being crowded with messengers and maids. The day had already felt too long, but it was only just beginning.

Moments after stepping foot out of the hiding place I heard a grunt. I spun around to see Tauren standing close by waiting for me. I wondered if Tauren noticed that Amira had just exited the same room only minutes earlier. Worry crept over me, a single bead of sweat dripped to just above my eyebrow. Nothing happened between Amira and I, nothing ever had. We were friends…if that. But I knew that it wouldn't appear that way, and even though it would be of little conscience to me, I worried about Amira. Her position and reputation. The best thing to do, I thought, was to act natural.

In all honesty, it wasn't so unnatural to be seen with Amira. I had known her all my life.

Not just because her father was a well-respected General who was close with the King, but because she had been raised here. She was like a sister to me. My family didn't see it the same way, but I always felt close to her. She was stubborn and had a carefree spirit. That's why I liked her. She wasn't afraid to be honest with me. She was the only person in court who could actually beat me at card games, would is more like it.

The General had been my tutor and weapons trainer. On occasion, Amira would join in training. I was expected to be skilled, but Amira was the surprise. She was a natural, even though her training had been discouraged by others around her.

Amira's mother, Lillian, had been the caregiver to the royal family, mostly to me and my older brother Isaac. Lillian had been like a mother to me. My brother and I couldn't have been more different. Isaac had gray eyes and dark hair. Although he was smart, his tantrums held little rival. I had been the sweet one, so I was told, and often scolded for it. Isaac was only a year older than me, but at the young age of eight Isaac fell ill and died of a fever that hit the kingdom harshly. The King and Queen were never the same after the loss of their eldest child.

Lillian fell ill just as Isaac did and passed away when Amira had only been four, leaving her and her older brother Lorin in the care of the castle while the General was away in battle.

Amira spent most of her childhood in court as a highly regarded lady. Unfortunately, she seemed to always find herself in trouble. Mostly sticking her nose in places that it didn't belong and voicing her opinion in all the wrong situations. She was seven when her father was killed in battle and she lost her social standing as a lady, but the King and Queen felt that they owed her father a great debt. They trained her as a palace servant and Lorin as the royal blacksmith.

Amira and Lorin were around my age, so as children, we often took to playing together. Especially since we had grown close during their mothers' service to the palace. This annoyed the queen because Amira's talent for finding trouble seemed to have influence over me. Lorin tried to keep Amira's nose clean, but he spent most of his time working. Throughout the years she learned to control herself, to comply.

At least, she learned to appear so.

But now we were older...

"There you are. I thought you were off lying drunk in a tavern somewhere." I said.

Tauren refused to speak. He could barely look at me. That only confirmed that he knew Amira and I were alone in the hiding place together. Tauren's intentions were obvious to me and it irritated me. Surely Amira could do better, but a handsome high-ranking body guard to the future king was about as high as her position could take her. She would probably feel lucky if she were aware of his affection toward her. According to my knowledge, Tauren had rarely spoken to Amira. I hoped he would continue to keep his mouth shut.

"Right. So, what's on the agenda?" I questioned my stiff bodyguard. When there was no response, I turned on my heels and headed back to my room to study the protocols and schedules. I didn't want to appear nervous, everything had to be perfect.

Throughout the day countless people entered my chambers, announced by Tauren using as few words as humanly possible. Menus, entrees, clothing, and guest lists swirled around my mind until it all became too much. The day had felt like a blur. The crowd of people began to slow. I held the speech in my hand, not realizing that the sun had set. A housemaid noticed me struggling to read and quickly lit the lamp and apologized for not doing so sooner. She not only appeared tired, she was exhausted.

No doubt all the maids and servants would be tired this week with all of the excitement.

I smiled and dismissed Hilda, my house maid for the night.

She offered to stay until I was asleep, which was custom for her to do so, but to me it felt like babysitting.

I always enjoyed Hilda's company. She has been around for as long as I could remember. She had always been a plump and rosy woman, the opposite of my mother. I could swear she always smelled of cinnamon cakes, which is what she always surprised me with on my birthday.

Whether it was still a surprise or not, I enjoyed them just the same.

It wasn't until that night, though, that I realized just how tired she looked. Her soft milky skin seemed to have dulled, fading greatly into the wispy gray hair braided and pinned to her head. Looking upon her face it was apparent that her once rosy cheeks had become rivers of wrinkles.

After thoroughly convincing Hilda that I did not need her to stick around- demanding that she get some beauty rest- a chuckle sounded from the depths of her large belly and she finally dismissed herself.

I rubbed my eyes and looked out to the night sky.

It was late, most of the castle had settled in for the night.

Most...

That's when I remembered.

CHAPTER FIVE

Last Night Out

Aryn

Sneaking out wouldn't be too difficult.

Not if I played my cards right.

With it being as late as it was, all I had to do was suggest a guard rotation and relieve Tauren of his duty. He had been on shift long enough and it wouldn't appear a strange suggestion.

My next guard would want to check in with me, but if I instructed Tauren to inform the on-duty guard that I was sleeping and was not to be disturbed, I could slip out unnoticed during rotation.

Tauren nodded his head in acknowledgment of my instructions. Luckily he was more than willing to depart.

Typical.

I hadn't snuck out many times before, but I knew that if anyone saw me dressed in my current attire, I would be spotted quicker than a cow in a field of horses.

My nightshirt and dusty old riding trousers should do. I blew out my lamp and rested my head on the door, listening. It was silent. The halls were like a maze. If I could just slip out and make it to the narrower hall across from me, I could make my way to the servant's stairs which would hopefully be empty at this time of night.

Either way, it would be dark.

Just before peeking my head out of the door, I glanced back at the mirror in my room, running my fingers through my tangled mess of hair.

That was a stupid thing to do. It was too dark to see me reflection and no one would really see me anyway.

Once finally possessing the courage, I stuck my head out to see if the coast was clear. It was but it wouldn't last for long, I had to move fast.

I swiftly swung out of my room and glided stealthily to the servant's staircase. No one seemed to occupy them, but it was hard to tell because of their narrow and winding structure.

It wouldn't really matter if I did get caught though. I could simply say I was going for a walk. But with the clothes I was wearing and with no guard or maid…Suspicious.

Just before entering the dark staircase, I noticed a pile of clothing outside of the rooms. No doubt they were filthy and ready for the laundry, but there had been a dark cloak that I thought might be useful, especially to cover the bright white of my shirt. No one's clothes were as white as mine.

I bent down, grabbed the cloak, and took a quick sniff, which I probably shouldn't have. It smelled…less than pleasant but could have been worse and it wasn't a bad fit. A little short, exposing my fine brown leather boots, but nothing a little mud and dirt couldn't fix.

I raised the hood over my head and began to trot down the stairs as quickly and quietly as possible.

Although it had been mildly warm in recent days, the night was getting cooler. The top of the stone stairs seemed musty, cold, and wet, but as I made my way down the air become cool almost causing me to shiver. I was more thankful for the cloak now and wrapped it tighter around myself.

It was dark and dreary, not that I was frightened, but I was used to wide grand staircases with no walls or barriers. Thankfully, I hadn't ever used these stairs. This felt like a dungeon.

The full moon shone through the cracks in the walls giving just enough light for me to see where to step. The small breeze that blew through the cracks allowed for a slight movement of air, alleviating the staleness lingering around my nose.

Once I made it out of the crumbling staircase it wasn't hard to find my way through a servant's entry and rush through to the gate.

Silence filled the air, save for the occasional cricket or owl. The moon barely lit the outskirts of the woods. I had found my way to the big rock- familiar from my childhood- which I had sworn was shaped like a dog bigger than a wagon. It had been a long time since I had been out here and I had been out so few times. It was more difficult than I would have wanted to admit to find the special place, but I found it.

Had I come too early?

Or possibly I arrived too late?

Of course, she wouldn't have waited for me.

I let out a heavy breath, feeling more disappointed than I realized.

Stupid.

"Boo." Hands covered my eyes from behind and a voice whispered coldly into my ear, but I kept my cool. At least I hoped it appeared so from the outside.

"Happy Birthday," I said, still facing the same direction allowing her to slip in front of me.

My breath nearly stopped when I saw her. Beneath her thin dark blue cloak, she wore a lavender dress. The pale-lavender dress bled into a dark blue, blending into the dark ground. The moonlight reflected off of the top of her dress, her face glowing in a way I had never seen before. Hair dark as night flew behind her loosely being blown by the wind.

I had never seen her dressed this way before. Or at least not in many years, but this was different. My pulse quickened as I tried to slow my breathing.

I was used to her plain and simple maids' dresses, which were more colorful and extravagant than the servant's clothes, but plain none the less.

The wind picked up letting her spicy yet sweet scent fill my nose. The aroma slightly burned and tickled my throat. I suppressed a cough, gulping loudly, feeling my Adam's apple rise and fall.

She spent a lot of time in the kitchens, I knew that. But somehow the scent stayed with her in a way it didn't anyone else.

"Are you ready?" Amira asked.

"For what?'

"It's a surprise," She said with her eyes nearly bulging with excitement.

"But it's your birthday."

"Our birthday… Sort of. Well, close enough." She giggled. How did she look so relaxed, and why had I all of the sudden felt so tense?

"So where are we going?"

"Like I said…surprise. Tag-you're it." She spouted out in a childlike tone and ran off into the night.

I took off after her, chasing glimpses of black hair and the silvery, pale-purple of her dress as she tucked and dove between trees with ease. She moved as a night breeze in the woods.

I had no trouble keeping up with her in speed but was impressed with how fast she could still run through the thick forest. Although it wasn't really surprising, she had always been fast. Especially the summer she hit a growth spurt before me and teased me for being smaller and slower than her. But of course it didn't take long for me to catch up to and surpass her.

I missed this. The two of us playing, maybe playing wasn't the right word, we weren't children anymore. I was reminded more of that as I watched the curves of her body as she ran in front of me. I suddenly felt short of breath and when I began to slow down I gulped loudly, realizing how dry my throat felt.

"Slowing down old man?" She began to come to a stop. "Almost there…I think."

"You think?"

"Where's your sense of adventure?" As she came closer to me I could see the spark in her dark brown eyes. They always had a shine to them, except when her parents died. Even then, she showed great strength. I admired that about my friend, envied it really.

There was no doubt I was physically strong. My body was lean but outlined in tone muscle. Maybe under many coats of fabric and cloaks, I might appear skinny, but under all of that was pure muscle. Not so bulky to make me appear wild, but I was well sculpted. Women often whispered of my fine body and gorgeous hair. It was embarrassing. But, truth be told, I didn't have much experience with women, not like I would get much of a chance. I was expected to marry based on the coin system, so I had no choice in the matter.

As of late, I found myself cornered by women seeking me out. My morals would never let me go too far with someone I couldn't marry…but that didn't mean I wouldn't take pleasure in exploring my 'possibilities'.

I tried not to focus on her strong scent or her chest noticeably rising and falling beneath her dress. Her cloak barely hanging on, was now lying slightly off her shoulder and showed the smallest amount of skin, exposing her collar bone. I noticed small bumps across her arms and worried she might be cold. She should be, it was a chilly night. Not too cold, but the chill in the air grew stronger as the night went on. In fact, I began to wonder why I wasn't cold.

"You look chilled, you'll catch a cold. Here, use my cloak. It's warmer." I began to untie mine and hand it to her, but she bunched up her nose and laughed.

"No thanks, it smells like dirty man feet."

I stopped, suddenly feeling more embarrassed than I should. The thought was fleeting as I broke into a deep laugh, bending forward slightly at the middle.

This was my true laugh. It was rare but came from the depths, overcoming me until I couldn't control myself. It grew louder and louder, my eyes began to squint as I bent down further. It felt good.

Amira began to laugh beside me but her face suddenly became filled with worry. She bit her lip and placed her hand on my shoulder as my laugh slipped back into a chuckle.

Her hands were warm. So warm.

Amira smiled gently at me, "I haven't heard you laugh that loud in…" She trailed off and looked me in the eyes which sent a chill through my body. No. It wasn't a chill. It felt like lightning. "How are you doing?" Her voice dripped with sincerity.

"Fine." I said in a chipper voice. She knew me. She knew that my sudden burst of hysterical laughter was just me releasing the smallest portion of stress I was dealing with. "I'm fine." I said in a more stern voice.

She stepped back slightly.

I hadn't meant to frighten her or push her away. She's always been my closest friend. "Fine. We're here anyway…I think." Still biting her lip on one side, she let a mysterious smile slide across her face.

CHAPTER SIX

The Wading Pull

Amira

Something was different about Aryn, I could feel it. I knew it was in part due to him assuming the throne soon. Like really soon. That and having to marry some random person. We had often joked about who he might marry. I would list off women nearly twice his age. It had been fun, but now I was beginning to worry. Aryn deserved a good woman, the kingdom needed a good woman.

If there was one thing I could do, at least I could take his mind off of the stress for one night. He deserved that. This would be a sort of party, his last night of freedom. I felt a little sad realizing this would probably be our last night alone together, we weren't children. Soon he would have a wife.

Even worse, Lorin has been mentioning possible prospects for me to consider marrying.

Anger boiled from within me. I didn't need a man, I was doing just fine on my own. I was used to being alone. I used to have my brother, but recently he spends all of his free time with Rachel. I had nothing against Rachel. Rachel was smart, attractive, and kind. It was strange that it wasn't just the two of us anymore. It wouldn't be long before Lorin would ask for her hand. I would be genuinely happy for them, but it bothered me and made me sick to feel that people seemed to simply live, marry, reproduce, and die.

Adventure coursed through my veins. I felt my father's blood was strong in me.

I took a deep breath and calmed myself. Aryn would be fine. Who wouldn't love him? I knew deep down he would make a great king, most definitely a great husband and father. Whoever was selected in the Choosing Ceremony would truly be lucky.

It was hard not to feel overprotective of Aryn, he was there to ground me when my world spun out of control and collapsed. He and Lorin were all I had, I just wanted what was best for both of them.

Amira smiled and grabbed Aryn's hand, pulling him forward.

I heard the faint sound of water crashing ahead and knew we must be close. I had never ventured out this far but had come close before.

Truth be told, I didn't know what I was looking for but had always been drawn to this side of the forest. It was forbidden to go out this way. Well, not forbidden…merely discouraged. There were horror stories and warnings deterring people from this side of the forest. It hadn't stopped me from exploring or dragging Aryn along with me when I had the chance.

I had always felt as if something were calling me to the forest. A pull which was hard to resist.

Just a few days before, while shopping in the market, I ran across an old blind man who told stories of magic. Curiosity peaked in me, though I knew magic was a myth.

The towns' people mocked the blind man and threw trash at him.

Few people stopped to offer coins or food.

In Astrean, especially this close to the castle, it was rare to see beggars. But I assumed his blindness had something to do with it. Although, he didn't seem to want anything. In need of a good meal and a bath, sure. Although he stood hunched over with a raggedy, brown cloak and clothes that look as though they haven't been changed or washed in a while, I sensed that strength and wisdom filled him. If you looked hard enough it was there.

When he faced me, I felt as if he could see me. He smiled and began telling the story of a hidden place where old magic once resigned. It was as if he were telling it just for me. The next day I looked for him but he was nowhere to be found and no one seemed to want to help find him.

This would be the perfect adventure for Aryn and me.

A last hoorah.

We made our way toward the sound of crashing water.

It was incredibly dark, but once we made it past the trees to the clearing, it was as if the moon was shining directly above the lake of water just below the falls. Its light reflected all around.

The moon seemed larger tonight.

It was breathtaking.

I stood there taking in the beautiful surroundings. Astrean was truly the most beautiful place in all the world, but this…this was breathtaking.

The lake, although dark outside, seemed to be crystal clear. It was black because of the night, but the moon shining above gave the water a silver hue, making it sparkle. The waterfalls above were huge. The water came crashing down with immense force and vigorousness, but from this distance, the disturbance to the calm water was but mere ripples to the shore's edge.

Flowers were in bloom, which wasn't too strange, but considering the time of year, I thought they would begin to hibernate.

A crisp breeze came off the water, but astoundingly it was rather warm where we were standing.

Strange bugs flew around us. Lighting up and disappearing it looked like twinkling lights in the night, like stars had fallen to this special place in Astrean.

I knew that these strange bugs loomed in the air of the forest but sensed that they were no threat.

I stood there for what felt like an hour just taking in the beautiful sights, but as I glanced at Aryn I noticed that he was looking at me. Warmth flooded my cheeks and I looked down noticing that my hand was still in his.

I quickly pulled away feeling silly but somehow regretting the lack of warmth that radiated from his strong, gentle hand.

The old man had said that this was where the magic originated. Legend said that it was where the Source first held the coin ceremonies.

It was magical, except it was nothing but a lake. There were no caves, no sanctuaries, and no buildings. Nothing to show that anything special had once been here. At least nothing but the beauty of nature. It disappointed me, but I hadn't gotten my hopes up much anyway.

To tell the truth, this was more than I could have imagined. I easily made my way to the edge of the water. Slipping off one shoe, I slowly dipped my toe into the water bracing myself for the chill, but it never came.

The water was warm. As if it were a gentle kiss.

I glanced back at Aryn, who seemed to still be staring at me.

A place this beautiful shouldn't be wasted.

I paused for a moment, slowly gaining the courage to do what I wanted most. The water beaconed me. I began uniting my cloak, slipping it slowly off of my shoulders. I was surprised the air remained warm. My hands began to tremble, but I calmed them. There was no need to be nervous. Not around Aryn. I began to undo my dress. I had bloomers on underneath that stretched from my waist to my ankles and a corset type top covering my stomach and chest. It was really no less than I wore to sleep and covered no less than what my dress had, except exposing my arms and shoulders.

I looked back toward Aryn who stood motionless. He gulped, his Adam's apple rose and fell making him appear much older than the boy I once knew.

"What are you doing?"

"What does it look like? You coming?"

He looked down at my dress on the ground, he looked as if frozen in shock. I fought back a sly smile, knowing how uncomfortable he must be.

"I can't very well swim in that can I? And besides, you've seen me in my night clothes before. It's nothing scandalous."

Instead of stepping into the water, I began to skillfully climb a pile of rocks until I was as high the trees.

"Get down, that can't be safe," Aryn yelled from below.

"Chicken!" I called down and then smiled right before I leaped into the water.

I made a small splash as I gracefully dove into the blackness of the water. Aryn wouldn't be able to see anything in the darkness. I knew he waited for me to come up for air but I stayed below the surface of the water. The ripples became smaller. He tore off his cloak, kicked off his shoes, and dove in wearing the rest of his clothes. He began swimming as fast as he could toward the spot where I had entered.

"Amira!" He screamed while slicing through the darkness.

I remained just under the surface, but far enough down to be unnoticed. I could barely make out his form beneath the depths of the dark water.

I brushed against his leg, which must have spooked him because he began to kick and swim back a couple of feet. I tugged on his foot, pulling him under slightly. He bobbed back to the surface kicking and splashing. I resurfaced, splashing Aryn and giggling uncontrollably. He was so easy to tease. So serious all the time.

"Mer! How could you do that?"

I sunk further into the water until only my eyes were above the surface. My long hair floating behind me almost blended in with the darkness of the water. The only light we had was that of the glowing moon.

As I splashed back to the surface I spit toward him, spraying his face with water. I laughed so hard, then Aryn swung his arms toward me, splashing me with a wave of water.

Laughter broke out between both of us. This was the Aryn I enjoyed.

Both of us were treading water only inches from each other, our laughter began to fade. The gentle waves of water were circling around us, rising and falling above my chest.

"Your clothes are drenched." I giggled.

"Yeah, thanks." He swam closer to the rock's edge and pulled the clinging shirt off of his body, tossing it to the side on the rocks.

It had been a while since I had last seen Aryn without a shirt. He looked...different. Good different. Sculpted.

"Pants too, unless you want to drown." I said trying to keep a straight face.

Aryn's face turned bright red.

"I mean unless you don't wear anything underneath, then please, by all means, keep them on." I couldn't stop my face from burning a bright red. I sunk a little deeper into the water allowing only my eyes and nose to appear.

"Fine." He began to try and untie his trousers but realized he needed both of his hands to do so, but he also needed them to stay afloat. He struggled to get free of his trousers, awkwardly bobbing up and down in the water and going under until he was free of them. Then he tossed them to the same place his shirt was.

He shouldn't have been too embarrassed. He wore underwear that spread loosely from his waist to his knees. The only thing he would be revealing was his calves. The water was too dark to see in any way.

The night was silent save for the steady crashing of water far off. The light bugs still fluttered around like specks of gold caught in the night sky, falling down to be on Earth.

I gracefully maneuvered my arms to stay afloat. I felt as if I were a swan dancing in the pool of water, while Aryn looked like a piece of driftwood floating simply floating there.

I turned onto my back, into a floating position. I laid on top of the water with my arms moving gracefully, I was almost dancing.

I was confident in the water; I was confident everywhere. I popped back up and splashed Aryn in the face.

"What's going on with you tonight? You're quiet. I mean, more quiet than usual. Don't spoil the party."

"Just…everything is changing. Nothing will be the same after all of this."

Just as I was about to reply I saw something glimmer in the distance and stared at the falls with curiosity.

"What? What's wrong?"

"I thought-" I stopped. I saw something. Something sparkled from behind the waterfall. "Did you see that? It did it again?"

"See what? Maybe we should get out of here. Someone might have seen us."

"No… it's not that." I bit my lip still staring at the waterfalls.

"Come on, let's dry off and head back," Aryn said as he glanced around the edge of the water and began to turn, ready to swim out of the lake.

Instead, I dove deeper into the water and began making my way toward the powerful falls. Something was pulling me closer.

"What are you doing?" Aryn called out, but I could barely hear him.

The current by the falls would have been strong, Aryn must have known that because I heard the worry in his voice as he called out to me. His voice became faint, drowned out by the wonder looming in my mind.

Aryn swam toward me shouting my name, but I couldn't stop…the crashing of the waves made a sound of great ongoing thunder.

To my surprise, the closer I swam to the falls, the more the crashing water let up until it became but a gentle stream. I was almost at the falls. Instead of the powerful pound of water crashing to the bottom, it was more like a deep steady rain. If anything, it felt as if the current would drag us in rather than under.

Mist surrounded us and steam rose from the surface making it difficult to see, but the light bugs still danced magically in view. The further I moved into the falls, the warmer the water seemed to feel.

The pull was strong, but it wasn't the current. It was something else. Something inside me. Like the calling of a familiar voice.

The loudness of the crashing water had quieted, making it easier to hear each other. I peered beyond the falls to the rock that laid beneath. I slowly made my way closer then looked back at Aryn who had just caught up with me. He began to suggest we head back.

I took a deep breath.

"Mer. What are you doing? Don't."

I dove into the water falls. A cloud passed over the moon allowing it to go dark for a moment.

After a few minutes, I had yet to resurface. I didn't know where I was headed, but I knew I was almost there.

CHAPTER SEVEN

Playing with Coins

Amira

I had found that there was indeed rock on the other side of the falls, but something led me deeper, further. When I finally surfaced I was astonished to see that I was in a cave. A large cave, which was surprisingly well lit. I waded my way a few feet. I noticed there was a bottom that seemed to incline, allowing me to walk out of the wading pool rather than climb out onto the surface.

It was strange, this cave almost seemed man-made. Although it was too beautiful to be artificial, it was also too perfect to have happened by accident. There were small cracks and openings above that let the lights from the stars and moon shine through. The water trickling from the side made the walls glisten, rough in some spots but smooth in others.

Gold, silver, gems, and sea glass shimmered in the walls.

I ran my hand along a small piece of sea glass that stuck out of the wall. It was odd, it looked like it had washed up and been stuck here. Although it didn't belong with the valuable jewels and gold within the walls I liked the few pieces of sea glass left behind. True, it was strange to see that sea glass was hidden in a cave with fresh water. It must have meant that people had been here before.

Sea glass had always been special to me even though it wasn't as valuable as gold. The small piece of sea glass I held in my hand now reminded me of my father. I closed my palm and held it tightly. Then, closing my eyes, I pictured his bearded face. He often came home from long voyages with small pieces of smooth, colorful glass. The General thought it was cute that I found such joy in the little treasures he brought home. He said they reminded him of me. Colorful and sharp, but smooth on the edges when worn down.

I was pulled from my thoughts and frightened by the sudden feeling of a hand resting on my shoulder…until I turned and saw Aryn. I had been lost in another world, the past. He smiled down at me and a warmth grew from deep within. I was glad he was here with me. He didn't say anything. There was something solemnly beautiful about this place and I could tell we both felt it.

This place seemed familiar, but it wasn't the cave itself, it was the layout.

It had a large open area that was long and led far back to a platform of stone. The stone formed an altar that laid in front of what seemed to be a smaller waterfall. But this was more like a fountain. Water trickled down in a soft flow from the top of the ceiling. Light sprang from the water.

It looked magical.

The Coining Ceremony, that's what this place reminded me of.

Not that I was able to go to mine. I felt my grip tighten on the smooth piece of sea glass I still held.

From as far back as I could remember, I had been anxiously anticipating my Coining Ceremony.

I always thought I would follow in my father's footsteps and be a general in the army. It was unlikely for women to be chosen, but not impossible. Although, my mother wished I would be chosen as a caregiver like herself, or perhaps something more extravagant. It didn't matter. I had no one to escort me to the Coin Ceremony on my thirteenth name day.

I had hoped Lorin would. Instead, the queen sent me a coin. Like it was a piece of mail. Servant…

At least I was able to be a high-class place maiden. Lorin had already attended his coining ceremony and had received soldier-- weapons. But the queen said it was interpreted wrong and that he was meant to be a weapons maker, not a weapons handler. It was hard to refuse the abrupt change, especially since he had no one to speak for him.

Although I hadn't been to my own coining ceremony, I had been to her brother's.

It angered me that my fate was handed to me like that. Instead, I felt that it had been stolen from me, just like everything else in my life.

"Does this place remind you of anywhere?" I asked quietly, as if speaking too loudly would be a sin.

"What do you mean?" His head tilted slightly.

"You don't see it?"

He looked at me as if I were crazy. Maybe I was.

"That's right. You haven't actually been to a Coining Ceremony. That's what this reminds me of."

"What do you mean 'never been to a Coining Ceremony'? You were at mine." Aryn stepped back with eyebrows burrowing.

"You may have received your coin that day, but that most certainly wasn't a Coining Ceremony."

On Coining Day hundreds of people would line up, having walked for miles and miles to receive their coin. Even though they dress in their best and bathe the day before, they all stink after a day or so journey. No matter how glamorous they try to look, it was nothing compared to Aryn's personal ceremony. His wasn't even in the same location, nor did he have to share his day with anyone else. His ceremony was far from traditional. I just wished I had a Coining day, long lines or not.

I could feel the tension rising and it made me feel bad for having said anything. He didn't ask for the life he was given, but neither had I.

"I'm sorry you never had your Coining Ceremony," Aryn's warm breath whispered behind me. He had always understood me.

I shrugged and returned a smile.

It was hard to be mad at Aryn. His hair that was straightened and darkened from the water was now beginning to dry and frizz into the childish curls I had always adored.

I peered back to the glistening walls and ran my hand over the surface. It was much smoother than I would have imagined. I began to wander the rim of the cave letting my hand glide along the walls as I slowly navigated.

Aryn shadowed me, tracing his hand along the path mine touched.

The cave was cool, but I could feel the heat radiating from his skin behind me. The contrasting heat burned and tickled my neck, sending a tingle down my body.

Gold and gems were scattered on the floor. It appeared that there had once been more. It seemed as though this place was left in ruins, but nothing could cover the beauty of this place.

I made my way to the glittering falls at the back of the cave and gently swept my fingers across the surface of the stone, the same size and structure of an altar.

"Introducing…Miss Amira of House Viribus, daughter of the great General Harran, Kingdom of Astrean. Please place your offering upon the altar and receive your destiny." Aryn said in a deep and political sounding voice.

"What are you doing?"

"You never went to your Coining Ceremony. So, we are doing it now."

"That's not how it works. This isn't the place, nor the time. And…I'm not thirteen."

"Come on, just for fun."

"My coin has already been engraved. What do you want me to do, dunk it in the water?"

"If it is magic, then would it really matter?" Aryn held half a smirk with either confidence or arrogance. I knew he was only playing.

"Please place your coin upon the altar and let the magical waters runneth over to uncover your destiny."

"What about the Dator?"

"Today, I'm the Dator."

It was hard to resist Aryn's playful smirk.

Why not?

I reached for my coin -made into a necklace like most girls wore- but couldn't undo the clasp.

Turning to Aryn, "Would you mind? Sir, Dator."

Aryn sucked in a deep breath and stepped closer. I turned my back to him and gathered my wild damp hair to the side. I felt him come closer and hesitate. He finally let out a breath and the heat that passed through his lips lingered upon my neck, warming my whole body.

He slowly worked the clap until the necklace became loose, both ends still resting in his hands and the coin upon my chest. His hands barely resting on my shoulders, sent a shiver through my body. With my back still turned to him, I reached to where his hands were and took hold of the ends of my necklace, as Aryn let go.

His hands felt strong from training, but there was a softness as well. I turned to face him. He coughed slightly, took a step back, and nodded toward the stone table.

I marched to the 'altar' and placed my coin under the running water and backed up.

"Now what? Aren't you, the Dator, supposed to hand me the coin?"

"Right."

Aryn pretended to bow before me, but it was a comical effort on his part.

Just as he reached to grab the coin a loud thunder-like sound erupted and the floor began to shake. The rocks and gems that laid upon the floor began to bounce and the ceiling started to crumble.

I was certain the place was about to cave in.

Another explosion of thunder echoed through the air causing some of the rock to loosen just above my head.

A ringing sound echoed in my ears, I felt dizzy and off balance.

I was hurled to the ground, unaware of what was happening. The light blinded me and my side ached.

When I opened my eyes again Aryn was on top of me panting.

For a moment, the ground remained still and the cave quieted.

Neither of us moved, as if we forgot how, frozen in fear.

I could feel the pressure of his body against mine.

Silence broke as the ground shook, sending boulders of rock crashing down from the roof and walls. Aryn leaned in closer to me to shield me from the debris, bringing his face mere inches from mine. I could feel his breath in sync with mine.

The air around us filled with dust, making it difficult to breathe. We had to get out, the cave had become unstable.

I closed my eyes, tears dripping down from the dust and debris. I could no longer see Aryn's face, nor hear his labored breathing. I felt his strong hands take hold of my shoulders, relieved that he was still near. He pulled me off of my feet, grabbing my hand firmly as he attempted to navigate away from danger.

We made it to the edge of the cave, both coughing violently gasping for fresh air. My hand shot toward my chest. "My Coin!" I screeched, trying to turn back. Losing your coin was almost breaking the law.

"Leave it!" Aryn shouted through the sounds of crashing rocks and falling water.

"I can't return without it."

"Worry about that later!" Aryn yelled, pulling me closer to him. He wasn't rough, he never was. His hold was firm but reassuring. I trusted him, fully. The coin could be replaced with little explanation. Lorin could easily make a spare. Aryn was right, it was time to go.

I knew the cave had become dangerous, yet my heart broke knowing I would never see that beautiful place again.

Still holding hands, he led me into the water. He nodded, taking in a deep breath and diving under. I followed instantly. The water crashed harder than it had before, making it more difficult to swim through. The weight of the falls pulled us under. My head spun and suddenly I didn't know up from down. Instinct told me to let go of Aryn's hand to free myself and use both arms to fight for the surface, but if I let go we might be lost forever.

A story my father once told me poured into my mind. It was about his ship being caught in a great storm and going under. He had abandoned ship just as the rest of the soldiers and crew had. The crashing waves sent him into a confusion, unable to tell up from down, yet he was a capable swimmer. He had described feeling chaos and fear, which was hard for me to imagine because my father was the bravest man I knew. He explained that as he sunk deeper into the water, just before the feeling of helplessness and despair took him, he saw my mother's face. It calmed him. Thinking it was the end, he let out a deep breath. The large bubbles of life that escaped him began floating away. Not away, but down. He realized that the bubbles weren't floating down, but up. He turned himself around and with the very last bit of life left in him, he forced himself to the surface.

That's how I felt now. On the brink of helplessness. I could no longer see Aryn in the blackness of the water but could feel his pull. We were both fighting in opposite directions. Even though he must have been nearly out of breath, he held my hand firmly in his.

It was all I had, the last breath in my lungs. I could feel my chest burning, desiring a fresh breath of air more than anything I had ever fought for. Closing my eyes, I let it out. As I opened my eyes again I watched the bubbles floating up. With all of my strength, I forced myself up, tugging Aryn's hand as I fought the dizziness of being tossed around by the power of the falls. The current still pulled us under, but I pulled on Aryn's grip which had suddenly begun to soften and slip away. He had been fighting the current, now he's fading into it. His hand slipped out of mine.

I had to reach the surface. I felt weak, dizzy. I didn't have much time left. But I wasn't leaving without Aryn. I swam down further, I could see nothing. Whether from the dark water or lack of oxygen I was unsure it was him until my hand felt his chest. I pulled at his arm, but the weight was too much.

I could no longer stay under the water. I darted to the surface sucking in as much air as I could when I broke from the water. I tried to catch my breath and sucked in one last breath before I dove beneath the surface once more. As if drawn to the heat of his body, I found him more quickly than I had expected. This time, instead of pulling at his arm I pressed my chest against his, wrapping my arms around him and kicking my legs with all my might. My legs strained, feeling tired, but I finally broke through to the surface with Aryn still in my arms. I held him…heavy and lifeless.

Was he breathing? I wasn't sure. I forced myself and him to the edge of the water. Once I reached the shallow edge I could barely drag him. I left him half in the water, but I managed to keep his head above the surface.

"Breathe!" I yelled as I held his head in one hand and beat on his chest with the other.

Nothing.

"Breathe… Aryn, Breathe!" I cried now, my voice breaking.

Breathe…please…you can't leave me! My hands began to tremble. I held him closer, digging my fingers into his skin.

I pulled him further out of the water so that only his lower half still remained submerged, his head lay on the mix of grass and mud. I beat my hands on his chest one last time before sucking in a breath of air, leaning over, and breathing what air I could into his still cold lips.

I can't give up, I can't lose him. He is my best friend.

I laid my head on his chest to listen for a heartbeat, tears began to sting my eyes.

Suddenly his chest constricted. He began to cough. It was violent, but he was coughing. Water gushed from his mouth.

I pushed Aryn up as he expelled the contents of his lungs. He was breathing. Coughing, but breathing.

With Aryn sitting up now, well leaning over his arm, I jumped at him wrapping my arms around his neck and clumsily falling over, knocking him back down.

"Oh, Stars! I'm so sorry."

He laid his head back in the mud taking in breath after breath until he began to laugh.

"How are you laughing?" I replied, only to add a hint of contagious giggling to the end of my question.

"You're laughing too." His voice sounded raspy and he choked and coughed between laughs.

It didn't matter. I was relieved. Mud or not, I laid down beside him, now more aware of our closeness. I stared into the starlight, Aryn propped himself on his elbow to face me. He remained silent. I kept my eyes on the stars, but I sensed him smile.

CHAPTER EIGHT

Dream Come True

Aryn

The night had been…eventful to say the least. Any time that I spent with Amira was anything but boring. But that was all over now. The walk back had been quiet. To me, it almost felt as if it were a silent goodbye, which was probably why we both kept our pace slow. We both knew everything would be different from here on out.

She made me turn my back as she dressed. I had a harder time finding my boots and shirt. It felt strange to be half drenched and half dry. Amira's long silky black hair cascaded down her back. It seemed to hold the water more than anything else, almost instantly drenching her top dress as she put it on. She tried leaning over to ring it out with her hands, but that didn't seem to help much.

The air had become cold and crisp in the night. I could see bumps rise upon her soft pale skin. She slid her cloak around her and pulled in close. I knew she was still cold.

"Are you sure you don't want mine too?" I turned to offer her.

"That nasty thing? Never." She raised her nose and held firm for a brief moment before bending forward to let her laughter release.

That had been the last time we laughed that night. Something gnawed at me, I didn't want that to be my last real laugh.

We parted ways as we made our way to the outskirts of the kingdom. I wanted to see her safely to the castle but also knew that if we were caught it was best to be caught alone. I traced my steps back to my room, although with more difficulty this time.

Maybe I wasn't as good at sneaking around as I had thought, but good enough to make it back in quarters unnoticed.

Judging by the moon, dawn would arise shortly and I had a busy day ahead of me. I allowed myself self to lay down and rest my eyes but felt myself slip into the night.

Flashes of the night before replayed through my head. Amira's face, her dress, the water, the cave, the shiny bugs that lit the sky...but it was the image of my own coin that crept into my mind. The Choosing ceremony was tomorrow. Someone's coin will be selected. A wife, a Queen, and me the King.

Soon, the sun rose and I found myself standing on the raised platform that had been placed outside, covered with tarps and fabrics shading the three thrones--four actually. A new one had been built for the ceremony. That's where the future Queen would sit once she was chosen. The makeshift outdoor platform of thrones for all to see.

The sun beat down on my head and shoulders. I couldn't sweat, not here.

The time was now.

My mother rose and made her way to the Ark in which the coins lay. It was a large chest made of gold with carvings throughout. From the top of the chest sprouted two large golden arms that made a sort of bridge, both meeting in the middle to form large golden hands lying flat, palms up. A small fountain was attached at the back of the chest, creating a small waterfall. Water was an important part of every ceremony. It symbolled cleansing and clarity. When I stood in front of the chest a coin would fall from the water to the hands. It was to appear as magic, but since I had practiced it many times I knew there was a lever on the floor that triggered a mechanical reaction, picking a coin at random from the box to travel up a hidden tube behind the fountain.

What was she doing? It was I who was to draw the coin. Without hesitation, I rose and quickly strode toward the chest. I was dressed in gold and red, more red than I had remembered being in the wardrobe when looking at it days prior.

It was silent, whether from the crowd's anticipation or from my nerves blocking any noise. Steadying my hand and inhaling a deep courageous breath, while standing in front of the chest, a coin fell from the waterfall. I hadn't even realized my eyes were closed as I held it in my hand.

With the sound of my father clearing his throat, my eyes shot wide open. In my hand was the coin. The coin that would reveal my forever bride.

I opened my palm, looking at the coin.

It was the crown. My crown. The same crown that braced my coin and that of my mother and fathers. Slowly, with my other hand, I flipped the coin. My breath caught. Suddenly I felt lighter, like I wasn't tethered to the ground. I knew this coin. I knew that family crest. I knew this girl. The only girl in her family.

Amira.

Light startled me and stung my eyes. I jumped, falling out of my bed. Wrapped in my blankets I struggled to free myself and come to a standing position. Confused and disoriented, I grabbed for my sword on my belt, but it wasn't there.

I heard giggling, but not the giggling of a young woman. It was the chuckle of an old woman. Hilda. I was there, standing in my room in only my underwear. I quickly grabbed a pillow and held it out in front of me, covering my royal gems.

"Oh, honey it's nothing I haven't seen before. You took quite the tumble this morning. Not enough rest?"

I blinked away my confusion. A dream. It was only a dream. But how? It had felt so real. The nerves of choosing the coin, the beat of the sun, the cool feeling of gold in my hand, then the…thrill. I wasn't sure what I had felt. It was as if lightning had struck, but it didn't hurt. I had been excited. Had I truly been excited that Amira had been chosen?

"Honey? Are you feeling okay? You look terrible."

"Gee… Thanks." I said as I reached for the shirt that had been laid out for me. Kings didn't dress themselves, but Hilda had long learned of my embarrassment of being dressed by my maids. That would have to change soon.

Shaking the dream had been harder than I imagined. It felt so fresh in my mind. I had become distracted by my thoughts. I didn't have time to be distracted. Today was the Choosing Ceremony. Festivities would last all day, all week really. Countless vendors, entertainers, booths of food, fighting events...all leading up to the main event. The choosing of the coin.

That wouldn't be until just before sunset. Of course, it was planned so that fireworks would go off shortly after the selection. I knew that the delay had also been a ploy of my mother's. Usually, it was free to enter the Choosing Ceremony, not this year. For every family, every daughter, there was a cost. The longer the festival went on, the more women would enter.

A greater selection, I told myself. Although I knew my mother had eyes on the gold.

So, the day began.

Maids piled in my room at the break of dawn to feed and clothe me, even though I had requested a little more privacy. They adorned me with gold, red gems, and fabrics. I felt like an object being decorated for the festival. If this ceremony didn't kill me, the heat of the sun and the dreadful clothes would.

It was strange, it must have been nearly seven in the morning. Merely an hour before the festival was set to begin. I had seen countless maids and servants and yet had not seen even a glimpse of Amira. I attempting not to worry, surely she was busy. I couldn't help but feel something was off. She would be here. She had to. Not only for work but to wish me luck today of all days. Something nagged at me. Had she entered her coin? Would she?

Sure, she had lost her coin the night before, but with her brother being a blacksmith she would have had time to get a spare.

Tauren had appeared bright and early in shining armor and a pristine uniform, still silent. Two others joined him by the door, soon followed by at least three more. I didn't know most of their names but had seen them around often. Honestly, they all looked the same to me. Security would be higher than usual today, brutes following my every move.

I had been used to being crowded my whole life, but even this seemed a bit much. My large quarters were overwhelmed, this made me glad that the festivities were outside. It would still be crowded, but maybe I wouldn't feel so boxed in.

The trumpets sounded in the courtyard signaling the soon arriving royal party. People from all over the kingdom, even some from surrounding kingdoms, had been traveling for days. There was no doubt that people had been arriving early, filling the palace and courtyard, even beyond.

Hearing the trumpets only seemed to make the maids nervous and begin to scurry faster. Hilda had been by my side all morning. I was thankful that she had brought her special calming tea that used to put me to sleep as a child. It seemed to help my nerves, although I couldn't help but wish she had brought along something stronger.

"Alrighty, shoo," Hilda hissed at the maids, "Everyone who doesn't need to be here needs to leave at once. It's time we get this fine Prince to his festival." Her eyes glistened as she looked at me. "And pray to the Source he might find his mate on this day." The plump woman nodded then dabbed her eyes with the bottom of her fine skirts. It wasn't lost on me that she was dressed to her best today. Everyone was.

Time became hazy in the moments to come. Soon I found himself standing closely behind my mother and father. The doors would open and they would lead the procession, followed by me. The man of the day. Normally the queen demanded the most attention, but today all eyes would be on me...Prince Aryn.

The trumpets sounded again and the doors flew open. Cheers erupted from the crowd. It was deafening. The King and Queen -arm and arm- lead the way, stopping at the top of the steps to wave to the people. They were then escorted to the side to make way for the crowned Prince. I took a deep breath and stepped forward, waving at the crowd with the biggest smile I could muster.

Now I would lead while the King and Queen trailed me.

This was just the beginning.

CHAPTER NINE

Festivities

Amira

The image in the mirror was startling. I hadn't gotten a good night's rest and it was evident on my face. I never had any use of face creams or powders, but the other palace girls lived by them. Normally I wouldn't care if I carried bags under my eyes, but I couldn't look this tired. Not today. I would just have to find the time to slip into one of the girls' rooms and attempt to fix myself up.

The smell of mixed perfumes filled the air making me feel dizzy. Even the maids and servants were pulling out their finest clothes and perfumes. As much as I detested everyone putting on such a show, I found myself wearing my best dress. I was covered in simple, yet elegant, fabrics of white and gold with lace flower embellishments woven throughout. From far away it appeared a simple dress, nothing eye catching. But if someone were standing close by while the light graced me, the golden flowers would appear to bloom from the dress. The stitch work was nothing less than perfection and the lines of the dress were brilliant.

I didn't sew often. I thought that the jobs given to women were too boring and pointless. Although I did enjoy working with my hands, it wasn't the tedious sewing that occupied my mind, it was the craft of it. It was one of the few things the maids were allowed to do in their down time. I hadn't had much of a gift for womanly chores or crafts, but this... this, I had gotten from my mother.

Perhaps that was what had inspired the dress I wore today. The colors, the roses, and the lace had all been incorporated into my mother's wedding dress. I had never seen it personally, but I still had some of the fabric that had been used. Lillian too made her own dresses. When I was born my mom used the fabric of her wedding dress to make a blanket for her me. I treasured that blanket. It was one of the few things I had left of my mother. I had spent years learning my mother's stitch work from that one blanket. Of course, it was older now. The colors had been worn down, stitches come loose, stains spotted the fabric, but I had vision.

I had meant to save the dress for something more special, perhaps my own wedding if I were to have continued working on the dress, adding beading and layers to make it stand out. When rummaging through my dresses that morning I just couldn't get that dress out of my head. It had been the one I wore in my dreams the night before.

Golden rays of the early morning sun were still just creeping above the waters outside. I quickly slipped into Hadassah's small quarters, another house maid that I befriended during my years at the castle. The room was dark. Either she was still asleep or had already gotten up and ready for the festival.

I bumped around until I found the small lamp beside Hadassah's bed. Once I lit the lamp I saw that not only had Hadassah not still been sleeping, but it appeared as if a disaster had occurred in her chambers. I wasn't worried though. It wasn't hard to guess what had caused this catastrophe. Knowing Haddy, she had been up half of the night trying on dresses, fixing her hair, and applying unreasonable amounts of makeup.

It didn't matter that I had often told Hadassah that she required no makeup. Hadassah was beautiful. Her hair was the same dark brown as mine, but hers was paired with piercing blue eyes and plump lips. She had had no trouble finding men that were interested in her, she held out for one in particular. The one she might actually have a chance with today.

The Prince.

For a moment I found myself, again, wishing that Hadassah would be chosen. She would be good for Aryn.

But my dream kept nagging at my gut.

After my first attempt to hide the shadows under my eyes, I realized that I had highly overestimated my abilities with cosmetics. Hadassah had done my makeup once before. I closed my eyes and tried to remember the order and techniques Hadassah had used, mimicking them until I finally felt decent enough to leave the room. I had little time before the festival would begin. At least I didn't have to clean up my mess in Hadassah's room. Haddy would neither notice nor care.

Shutting Haddy's door behind me, I felt a tug at my gut to go see Aryn. Shouldn't I go check on him, wish him luck, or tease him about his dress clothes? It was still early enough for him to still be in his room, or somewhere in the castle. Instead, I scurried to find a job to do. I had been avoiding my chores all morning, something I couldn't get away with any other day except today. If I were stopped by one of the elder House mothers, I could simply say I was primping for today. Most of the girls had either decided to enter their coin, or at least used today as a way to find an eligible bachelor.

Most of the girls here found marriage as an escape from working, I felt it was the other way around. There was nothing stopping the girls from accepting a marriage proposal and leaving the court, so long at the queen approved. In fact, she encouraged matches in her court, sometimes even arranged by herself. Marry off the older girls to keep younger, prettier ones around the court. The few that were not married off- whether by choice or circumstance- went on to become House mothers. Although the queen had never pushed a match for me, I doubted it was Queen Beatrice's wish that I grew old in the castle as a House Mother.

The trumpets sounded, sending the workers into a frenzy. It was time for the festival to begin.

I swiftly weaved and ducked between busy people trying to make my way outside.

Fresh air and finger foods were what I needed.

Before I could get my hands on any appetizers I heard the trumpets sound again, announcing the Royal arrivals. Everyone hurried and pushed against each other lining the ways trying to get a glimpse at the royal family. The girls especially wanted to see the Prince and were doing nothing to hide their eagerness. Rows of people towered before me making it impossible to see anything. Not like it's anything I haven't seen before.

I hiked up my skirts and searched for higher ground.

I found a hill off to the side with two or three merchants set up for the day. Over all, there were seldom any people there. Most people would try to eat the free food and entertainment before seeing the merchants and these didn't seem to be selling anything worth anyone's time. I felt a small wave of pity, especially for the elderly lady selling handmade jewelry. By the looks of her table, she would not make much today.

I hadn't brought much with me, just a small coin purse with few coins. The last thing I needed was to waste all of my savings on sweet foods and card tricks.

I approached the frail lady and gave her a genuine smile.

"My, what a lovely young lady. Here to seek a chance at the Prince I imagine?" Tilting her head curiously looking me over from head to toe. The thought made me cringe. I clenched my teeth but kept smiling. I glanced through all of the small pieces of jewelry, knowing that they were mostly worthless, I figured I could find something worth buying. My hand had begun to reach for something, a small pair of pearl earrings. Whether or not the pearls were real was the question. I reached back into my coin purse and offered the lady 3 coins, probably three more than the earrings were worth, but my heart ached for the woman. The lady swatted my hand away.

"Excuse me?" I said breathlessly.

"Three coins is far too much for those worthless earrings." The lady responded.

I took a slow step backward, confused with the way the woman had refused the coin that I offered.

"You are much too beautiful, with a kind and brave heart. You deserve something special." The woman searched her pockets until her eyes widened. She held an object in the palm of her hands, one she must have had hidden from buyers.

Curious, I leaned forward. Her frail hand held some sort of pendant necklace. A single clear crystal hung from a gold chain. It was simple, elegant, easily looked over, but it was a fine piece of work. She grabbed my hand and placed the pendant in my palm. The clear of the crystal and the gold of the necklace paired with my dress perfectly. As if it were made to match. Something about the necklace seemed familiar. Hadn't I dreamed of the same necklace last night? I suddenly felt dizzy again. I reached for my coin around my neck, but it wasn't there. That part about last night had been real.

I grasped for my coin bag to offer the woman more than three coins.

"Please, a gift. For you."

"No. no. I couldn't." Before she could offer again a large man bumped into me, nearly knocking me nearly off my feet. The man grabbed my arms and steadied me.

"Wow, I must be one lucky man running into a beautiful woman such as yourself."

He alarmed me, not simply because he had nearly run me over, something about him was off. It was his clothes, his accent, and the way he presented himself. He was strikingly broad, handsome, and appeared as if he were trying to fit in. Despite how hard he tried, it was easy to see that this man was not from Astrean. I wanted to let it bother me, but his presence could easily be explained by the festivities. Many people were allowed to travel from kingdom to kingdom so long as they were strictly regulated.

I smoothed my dress and excused myself. When I looked back the older woman was gone, yet her table remained.

Louder cheers erupted from the crowd.

I found an opening and peered out to get a glimpse of my dear friend on his special day.

He was wearing the same thing that he had worn in my dream. He looked exactly the same. Flashes of the dream continued coming back to me, it had felt so real that it became confusing. I felt faint, I needed a drink. Perhaps the heat was getting to me.

Music, laughter, and fragrances filled the air around me. I seemed better after finding refreshments but felt heated at the inflamed prices of something as simple as a wine. I wasn't the type of girl who would flirt with a guy to encourage him to buy me a drink, but today the thought tempted me.

The burning smell of spiced meats scorched my nostrils, making my mouth water more. Maybe this festival wasn't so bad after all.

A drink or two, some spiced meats, and some sweets and I wouldn't spend any more coin.

A clanging sound of sloppy musical instruments caused me to cringe as I turned to see who could possibly be making such a racket. To my amusement, I found a small group of homely children with what looked like instruments that had been tossed aside or put together with scraps. I glanced around to see where their parents might be but with their dirty clothes and bony composure I concluded that their parents would not be found.

My heart sank with pity for the children, and yet their eyes were filled with profound joy and wonder. They were truly having fun and enjoying the festival. For them it came with potential for plenty of food scraps and entertainment. Still, there must be something I could do.

My hand immediately found its way to my purse…again. I pulled out the remainder of my coin and handed it to the eldest child, he was no more than ten. They needed it more than my belly needed sweets. I briefly wondered if he would be allowed to participate in the Coining Ceremony when they turned of age. Maybe fate would have him become something that took him far from the streets of poverty.

I wanted to do more for these children, but there was little I could do at the moment. Once the crowd of people left, probably days from now, I could ask around for homes or work for them. I feared Queen Beatrice would do very little, if anything, for the poor children who had drifted toward the capital…but Aryn, he would be King by the end of the week. Surely, I could convince my friend that starting a home for lost children could benefit the kingdom. They had as much of a right to a fair life as anyone else.

I always wanted to save enough money to buy my own dowry. Once I did I would be free. No one in my situation seemed to feel like a slave, except me. I had always assumed I would join the army as my father had. It was rare they let women in unless their coin dictated so, but if my coin couldn't provide passage to the army, money might buy my way in.

Seeing these children sparked something in me I had never truly experienced. Perhaps, if I couldn't find my way into the army I could run the children's home. It seemed funny how different the two ideas were, but most of all I just wanted to feel useful. I wanted to make a difference in the world rather than be just another girl.

My father taught me that bravery, wisdom, and compassion could change the world.

I listened to the children play their instruments, or whatever they were, until I could handle the clanging of metal no longer. I smiled at the children and waved goodbye. A small girl, maybe 6, ran up and gave me a hug. Surely the dirt from the girl would ruin my dress, but I didn't care. I bent down and hugged her as well.

"I'll see you again," I said gently, tucking a piece of tangled hair behind the girl's ear. Very soon, I hoped.

The festival would last all day, closing with the coin choosing in the evening. Even after that, the festivities would last through the week to celebrate the engagement, Aryn's birthday, his being named King, and the wedding. Although, even if people weren't excited about King Ezra stepping down- which was unlikely- people used any excuse to celebrate.

Women constantly flocked to the Ark to enter their coin. All were dressed in their finest, and many huddled in prayer with their families hoping that saying some chant and soaking themselves in oils would help them be picked.

Others had their fathers, mothers, or brothers enter the coin for them.

"Huh." I let out unexpectedly. If they weren't brave enough to offer their coin, they surely weren't fit to be queen.

The new queen had to be strong, strong enough to stand up to Beatrice.

CHAPTER TEN

Show Pig

Aryn

This day could not have been any longer. Although I was surrounded by so many people and guards that I could hardly breathe, I somehow felt alone. Something was missing, someone was more like it. I hadn't realized how much I had expected and yearned for a pep talk from my best friend. Even Lorin had stopped by to wish me luck and pat me on the back. The way he was talking, I was sure Lorin was close to asking for Rachel's hand.

I was happy for my friend, he was like a brother. I tried to push thoughts of jealousy from my mind. Lorin was allowed to choose who he would marry. So long as she accepted, but I saw the way they looked at each other.

I started to feel too romantic. Romance wasn't a part of royalty, and I was to be King. Duty came before all.

The one good piece of encouragement that Lorin gave me was that today the women would be flocking to me. That, I didn't mind. This would be last day I would really be able to look at women. Though I held so much power, I felt immensely powerless.

Finally, I saw a familiar face.

Her hair and dress looked more put together than the last time I saw her. After making small talk with eligible ladies and rich lords- which seemed pointless because I didn't have a choice to begin with- I welcomed a change.

The Queen tilted her head as I stepped away. She wouldn't dare reprimand me in public like this. The thought of going off without her permission brought a slight smirk to my face. One that was wiped away when I felt the rush of guards clinging to my feet. I couldn't even have one conversation without people babysitting me.

I began to approach her, feeling less confident than expected.

The palms of my hands became sweaty, but not from the heat.

"Hi…" I had meant to introduce myself, make small talk, and say something clever… But all I had was 'hi'.

She was startled. She became stiff, her face drained of color. She stuttered, then bowed in such an awkward way it made me chuckle.

"I'm Prince Aryn."

"Yes. I mean, I know. I mean, your majesty. I'm sorry." She looked down, wringing her hands. She still had the same fresh scent that I had smelt previously. Her hair was less frizzy, as if she had spent extra time with it this morning, but a few hairs escaped. The shyness and imperfection of this girl made my heart warm. Already, the sun from the day appeared to have added more freckles to her face.

"Your name is?"

"Oh, me? Fiona. Fiona Kuval." She said nodding once again.

"Kuval?" I said with surprise. "What is a lady of Kuval doing as a palace servant?"

"Oh. Um… My Uncle suggested it. I'm to become a court lady if the queen approves."

"Ahh…" I said nodding my head. That meant that no one had claimed her as a wife, so her father must have sent her here to find a husband as a lady of the court. Although she didn't look like the other ladies my mother took in, she had status, so she had little to worry about.

The Kuvals had originally come from a long line of Tarkans. One of the chosen families from Tarkus to come to Astrean. Their family had done well for themselves. If memory served me well, the Kuval's had just come into a heap of wealth. Which begged the question, why was she here at court?

"Could you do me a favor?" I questioned.

"Anything your highness."

Your highness. I hid my grimace.

"Today is… rather formal. Could you maybe walk with me? As just

Aryn." I looked back at my guards. "Well, Aryn and his…obsessively close friends who follow his every move."

Fiona giggled, her cheeks turning pink.

I offered my arm. Hesitantly, she took it.

She was silent for a while. It seemed like she was afraid to speak. I could tell she wanted to say something.

"What is it?"

"Nothing." She replied quickly.

I stopped and turned toward her. I wasn't planning on moving until she spoke.

"It's just… Why are you walking with me?"

"Because I'm the Prince and I do as I please."

"Of course, I just mean…why me?" She looked down and bit her lip.

"You look…honest. I can use honest."

"I can imagine."

I felt less lonely realizing that she must have known how I felt. Everyone I talked to today wanted something. They were speaking with the Prince, the almost King. They were putting on shows to look good. Everyone wanted to be the Kings friend. I gritted my teeth as I thought of their idea of 'friend'.

I enjoyed the few minutes I was able to spend with Fiona, but I couldn't help glancing around to see if I could find Amira. I hadn't seen her since last night. I needed to see her.

"Prince Aryn, maybe we should head back to the tent. You should be preparing for the Choosing soon." Tauren said.

"Oh, look. You talk." I teased.

Tauren didn't flinch.

Aww well.

I hadn't noticed the sun starting to go down. There appeared to be only a couple hours left of sunlight. Meaning, it was time for all the long speeches, traditions, and formality before the Choosing.

I said my fair wells to Fiona, it was nice to see her. I actually liked her being quiet. Not that I preferred women to be quiet, in fact, I found that strength was one of my favorite qualities in women. But I liked that she listened to me. Very few conversations felt real. Fiona felt real.

I made my way to my tent, where I would most likely be fed, groomed, and pampered. Then given the instructions and protocol for the Choosing Ceremony for the hundredth time. Along the way, I stole glances all around me. I didn't know why not seeing Amira bothered me so badly. My mind kept going back to the dream I had the night before. What did it mean?

I excused my servants and guards to spend a few moments alone, pleased that they allowed it, even though I knew they were all just outside my tent. Still, to finally be alone.

I sat back in a chair that they had brought into my tent. I released a deep breath and slouched into the chair letting it encompass me. I lifted my feet onto the table in front of me, knowing the trouble I would get into if my mother saw me.

Finally... Peace and quiet.

I must have begun to drift off to sleep because the tapping on my shoulder nearly sent me rolling out of the chair. It wasn't often I was caught off guard. And who would tap me on the shoulder unannounced?

Of course, it was her. She was the queen of sneaky.

The shock from being awoken suddenly was scarce in comparison to the shock of seeing her dressed so...beautifully. I was at a loss for words. For a moment I felt like I was dreaming again. My eyes glazed over and I stood motionless.

I felt a sharp pinch on my arm.

"Aryn? Hello?" She had pinched me. Actually pinched me. So, I wasn't dreaming.

"Amira?"

"Of course, did you think I wasn't going to come say hi?"

"How...how did you get in here?"

"Are you kidding? It's me."

"Right."

We were both quiet for a minute. That seemed strange. Since when is Amira quiet?

"How are you?" She asked.

"Good. I'm good." Why did she look so different today? She looked like a bride. She was even wearying makeup. I felt weird that I knew that, but I knew her face well.

"I'm sorry I didn't come by sooner...I overslept."

My eyes narrowed. Since when did Amira oversleep?

"Mir-"

"Ren," She cut me off, "look. I wanted to-"

"It's almost time." Tauren busted in before either of us could say anything.

"Could we have a moment?" I demanded.

"Queen Beatrice says it's time." He replied in the same demanding tone I had used. It was infuriating.

There was something in Amira's eyes. She seemed nervous. Had she put her coin in the chest?

Suddenly my heart pounded faster at the thought. Why had the idea excited me so much?

'It's nothing, you should go. Good luck…Prince Aryn." She said with a low bow. I couldn't tell if she was being sincere or not.

I fought the urge to stay, to ask her if she had entered her coin. However, people started crowding in my tent, straightening my collar and sashes, positioning my hair just right. One lady even tried to put powder on my face but I quickly waved her away.

"Now," Tauren demanded.

I didn't like being talked to like that, but it was time and I knew it. The sun stung my eyes as I exited the tent. The light was blinding. I was lead onto the royal platform like a show pig, and I played the part.

CHAPTER ELEVEN

The Tales of the Seven Kingdoms

Aryn

The pounding of my heart sounded as if it were the beating of drums. The heat of the sun bore down on me. My palms were damp with sweat and I wiped them on the drapes of clothes I wore. A Prince does not sweat, I thought to myself, unless in competition or battle. It would help if I could take off some of my dress clothes. There seemed to be enough layers to last someone a week.

My mother and father were already on the stage. Most likely, my father had been there throughout the entirety of the day having people fan him and bring him any measure of food and wine. My mother, on the other hand, had probably been on the move all day. Between sizing up the eligible women, smooth talking her allies, and keep an eye on the entire affair, she was a busy woman. I could at least respect her work ethic. Maybe ethic was the wrong word, but the woman was strong and wise if nothing else.

It was strange to see my throne in the middle of the other two. Usually, the King's throne was the center while the Prince sat to his right and the Queen to his left. Today was the first time the thrones had been switched. The King's throne now sat where mine once had. The snarl on my father's face clearly showed that the set up was my mother's doing. And that's how it would be from there on out.

I wondered for a moment where my bride would sit. For today, there was an elegant throne placed off to the side. Since she would not be a royal until the wedding, her place was not yet with the royal thrones. It was an ideal setting, almost giving her a different spotlight. Whoever was picked would become a sort of celebrity.

I took my seat on the throne. There would be a long, boring set of rituals and speeches. As if the festivities of the day hadn't been enough. The Dator was the one who was supposed to do the introductions and speeches. I was to give the retelling of the Seven Kingdoms just before the time to select the lucky coin. Speaking in front of people came easily to me, but that didn't stop me from rehearsing months in advance.

After the Dator introduced the most important people, he made a surprising announcement. This was his last attending ceremony. He introduced a younger man, maybe in his thirties. He wore the same white robes as the Dator, but it looked strange on him. I had seen this man around the castle but not known who he was. Unlike all previous Dator's, this one was young and handsome. It was strange to see a young man with a straight back and no wrinkles. Usually, Dators were at least fifty when chosen and remained a Dator until death or retirement.

Why had I not been informed of the change? It seemed rather strange that I had no hand in selecting this new Dator. This was not the time for a spectacle, and I refused to show surprise. It did ease my mind that I could, at least, understand this man's words. The previous Dator was so old, his voice was hushed and trembled. I strained to hear him and feared I would miss my cues. Maybe that was a part of the reason for the sudden change.

I fought to pay attention to all the formalities. I struggled to keep my eyelids from drooping, trying not to fall asleep in my chair. I soon saw the Dator turn toward me and hold out his hand. Stars! Was that my cue?

I rose confidently. Even if it wasn't my cue, I could easily act like I was about to interrupt, or even just ask for a glass of wine for my parched throat. All eyes were on me. I nodded at the new Dator, then greeted him formally. As I stepped in front of the massive crowd my eyes casually searched for Amira, but I was not able to see her among the crowd.

"Thank you. Lords, Ladies, and People of the Kingdom for bearing witness to this most special of days."

I waited for the clapping to slow.

"Before we begin, it is custom to recite the Tale of the Seven Kingdoms. A favorite among us all. This story is a part of the history of the people…"

The crowd erupted in cheers. The whole point of telling the story was to inspire people. It was to remind them that everyone had a place in the Kingdom. With rebel groups causing mayhem, it was of the utmost importance to reiterate the importance of the coin system.

"On this day we honor our Creator. The source of all. He created a perfect world, Straterra, and came to live among his people, but some envied his mighty power. After a thousand years passed, hatred, envy, and war emerged from the land. The people took to separate lifestyles, drifting away from each other. Each group of people thought they were better than the others. They believed their people should rule.

When the Creator had enough of the fighting he devised a plan. He traveled the vast land to seek three righteous families from each of the six groups of people and told them to travel to the center of the land, a place called Tarkania.

Upon the meeting of the eighteen families, the Creator raised his staff and spilt the land into six separate continents.

The land in which they stood became known as Tarkus. The people of Tarkus were full of wisdom and knowledge. Libraries spread across the land. The people encouraged education and the retelling of history.

To the left fell Picis, consisting of the bay of Straterra. The people were well practiced in the art of fishing and boat crafting. At first, they fared the best. They were the only people who knew how to travel in water and eat from the sea.

Venatures fell to the far right. This land consisted of hunters and warriors. Strong men and women skilled with weapons in a land teeming with animals.

To the far North lay Montis. Montis was a cold, harsh, mountainous environment. These families were harsh and could survive the cold weather. They mined the mountains for precious materials.

Just above Tarkus was the land of Arurum. These were the crafters and entertainers. Since they split from under Montis, many gems and fine metals were left among the shores. They prided themselves on being the wealthiest and most beautiful of people.

The last kingdom, Medici, stretched to the Northern part of the East. The weather was pleasant and vegetation plentiful. With the herbs and plants surrounding them, they became the healers."

The crowd seemed to be listening intently, despite the few cheers and shouts. I took a moment for a dramatic pause. I was well studied in public speaking. It was the area in which I excelled the most, yet even with its benefits, my father was less than pleased.

"The Creator's purpose for the great split was so that each group of people could rely on one another. The people of Picis provided fish and boats, Montis produced metals and gems, Arurum administered fine goods, Venatures contributed meats and cloaks, Tarkus held great information and wisdom, and Medici accommodated herbs and knowledge of healing. Each kingdom needed the other.

That was until the fighting broke out again. The people placed value on what they sold. The fight for power grew.

Picis fared well, selling their crafter boats and regulating the trade of the Sea. But rising prices and regulations made trade difficult.

First, the Kingdom of Montis fell. Although it was perfect for shelter and provided great protection, the weather was often unsteady and vegetation rare. Without trade, the population fell and people became desperate for outside sources of food. Their hearts became cold as the stone mountains that surrounded them.

Aurum had once been the richest of all the lands. People dressed to extravagance and lived for entertainment, but beauty is fleeting and unavailing.

The other three kingdoms soon followed behind.

The great Creator continued his plan to start anew.

The Creator gathered the chosen families and created a seventh and final kingdom, Astrean."

The crowd broke into cheers again. Obviously Kingdom moral still remained. As I spoke I kept my eyes on the crowd and my shoulders straight. I was proud of my decision to not read from a scroll. I had the crowd in my hands.

"Astrean, the wealthiest and most beautiful of the Seven Kingdoms." I paused for applause. "Blesses, beloved, and plentiful in all things." The cheering had become less enthusiastic than before, leading me to speed up the ending. "But all was not well. Again, the fight for power grew. The Creator had taken a step back, unwilling to lead the people. With the people clueless as to who should lead, the Creator devised a plan.

To make the land run smoothly, each person should hold a specific purpose. He brought all of the people to a magical cave and told them to bring a single golden coin each. One by one the people placed their coin under the water that flowed from above. When the coin was once again held it would reveal their destiny.

That was how this began, and how we still see things today. With our destiny shown to us, we may all live in peace and harmony, knowing each person serves a purpose in the kingdom. I take immense pleasure to know that I have been chosen to rule over this great land and promise to be the great leader that I was destined to become."

Cheers came from the crowd again, but it was easy to notice that most of the cheering came from ladies. I took a step back and nodded toward the Dator to continue his duty.

"Prince Aryn Cynrick Raeghann Karoly, Son of His Majesty King Ezra Durrell Evrard Karoly and her highness Queen Beatrice Arrarius Karoly. The time has come to choose a bride for Astrean." The crowd applauded, shouts filled the air. The Dator raised his hands to settle the commotion. I stayed as still as I could manage.

A dizziness crept over me. It felt like déjà vu.

"Prince Aryn. If you will, please stand before the Ark of the Coins to receive the coin of your chosen mate."

I had expected the crowd to applaud and shout again, but not this time. It was quiet, save for the shuffling and movement of the people in the crowd. I sensed that they were as anxious as me.

I slowly turned my back to the crowd, the only way I could stand in front of the chest. I had practiced many times before so that my foot hit the hidden lever precisely without anyone to suspecting anything. Even though the mechanics of it were rigged, the coin was still chosen at random. Destiny would decide which coin landed in the golden palms. I swallowed hard, my Adam's apple clearly visible making me glad I was facing opposite the crowd.

My foot found the lever easily and hit its mark. The water falling from the fountain was mesmerizing. Spilling out from the water was the coin. I nodded once toward the Dator. Getting the go ahead, I reached for the coin. I gripped it tightly, slowly opening my hand to reveal its secret. I saw the royal crown, same as mine. I already knew whose crest would be on the other side. I turned to face the crowd, proudly revealing the family crest on the back side of the coin. I passed the coin to the Dator and he held it high.

"House Kuval."

Shock spread through me. My knees trembled and my head spun. That wasn't right. House Pallas. Amira Pallas. I pulled myself together, not allowing myself to even flinch. I clenched my teeth and swallowed hard.

It had been just a dream.

This was a reality.

CHAPTER TWELVE

The Choosing

Amira

That was it. The Choosing was over. The princess had been selected. Time appeared to slow down. People were cheering, but I heard only silence. I made my way closer to the platform just as the ceremony was taking place. I felt a need to be near Aryn. For support, possibly. My hands had begun to tingle right before the selection. I tightly gripped my hands together. I found it hard to breathe.

Then, she was chosen. A girl. Just some girl. I didn't know her, but she had seemed familiar. I thought I had seen her around the castle, but I knew all of the palace ladies and servants.

Pretty. I guessed. If you liked redheads.

As the girl approached the platform, my gaze fell back on Aryn. Maybe I had imagined it, but he seemed to have gone pale. A smile filled his face, but I could tell it was forced. Aryn had a smile like no other. With one almost unnoticed dimple on his left cheek, his smile was always a little lop-sided. Heavier on his left side which made his eye squint slightly. The smile he held now was perfect. Too perfect. I wished I could read his mind. All I wanted was for Aryn to be happy.

The girl, Fiona, seemed genuinely happy and surprised. There was something regal about the way she held herself as if she had been raised a lady, but she also appeared humble. A Kuval…out of all of the houses. Of course, a girl from a wealthy house had been chosen.

The rumors of sabotage tickled my brain. Whispers had been circulating for as long as I remembered. Reports from unseen figures held speculation about the royal family. I hadn't always been religious, wishful at times, but rational.

The idea that coins could be chosen at random always seemed ideal to me, at least there was some chance for those who had wanted to advance. Maybe it wasn't some all-knowing sorcerer choosing who would rule, but at least it was left to chance rather than people. Although, if it were left to chance, why were the chosen royalty always from either nobility or wealth. Studying wasn't my favorite thing. That was Aryns's alley of interest, but that didn't mean I couldn't recall most of Astreans written history.

Why was it that farmer's daughters, fishermen's daughters, or even palace ladies were never chosen? It seemed that every royal ever chosen brought something to the table or castle.

Maybe I was reading too much into this. Maybe that was why she was chosen. If there is some divine intervention involved, maybe the Kuval girl was right for the job.

My face scrunched and my lips turned down. I hated referring to Aryn's future wife as a job title.

Celebration was in the air. Even families who had not been chosen were still in a festive mood. These festivities often resulted in marriages soon to follow. It was the perfect place to make trades. Goods and daughters. The thought disgusted me. I stood among a breeding ground. The cheering, rushing of people, and slushing of alcohol all around made me dizzy.

I needed fresh air, but the streets were crowded for miles around.

Perhaps I was more tired than I had anticipated. Maybe I just needed to lay down, I hadn't gotten much sleep the night before.

The commotion had unwound my carefully braided hair and the skirts of my dress had become filthy from the streets. Why had I worn something so fancy? This dress was supposed to be special. I should get back to my room and scrub the dirt from the hem. Maybe if I let it soak it would be good as new. I felt frustrated and wondered why I hadn't just sold such a fine dress. Surely that would have helped me to earn wages toward my dowry. The sooner I paid it off, the sooner I would be free.

I craved adventure. A life outside of cleaning, sewing, and reading by the fire. Although I would never admit it, I envied my brother. Yes, he was forced to work in weaponry, but he enjoyed it. Even with the restriction of his place, he had more freedoms than I could ever hope for. Maybe that's what drew me so close to Aryn. We were both trapped. In a world where we were mere puppets. I craved nothing more than to cut myself loose of the strings. No one should make choices for someone else.

I had made it back to the palace. The sun was beginning to go down, but the glow from outside still filled the windows. Fires were set to keep festivities alive. Soon the royal party would move inside to the throne room where there would be more feasting, dancing, and celebrating. Maybe if I cleaned myself up I would find Haddy and enjoy the party indoors. That would give me a chance to see Aryn and maybe sneak a word with him. At the very least I would be able to size up the Kuval girl more closely.

I rounded the corner of a hallway on the way to my chambers and bumped into a large man with guard's armor. It felt like running into a wall. I stepped back in a hurry, tripping over my dress and falling backward.

"For the love of stars!" I cried out landing on my butt.

A hand reached down to help me up.

"I'm so sorry Lady Pallas. Forgive me. I was…" He stammered.

"Tauren?" What are you doing in the castle? Shouldn't you be in your little guard huddle babysitting Aryn." I winced when I said Aryn, hoping he hadn't noticed. I shouldn't speak of him so casually, no matter how casual our friendship was.

Tauren didn't seem to notice. In fact, he seemed nervous. I could swear I had seen him blush. The thought warmed me. The guards often flirted with the ladies when they could sneak a chance. Tauren had always been sweet with me. A side he didn't seem to show anyone else. I was surprised he wasn't already married. He was handsome and held a good job. Actually, he was more than handsome. He was downright rugged and savory.

With semi-long dark hair, tanned skin, and bulging muscles he could have any girl he wanted. True, he was a man of few words, but with arms and a chest like that who needs words? I felt my cheeks flush as well.

"Lady Pallas. You shouldn't be here. I thought you would be out celebrating with the other ladies." His voice was so stern. Was it curiosity or concern I heard in his voice?

"Other ladies?"

"They are…well…mingling outside of the castle."

"I'm not really a 'mingler'."

There was a heavy silence between us. It was like he wanted to tell me something, yet he stayed silent.

Pushing past him, "Excuse me. I should get going."

I felt a strong grip on my arm. My eyes widened. Guards were not allowed to touch a lady. Flirting was frowned upon, but touching was forbidden.

Tauren's eyes widened and his jaw separated slightly, a small breath escaping from his lips. He quickly removed his arm and clenched his jaw in knowledge of his mistake.

"I'm sorry lady Pallas. I only meant to..." He chose his words carefully, "I think you should stay in your room tonight." His brows furrowed. Why had he ordered me around?

I backed away from him in disbelief.

He stepped closer, but only slightly. He just stood there gazing into my eyes.

"Amira, I just want you to be safe. Promise me. Please."

I couldn't believe the way he was acting. I backed away further and turned on my heels, not looking back.

"Amira. Please." His voice was stern.

I hated being ordered around and now...by a guard.

I was headed toward my room, but something stirred inside of me.

I redirected my path to the throne room. I didn't care if I looked a mess, or if I felt tired. The last thing I wanted was to be cooped up. Surely by now, the party had moved indoors.

I was right. That was evident from the blaring music shaking the candles that led toward the large throne room used for a ballroom that night.

I slipped in unannounced. Attention would just make me feel like I was on sale at an auction, which was why most of the unmarried women here were dressed so nicely. If they hadn't been chosen as the princess, they would ensure they wouldn't leave empty handed.

I weaved through the crowd. I wasn't much for dancing unless you counted my fingers dancing along the buffet table.

Suddenly, the people around me slowed down and came to a stop. They cleared back against the walls, creating space in the middle of the room. A slower song was playing. Curiosity itched at my inner gut. Grabbing one more tart from the buffet table, I made my way to the front of the crowd.

They were dancing. Aryn and Fiona. All eyes were on them. They looked...nice. I squinted my eyes. That was definitely not the same dress she wore earlier and her hair was styled differently.

It was hard to read the expression on Aryn's face, but the girl was elated. The way she looked at Aryn... She was infatuated. It seemed sincere, like maybe she wasn't just after the throne. Aryn dipped her after a spin and there was a clear blush rising in the girl's cheeks. She liked him. Of course, she would. Why had I been so worried? What's not to like?

It was the way the Queen looked at the girl that scared me. Queen B would devour that little girl. Well, she wasn't little but she appeared so in Aryn's arms.

The Sun had set hours ago, my belly was now full, and I decided I wouldn't be able to get the chance to sneak a word with the Prince so I felt like heading back to my room.

At least, that's where I meant to go.

CHAPTER THIRTEEN

Interrupted

Aryn

Everything was a blur. I had been swept up in the celebration. Crowds of people congratulating me, people shuffling me about. The attention became dizzying.

After Fiona had made it to the platform and was told where to stand and when to wave, she was introduced to the kingdom. Even my mother and father greeted her before I had a chance to say even the slightest 'hello'. It felt strange to me that someone I knew was picked, then again, hadn't I just hoped that Amira would be chosen? And, I didn't know Fiona all that well. While still waving at people and acknowledging the cheers of the kingdom, I had a chance to look at Fiona. To really look at her. Not just her physical features, though I was presently surprised with her beauty. With just the two times I'd been beside her, she had genuinely seemed kind, caring, and smart. A little insecure, maybe. But her insecurity was refreshing compared to the women in my life who held strong opinions of themselves.

In fact, I found it cute how her face blushed a soft rose color. She pulled her hair together and moved it to her other shoulder. I could see that her ears were red as well. At least she seemed to understand how the attention could be overwhelming. I had hoped I wouldn't be paired with someone who loved the glory. I wanted a companion, not an ornament on my arm. Fiona could be that for me.

Before I had the chance to steal a private word with Fiona she was whisked away to be polished by her new handmaidens.

The sun was going down and time for the celebration to move indoors was near.

I was ready for the party to be over, not that I wasn't excited, but I wondered if perhaps I would be allowed a moment of peace with my bride to be before the nuptials. In other kingdoms, marriage was a business arrangement. Although this marriage wasn't arranged, it still felt like a business deal. My whole life was a business deal.

The Throne room was crowded. Packed with all the important Lords, Ladies, and wealthy families of the city. The palace maidens, the ones that were not otherwise engaged, were dressed to their best in hopes to fashion a match for themselves. The whole party, my party, was a business deal.

I stood by the door with my guards in tow. The shuffling of rushed heels filled the small hallway leading to the grand doors. I was finally met by Fiona and her maidens, along with even more guards now protecting the future Princess. The future Queen.

She was dressed in gold, jewelry dripped from her neck, and her hair was pulled away from her face in a more royal fashion. She certainly looked stunning. She also appeared nervous. I took her hand and gave her a reassuring nod just before the trumpets sounded and the doors burst open.

I let go of her hand and offered her my arm. She gently placed her hand in the tuck of my elbow as I lead her down the carpet to the thrones. This time, the King and Queen's thrones were placed in the middle with mine to the right and Fiona's to the left. That was odd to me. This was our engagement party, we should sit side by side. Since I would be ascending the throne at the end of the week, I should be in the middle. I had assumed my father and I would sit in the middle. My mother on the left, my father, myself, and then Fiona on my right. Rather, it was set up as if I was the prince and Fiona my sister.

Although Queen Beatrice stood applauding the entrance of her son and soon to be daughter in law, I could see the snarl on her face. Whether from the choice of the girl, or the fact that she had out shown the Queen was the mystery. The Queen looked beautiful and regal in her black and gold dress with sharp lines and diamonds. That was nothing compared to the young, fresh, redheaded beauty who would be ascending the throne.

Once we made it to our thrones the music began and the people danced. Dancing, drinking, and eating went on all night. Sitting on the opposite end of Fiona, I could feel every inch of the distance.

Finally, I rose from my throne. The crowd froze and the music stopped. The room fell silent. My mother's eyes burned with curiosity as she gripped her seventh wine glass of the night. I had been counting. My father was impossible to keep count of, but I knew how he would be at a party. My mother was the one to watch. Her moods were dependent on how much she drank and she rarely had too much in public. Tonight, she was pushing it.

I walked to my fiancé and held out my hand. She too had been gripping a wine glass most of the evening but had only taken a few sips.

"A dance with my soon to be wife?" I bowed slightly and extended my hand. No matter how much I tried to keep my hair from my face, even with my small crown upon my head, a few loose curls fell just above my eyes.

Fiona's eyes darted to the Queen and back to mine. Her hand shook as she handed the glass to a maiden serving her. She took my hand and stood. The room remained silent.

The sound of deep, drunk laughter cut the silence. My father burst into laughter and began patting his knee. He raised his glass and tried to stand from his seat, although it was obvious he was too large and had drank too much.

"A toast to my son!" The crowd erupted in applause and the music began again. The King sat back down and barked for another drink.

My father's toast to me had caught me off guard. Something warm filled me. This truly was a celebration.

The crowd made room for us to dance. All eyes were on us.

"Take my hand, I'll lead you," I reassured Fiona. Despite wearing heels, she had to look up to see me. She placed her hand in mine. Her hand was so soft and small. Even with the work she had done around the castle, her hands remained as smooth as silk.

A chill rain up my spin. It was a good chill. Excitement. Although she had been doused with perfumes, I could still smell the scent of sweet mint around her. I closed my eyes and breathed it in.

Fiona bit her lip as we spun around. Her eyes darted around the room, glancing at all of the people looking directly at her. "Focus on me. It will help. I promise. Pretend no one is here. It's me and you. I'm not a prince.

I'm Aryn, just Aryn. I saw you, a beautiful maiden and asked your hand for a dance. Just you and I under the moonlight." I smiled. It wasn't a fake smile. In fact, it was hard to contain it. She smiled back, cheeks blushing. From then on, her focus was on me.

Fiona and I only had time for a few dances before we were interrupted by more people congratulating us. A nobleman had pulled me aside to discuss a few things, which I hardly paid attention to. I knew everyone here was trying for as much time alone with me as they could manage, trying to remain on my good side for when I took the throne in a few short days.

What worried me was that I had spotted my mother talking with some of the Kuval family. Maybe she was seeking information to disqualify Fiona. But, the fact was, she had already been chosen. No turning back now.

I knew little of the Kuval's. Fiona's mother was fair with pale skin and blond hair, while her father had deep red hair and a fierce beard that made him seem almost wild. They had been a family of old money, who lost their fortune but recently regained it and then some. Like me, Fiona had no siblings. It seemed there was little to learn from the Kuval family.

Now my mother had taken Fiona aside. Fiona appeared to be terrified but maintained good posture and a straight face. It was her eyes I was trying to read from afar. I wouldn't dare let my mother intimidate my bride. I excused myself from the Lord I was talking with and made my way to Fiona.

"Mother, Fiona. How is everything?"

"Fine, dear. Everything is splendid. Fiona is tired and will be sent to bed, as I assume we shall all retire soon. You have a big week ahead of you." She stared down to Fiona, then kissed my forehead as she had when I was a baby. The gesture surprised me.

"Very well. Good night mother. Fiona. May I walk you to your room?" Of course, she had a room at the palace, she was a maiden here, but now she had a chamber all to herself. The Princess suite. I hoped it wouldn't be too much of an adjustment to move away from her family, but she had already lived here for at least a few days. It seemed so easy. She had already said goodbye to her family and moved her personal belongings to the castle.

"That won't be necessary," My mother said, "Her guards will escort her. You two shouldn't be seen alone together until after the wedding."

"Of course." Fiona said, bowing to the Queen. My mother lifted her head slightly, raising her nose and narrowing her eyes.

"Of course." I replied, looking back at Fiona. "Good night to you. May you have a pleasant night's rest?" She smiled sweetly and bowed. I bowed my head in response. It all felt very formal. She was taken away by her maidens and guards.

"Time to retire, I suppose." I waved to my guards that had been only a few steps from me the entire night. Tauren had taken the early shift and was either on break or off duty, this made me more relaxed. Some of the other guards were a little less uptight.

I made my way back to my room. One of the guards did a quick sweep of the room before I dismissed them and gave instructions to not enter the room unless in distress. I hated being babysat. Although, I knew there would be a minimum of two guards directly outside my door all night and several more posted around the hallways entrances.

As the door shut, I lit one of the lanterns and began undressing to my night trousers. I insisted that my maids take the night off. I could undress myself. The room was dark, quiet. It was near midnight. I moved the lantern to my night stand and pulled back my bed sheets.

"Boo!"

"What the…" I closed my mouth before the guards discovered that I was not alone.

A silhouette of a woman lay on my bed.

It had frightened me, but I had recognized her scent long before I could make her out with my eyes.

"What are you doing in here?" I whispered.

CHAPTER FOURTEEN

Hidden Walls

Aryn

"I wanted to check on you, this was the only place I could hide. Do you really need this many pillows?" Amira snickered tossing one in his face and moving to the far edge of the bed to put some space between us. I felt a little less uncomfortable now.

Realizing that I didn't have a shirt, I moved to my chest which held my night shirts. I quickly grabbed the first one I saw and slipped it over my head. "So, you thought you would sneak into my room? What if you had been caught?"

"I would have just said you sent me on an errand," She smiled narrowing her eyes, "And you would have stuck up for me." She was right. I'd always cover for her.

I sat on the top corner of my bed, careful to keep distance between us. We both knew how it would look if someone came in and we were in bed together. I would lose my credibility and Amira, possibly her life. At least, life as she knew it if nothing else.

"So?" I questioned, knowing there must be a reason for her intrusion.

"So... How are you?" She sat pulling at the strings on one of my fancy pillows. She wore a fancy dress. Her hair was a mess that only made her that much more beautiful. She wasn't the same little girl I grew up with.

"Fine. Why?"

"Fine? That's all you have? No. I'm your deepest, closest friend. Spill the details. I want to know everything."

Something didn't seem right with Amira. I couldn't quite place it.

Of course, she would be curious about how I felt, but the air was heavy around us tonight. Even though I sat so close to her, she felt further away than usual. Amira was always 'far away' in thought, but never like this.

"What are you thinking?" I laid on my bed with my head propped up by my elbow. I had never had a woman in my bed, even though it felt strange, I was more comfortable with her than anyone else. My mind flashed to images of my honeymoon that would come in simply a few nights. It caused me to sit back up and clear my throat.

"It doesn't matter what I'm thinking. What are you thinking?" She crossed her arms and held a firm tone.

"About Fiona?"

"Sure. About Fiona, about any of this."

"What do you think of her?" I asked.

"It doesn't matter what I think. I'm not the one marrying her." She relaxed a little and scooted to the top of the bed to lean against the pillows covering the headboard. We were closer now. I could smell her spicy cinnamon scent and it tingled my nose and sent a current through my body. I tried to appear relaxed, as if my body wasn't responding to the beautiful woman in my bed. I leaned back against the pillows on my side facing her. We lay together in the same bed separated only by space. "I think you can do better," She bit her bottom lip, and her eyes grew wider. "but I think you could also do worse."

"I think she's nice," I said with an encouraging smile. Was I reassuring her, or myself?

She stood abruptly. "Well, that is lovely. I'm glad."

I stood to the opposite side of the bed. "What? What did I say?"

"Nothing. You didn't say anything. It's late I should go. I just wanted to check on you, and you seem fine. So good night." She made her way to the door just as it swung open.

"Amira! What are you doing in here?" Tauren warned.

My heart nearly stopped. "You should have knocked!" I demanded, trying to appear natural.

Tauren glanced back and forth between Amira and me. He settled his glare back on me. My chest rose high and my body tensed. His hand still clung to the sword attached to his belt. Surely, he wouldn't hurt Amira. Was his intention to hurt me, the Prince? His hand fell away from his sword and made a fist at his side. Tauren began to take a step toward Amira, but I stepped in between them.

"What is your business here guard?"

Tauren kept a straight face and never took his eyes off of Amira. "You need to get to your room before—" He stopped.

Amira stepped forward. "Before what?"

"You shouldn't be in the Prince's quarters anyways. Especially not tonight. I'll escort you back to your room immediately."

"What about the other guards? Won't they see me?" Amira tilted her head.

"Just come with me." He grabbed her arm.

I shoved Tauren off of Amira, even though Tauren was as solid as a statue.

"Keep your hands off of her. And where are the other guards?" I shouted, "Guards!" No one came. Something was wrong. I stood in front of Amira blocking her from my guard.

She stepped aside. "Tauren! What is happening?" She said so fiercely I could almost see that Tauren flinched.

Tauren looked down, almost as if he were lost for words. "The castle is under attack."

"Where are the guards? Why have the alarms not been sounded?" I yelled running for my sword and boots.

"Aryn what are you doing?" Amira screamed.

"This is my castle, no one's taking it. There are innocent people here." My eyes grew wide with fear. "My mother and father?" I questioned Tauren. If the castle were under attack, my parents were the highest targets.

"I don't know…" He was still choosing his words carefully, it was easy to tell. "I came to get you and saw Amira here. She should be in her room. It's safer there."

"She needs out of the castle, she's not safe anywhere here."

"Excuse me? Me not safe? I'm just a girl. You're the Prince. Tauren, get him out. Take the secret tunnel. Give me your dagger. I can hold them off."

I glared at Tauren, while he steadily held my harsh gaze. Tauren laughed for the first time that I had ever heard. Was this man drunk? "No. I'm getting you out of here." Tauren said swooping her in his arms.

Something arose in me. I wasn't sure if I could trust Tauren with

Amira. I wanted her close to me. What would I do if something happened to her? I tightened my grip on my sword. Amira struggled to break free of Tauren and got a few hits in, which seemed to impress more than hurt him.

"Fine. There's a passage door behind my bed. Pull the bed away and it lies beneath the curtain. Take it as far as you can. There are several turns and doors keep taking lefts and you should find your way to the kitchen. Get her out of here. Do you understand?"

Amira bit Tauren's hand and freed herself. "I'm not going anywhere. Aryn. You need to get out. You're the Prince, the leader"

"That's right, I'm the leader. It's my job to make sure my people are safe. At any cost."

"You would risk your life for a servant?" Tauren stood amazed.

"I would risk my life for any of my people. What kind of Prince would I be if I didn't care about my people?" I paused and looked at Amira, "My friends."

We stood in a triangle facing each other trying to make sense of the situation.

Tauren handed over the dagger strapped to his belt. "Here take this." He drew his sword and backed away to the door. "I'll hold them off, you two get out of here." He looked longingly at Amira, then shifted his focus to me. "Protect her." He threatened.

"What? I can't leave. I need to get to the King and Queen." A sudden realization hit me. "Fiona. I need to get Fiona."

Footsteps stomping through the hallway signaled the approach of men.

"They will kill you Aryn," Tauren muttered. It was the only time he had called me by my name. I drew my sword. I couldn't leave my people. I wasn't a coward.

"Aryn!" Amira screamed and pulled on my arm. "We have to go. Please." Something about the look in her eyes. It wasn't terror, she was pleading with me. What would happen to her if I stayed and was defeated? She could be killed. Or worse.

With one more glance toward Tauren, I heaved my large bed away from the door and Amira slipped through. I followed after her. I was surprised she remembered the back tunnels. I had almost forgotten them. It made me feel silly that I hadn't taken them the night before as I snuck out.

I had hidden in the tunnel one time while playing hide and go seek with Amira and Lorin. Lorin had finally given up. Everyone was in a frenzy. Even the guards didn't have eyes on me. It was finally Amira who noticed the curtains behind my bed had been moved. She pulled it back revealing a secret door. I was never allowed to use the tunnel again after that. Somehow, she had still remembered it. Perhaps that was how she snuck into my room tonight.

As I slipped in following Amira, I heard the bed being pushed back in place. So long as no one noticed, the passageway would be safe. Unless Tauren spoke. I still didn't know if I trusted Tauren, but I trusted that he cared for Amira. The idea turned my stomach in knots.

I stopped and looked back as I thought about Fiona.

"What are you doing?" Amira did a bad job of whispering.

"What about Fiona?"

Her eyes narrowed. "She has her own guards now. There were like six last time I looked, and that's six more than you have."

I heard a noise that sounded like it was in the tunnel. The tunnels were cold and dark. Amira had grabbed my lantern by my bedside, but when she heard the noise she blew out the light and shoved me into a corner. I huffed because the wall behind me was rugged and rocky. That, and Amira was stronger than I expected her to be.

She held a finger over my mouth. Her hand was so warm. I shuttered at the touch of her finger across my lips. She pressed herself against me. I could feel the curves of her body. Every muscle in my body tensed, but I suddenly felt weak.

"I think it's clear." She said, as she backed away.

I didn't respond, I just stepped away from the wall and felt for her hand. Once I held her hand in mine, I led her slowly through the dark tunnels. Without the light from the lantern, it was almost impossible to see, which slowed our pace greatly. My eyes struggled to adjust. The tunnel had come to an end. So long as we took all the right turns, we should be near the kitchen. Now the hard part would be sneaking out in plain sight.

CHAPTER FIFTEEN

Nightmare

Amira

We had made it to the kitchen. My heart was racing. I told myself it was fear, but underneath I imagined it had been excitement. I was dressed too well to be a kitchen servant and Aryn, although in his night trousers and night shirt, stood out like a candle in the dark.

"Wait here." I said glancing at his sword and deciding not to take it from him. I still had the dagger Tauren handed me, but I never went anywhere unarmed. I also had a small dagger hiding under the skirts of my dress. I slipped through the hidden door in the pantry before he could stop me. It was dark. Quiet. No one was around. If the palace was under siege, it was a sneak attack. There was no telling if anyone had been captured or killed.

Once out of view from Aryn, I hiked up my dress to switch the daggers. Mine was lighter and easier to maneuver, but having a spare wasn't a bad idea. My small dagger wasn't much, but I was a small target and if I were quick enough, I could deal a devastating blow. Not that I had ever struck a person before.

The laundry room was near the kitchen. If I could sneak to the laundry room I could get some robes and cloaks so we might conceal ourselves better. I slipped along the walls as quietly as I could, wishing I had worn different shoes. I slipped my feet out of the heels I had worn that day. Barefoot wasn't safe, but it was quiet. And I liked to be barefoot. It was easier to maneuver.

Footsteps approached, from the sound I could tell it was only one soldier. What I didn't know was who they worked for. He made his way to the kitchen, lighting a few lanterns with the torch he held in his hand. With quick thinking, I stepped forward and hid my dagger behind my back. He appeared to be a palace guard, one I had never seen before. I was still unsure of his intentions, but never liked to show all the cards in my hand at once. To him, I would appear merely a lady of the court, perhaps out for a midnight snack. Harmless.

His curious eyes met my hard gaze. He looked me up and down, pausing for a brief moment on my chest. I felt disgusted and my grip tightened firmly around the dagger. He stepped forward and lowered his sword. A cheeky grin covered his face.

"Why now, what do we got here?" As he took another step closer, I moved further back. "I don't mean you no harm, my lady." He placed his sword in its sheath and switched the torch from his left hand to his right, allowing the flames to light parts of his face more clearly. He stepped closer, holding out his hand. "Aint no need of being shy. Plenty of girls are shy when they first meet me. They always warm up." He was close enough to place his hand on my face, sizing me up.

I had already sized him up. I knew the kind of man this was. His rotten breath now heavy upon my face. He slowly lowered to the ground to set his touch down. He had other intentions for his hands. He rose even slower than he lowered, pausing with his face but an inch from my chest. I held my breath. If I had inhaled, my chest would have risen closer to his face. He stood tall and raised his hand to cup my breast.

"I wouldn't do that. I'm a lady."

He smirked, "That's what they all say." He began to undo his trousers.

"Don't!" I was glad Aryn could not see or hear us.

The man pushed me into the wall and covered my mouth. "No need for screaming."

"I'm not the one who will be screaming." He didn't listen, he began to kiss my neck. I fought the urge to close my eyes. Instead I plunged my dagger into his side purposely missing any vital organs. Knowledge a lady wasn't supposed to have in the first place.

He backed away shocked, covering his wound and looking down at the blood. "You little—" I cut him off by driving the hilt of the dagger against his head, knocking him to the floor. He lay face down. Blood trickled around his body, forming a small puddle of red on the stone floor.

Hands trembling, I stood frozen. I willed my body to keep moving…to run away. Still, I had to know if I killed him. I circled the man, searching for other weapons he may have carried. I wouldn't make the mistake of being taken by surprise. I bent down, keeping as much distance as I could between us. I placed my fingers on his neck.

He still had a pulse. It shouldn't matter if he were dead or not. He was scum. I released a breath of air, unsure of how long I had been holding it in. I noticed a brand on his arm. Unable to fight the urge, I lifted his sleeve. A fisherman. Not only was he not a guard, he wasn't even a soldier. My eyes darted across the room and I found his sword. "I'll take this."

I placed my dagger back beneath my skirts and held the sword close as I snuck around to the laundry room. As I neared the door I saw blood trickling from the frame. My breath caught. I readied my sword and slipped into the room. It was dark, but not dark enough that I could not make out the scene in front of me. The blood wasn't from a guard or an enemy. I fell to the floor and dropped the sword, without thinking about the sound that resonated loudly from the metal hitting the stone floor. Tears stung my eyes and my heart clenched. I couldn't find my breath.

"Haddy—" The name caught in my throat. I reached down to check for a pulse.

Nothing.

It was pointless to check. Her throat had been slit.

Haddy wore a white gown and robe, both soaked in her deep red blood. Her eyes remained open, haunting me. Haddy's robe had been torn off and her dress shredded, exposing her dainty legs. I clenched my teeth as hard as I could, suppressing a scream. Not of fear but of anger. The horrors that had been done that night stopped at murder, but that wasn't all that had happened to my dear friend.

Thoughts rushed and crowded my mind.

The Prince. I believed in him. He needed to get to safety.

I carefully closed Haddy's eyes and draped a fine linen over her body. I paused before the linen covered her face. I glared at the blood-soaked coin around Haddy's neck. Carefully maneuvering my fingers to unhinge the clasp, I allowed the coin to fall into my hand. I held it tightly and finished covering my friend. She deserved a proper burial, but there was no time. Swallowing my grief, I moved forward. I grabbed an old cloak for Aryn and one for myself. My once beautiful dress of white and lavender was now blood soaked along the hem. I turned to leave the room, but not before finding a good pair of work shoes that would have to make do, even if they were too large.

I blew the flames from the lanterns, making the room grow even darker and saying goodbye to my sweet Hadassah.

All was not quiet. From behind came a shuffling sound and the light of flames. I turned quickly placing my sword to the intruder's neck.

"Mer. It's me. What happened?" His eyes grew large as the torch he carried dimly lit the room. His eyes fell on the blood at the bottom of my dress.

"I told you to stay!"

"I didn't hear from you. I thought…"

"Put these on, we must leave."

"Mer, what happened?"

"What do you think?" My voice screeched higher than usual.

A moment of silence passed between us. A thought arose in my mind like the flicker of a flame. The flame of the torch reflecting my hatred. "First I need to take care of something." I headed back to the kitchen. Aryn caught my arm.

"He's passed out Mer. We need to go."

"Not until he's dead." I tried to break loose.

Aryn grabbed both arms and looked deep into my eyes. "First we get to safety. You have seen his face. I think we can make it to the throne room. If mom and dad are safe that is where they will be. It will be heavily guarded. We go there. He will pay. Publicly, not in the darkness of a kitchen."

My heart was racing and my eyes were wet. Our first plan was to make it out of the castle. He was right, we didn't know where we were going. Maybe if I could make sure the prince was safe, I could sneak back and take care of the fisherman.

I had seen how the fisherman posed as a guard. Something felt wrong to me. They made it in undetected. They might have had help from someone in the palace, maybe all of the guards were revolting. Nothing was certain, but I knew to trust no one.

"Do you trust me?" Searching Aryn's eyes, "If you trust me at all follow me. It's not safe in the castle."

CHAPTER SIXTEEN

Wondering Souls

Amira

The safety of the prince was of the utmost importance, yet I could not seem to leave my brother behind. Even for a few short hours.

The night was dark and surprisingly quiet, the attack was still just beginning. Shouts began to fill the night and lanterns were being lit, making it harder to hide in the shadows of the night. Lorin's quarters were just above his shop. It was nothing fancy. A small bed and a fire with a pot to cook with. It was small yet cozy. I had begged him to find a new place, somewhere safer. With the smell of smoke and fire lingering in the air, I lived in fear that his room would one day catch fire. Luckily, he had started to see my way. At least, he knew it was no place for a bride. Perhaps that was why had had not yet proposed to Rachel.

We approached the workshop but the doors were locked.

I knocked. "Lorin." I whispered.

If we were to escape we could use Lorin and his weapons. Maybe even a man or two who he truly trusted. "Lorin." I shouted a bit louder.

A thud came from upstairs. I gathered my sword carefully, knowing the two daggers were tucked safely under my gown.

Light filled the cracks of the old wooden door. The lock sounded and the door crept open. Lorin stood in his nightshirt, undone pants that he must have thrown on, and untied boots.

"Mer, what are you—your Highness," His eyes bulged and he bowed. "What can I—"

I pushed the door open further and slipped in.

Lorin's gaze passed from me to the prince and his face grew pale.

Aryn was dressed much like Lorin, a nightshirt and half undone pants with untied shoes, and a cloak. I was dressed in the gown from last night but now covered in blood. It was clearer to see in the dim light of the workshop.

Lorin rushed closer, pulling me into a hug. I was unsure what he was thinking. No doubt he was conflicted between wondering if I was injured or was having an affair with the prince... Or both.

"Are you hurt?"

"No...I'm fine, but... We need your help."

"I see," Lorin said solemnly looking toward Aryn.

"No. Skies no. The castle is under attack."

"What? Where are the alarms?"

"It was an inside job—"

"What about the King and Queen? Your Highness are you alright?" Looking toward Aryn again.

"I'm fine...but that's all I know. My bodyguard got us this far. We need weapons and men to storm the castle."

"No! We need weapons yes, and help...but we need to flee. At least until we know what's happening. Something is off. Something is wrong."

"I agree with my sister. You need to get to safety."

"I'm the Prince!"

"I understand that your Highness, but with all due respect. You are also the future ruler of this kingdom and I will stop at nothing to see to your safety. Quick, grab what you need. We'll need to slip out."

Aryn stood with his mouth open and eyes wide.

I bumped him and handed him a sack. "Go upstairs and gather some food for the night. We'll get everything else."

He stood motionless.

"Go now!" I yelled.

I didn't have time to play "Your Highness."

"Do you know anything about this?" I asked Lorin. He shook his head.

"How—" He scratched his head. "Are you sure about all of this? It's not just a drill or an act?" Just then the alarm finally sounded. I looked at Lorin with a stern face.

"Okay then. We don't have much time. You need to change. I…have a dress in a chest in my room. You can put that on for now."

My eyes grew wide. I fought the urge to scold my brother. Now was not the time.

"No questions, just get dressed."

I nearly ran into Aryn as I ran upstairs. "I'll just be a minute."

Aryn came downstairs with a sack of food.

"I'll take that, your highness."

"Don't… Just call me Aryn, please." Aryn began to turn his back and grab the sword he had accumulated earlier.

"Wait, Aryn. This is for you. It was for your birthday. Technically I was commissioned to make this for you, but I did make it special." He handed him a sword. It was unlike anything Aryn had seen or felt before. It felt strong yet seemed to weigh nothing. The handle fit his grip perfectly and was lined with jewels and carvings.

"She's beautiful."

"Treat her well, my friend. She's a beauty, but she's got a bite to her." Then he passed a glance back to me as I rolled my eyes.

"Boys, boys. Please. Let's go." I said as I jumped down the stairs in a clean, yet simple dress. I tried not to imagine that it had been left here by Rachel. I cringed.

Lorin blew the lights out as we snuck through the doors. We could head the same way we did the night before. Maybe make camp somewhere until morning. We had just approached the brush when we suddenly heard hooves coming toward us at a steady pace.

"Go!" Lorin whispered.

"Not without you." I gripped his shirt with my small hands, but he pushed me away.

"They know someone's out here. I can explain myself. But they can't see you. We don't know whose side they are on." The sound of hooves against the cool ground became louder. They were getting closer.

"Halt! Who goes there?" A small company of men, three or four, came closer with their lanterns lighting the night.

"Go." He shoved me away one last time.

Aryn grabbed my arm and pulled me down behind a tree, crouching above me and pulling his cloak over both of our faces. He covered my mouth with his hand. I was tempted to bite down but resisted the urge.

"I...I heard the alarm. I was scared. I fled. I apologize. I should have stayed behind to fight." Lorin fell to the ground with his arms raised for surrender.

"Seize him." The guard shouted.

I tried to fight Aryn off, but he held me down and stared into my eyes. His pleading look broke my heart.

"We will come back for him." He said gently. Once I settled Aryn sat down next to me. "I'm sorry."

"They are long gone, we need to go now." I said, quickly raising myself from the hard ground. I began walking, not waiting for Aryn to follow. I had been out in these woods before, but neither of us knew where we were going. We kept walking, even when it was too dark to see. Several times I felt him reach out for my hand, but I moved it away. Why did he make so much noise while he walked? He sounded like an elephant stomping on dry leaves and twigs.

We walked for hours with no real idea of which direction we were headed. One thing I noticed, the woods were becoming lighter. We were nearing an edge. Morning was just a couple of hours away. Had we really been walking that long? Neither of us had spoken a word since we began this trek through the trees.

"Hello?" A frail man's voice called out and a lantern's light peaked through the trees. "Is someone there?" We both crouched down until the man was in view. He pulled a wagon filled with vegetables and spices. He carried it behind him as if he were the horse. His back was crooked and he seemed tired. Two lanterns hung from posts on the small wagon.

I stood sensing he was of no threat to us. "We don't mean to startle. Were travelers...from the festival. We just... We got lost."

Aryn must have caught on because he hid his sword behind his cloak and held up his hands. "Please, let me help you. You must be coming back from the festival as well." From the looks of it, he hadn't made much profit, his wagon was still full.

"I don't mean to be any trouble. But please. If you are hungry help yourselves."

"No, we couldn't" Aryn replied.

"At least it would lighten my load."

Aryn smiled sweetly and took the cart from the man.

"Hey." He protested.

"Where to?"

"You really don't have to."

Aryn nodded toward the old man.

"This way. It's not much further. I'll have my wife cook you two up something special. Do you have a place to stay?"

I looked at Aryn.

"Fine. Then you can stay with us. Can't have a lovely couple such as yourself out here all night." He thought we were a couple. I played along and kissed Aryn's cheek, then hugged the man.

"Thank you so very much."

"I'm Edwin, and you are?"

"Hadassah." I swallowed hard then smiled, nudging Aryn.

He coughed. "Oh, I'm a… Ari—Arden."

"Arden." The man questioned looking him up and down.

"Clark, house Clark," I replied.

"Ahh. A scribe."

We both nodded.

"I was a servant at the palace. That is until I met Arden." I smiled.

After about an hour of chatting and walking, we made it to a small town. Mostly farms. The houses were spread far apart and there was little in between them. At least it wasn't likely that we would be noticed, or that word would spread.

Finally, we had come to a small house on the edge of town.

CHAPTER SEVENTEEN

Change of Scenery

Aryn

Edwin barged through the door, color filled his cheeks and a smile lit his face. Without hesitation, a rosy plump lady with grey hair braided behind her back leaped toward Edwin. He gently grabbed her withered hands and brought them to his pale lips as he kissed them. Her hands then reached up and cupped his face as she planted a kiss on his lips. They looked like a couple of young lovers who had been without each other for a time. The age on their faces seemed to melt away as they embraced.

The older woman stepped back and chuckled as if she were embarrassed. She made a noise clearing her throat and gesturing toward me and Amira.

"Ah. Yes. Yes. Sorry, my dear. I found these young ones lost, wandering the woods after celebrating the festival. I didn't think you would mind having a couple of extra for dinner." He said sheepishly. "Hadassah, Arden, this is Margret, my beautiful bride."

Margret blushed then wiped her flour-covered hands on her apron. Reaching out to Amira, she grabbed her hands warmly. "It is a pleasure to have such a lovely couple join us," She then studied me for a moment before taking a step closer and grabbing my chin in her hand for closer inspection. I held my breath. Perhaps I should have disguised myself better. "A fine couple indeed." She looked back at her husband.

I wasn't used to being touched like that. Studied. Yes, I knew it would be dangerous for the town's people if I led on to who I truly was, therefore I must adapt to the circumstances. Although, I preferred to remain quiet.

"That is very kind of you," Amira replied.

"These two youngins helped me bring the wagon in." He stretched his head and glanced toward the door. "We ended up having plenty left over. Thinkin' maybe we can cook it up in the afternoon and host a town celebration. It'd be a shame to waste the harvest."

"That's a lovely idea dear." Disappointment was hidden in her face. Edwin passed her a small bag of coins that barely jingled as he handed it to her. She smiled politely. "Good work dear. I imagine next year's harvest will outdo all others. This lot will do just fine to get us through the winter." She said nodding. I felt a sting of pain. She seemed content, but I saw from the size of the coin bag that it wouldn't be enough. Was this how the people lived?

I looked around the small cottage. It was comprised of only two rooms. Edwin and Margret were standing in the main room filled with a small kitchen, a table with two chairs, and a couple of chairs seated by a drafty window. There was one door which led to another room. I assumed it led to their bedroom. The floors creaked, a chill leaked through the old boards, but a small fire seemed plenty to warm the small space. Their whole house seemed smaller than my washroom.

Speaking of a washroom. "I don't mean to be an inconvenience, but would you mind showing me your washroom." The two glanced at each other.

"We have a shed out back to use. It's not far from the house. If you wish to wash up we can bring a tub out and warm some water for you. I'm afraid we usually wash in the kitchen, but maybe we can set the tub in the bedroom for some privacy. We have a well out back to fetch water."

I felt ashamed for assuming they had the same privileges as me. "Thank you, it's late. Perhaps in the morning."

"You shouldn't have waited up for me, the day is nearing and you haven't had any sleep." Edwin expressed with worry.

"You know I can't sleep if you're not here. We will simply get what rest we need, then begin the day. We have a big one ahead of us if we are to make use of the leftover harvest. Ed, why don't you head to bed and I'll make a pallet for these two to sleep on," She looked over at the two of us, "It won't be much, but it beats sleeping outside."

"That sounds lovely Margret. Why don't I help you?" Amira glanced at my cloak. I understood what she was trying to say. I carried a sword with me, finer than any in the world. Much too fine for a scribe to carry. I would have to hide it.

"I think I'll use the shed, if you don't mind my absence."

"Of course not, sweetie," I reached for a lantern and left out the door. "Pretty boy you got there." I overheard as the door shut. I then heard Amira laugh.

I made my way past the shed the old woman spoke of. By the light of the lantern, I found a distinct looking tree. Instead of growing straight, it seemed to spiral up. I dug a hole and buried the sword. I couldn't return with dirt covered arms so I made my way to the well and cleaned myself best I could.

When I returned, the room was empty, save for Amira. She had laid down on the floor near the pallet and used her cloak to cover her, she still seemed to shiver despite the fire.

"Mer—"

"Shhh." She whispered. "Haddy, remember."

"Right." I said stretching out and running my hand through my hair. "Umm... Haddy? Why are you on the floor?" Even by the light of the fire, I could see her blush.

"I can sleep on the floor just fine, you, on the other hand, couldn't handle it."

"I can sleep on the floor. You're a lady."

"And you're a prince."

I tried to hide my sheepish smile. "We could... You know... It's quite cold. We could share. I mean if you want. Or I could sleep on the floor. It's just...if they come out, they might wonder why we aren't sleeping together. I mean sleeping next to each other."

"Okay. Fine." She sat up and made her way to the edge of the small pallet of blankets that I figured could barely hold two people. She recovered with her cloak and faced the wall. I knelt down on the floor and laid down on the very edge, giving Amira enough space to be comfortable. I then grabbed the warm quilt and covered myself. I draped the remaining half of the quit over Amira.

"Good night Mer."

She didn't respond.

She was right, even on the pallet I had a hard time laying on the floor. Sleep didn't come easy, but eventually, it came.

A sweet smell filled my nose, awakening my senses. The sound of pots and pans brought me stumbling to my feet. I had forgotten where I was. It had all seemed like a dream.

"Arden. You're up… Finally."

"How long did I sleep?" I said regaining my balance.

"It's about an hour until noon." The old lady replied.

The kitchen was filled with smoke, the doors and windows were open, letting the smoke out of the house. The sun had been up and the weather turned warm again, leaving the slight chill of fall in the breeze. Amira was nowhere to be seen. Neither was the old man. I was confused and a puzzled expression grew on my face.

"She's helping Edwin in the field. Sit, have some food, you'll need your strength." I sensed there was something more she wanted to say but refrained from doing so. "It's quite warm out. We have a small creek running near the woods. It has enough privacy if you care to bathe. Perhaps Haddy could join you when she returns."

I coughed. "Oh. Ah. Thank you. I might head out there in a bit. This smells lovely. What is it?"

"A little bit of everything." She said bringing me a plate of a small portion of eggs and what looked like grits… I hated grits. It was rarely served in the castle, only when the royal family took part in a public fast for the people. Even then, we normally had a banquet afterward. "Just don't touch anything else. It's for tonight."

"Tonight?"

"I've cooked all kinds of treats, and some of the local neighbors have as well. We've planned a celebration to be held at the Kirkland's barn."

"Celebration?'

"I figured you knew." There it was again. Something about her I couldn't read. "A Princess was chosen. At least that's what I heard. But, you can't always believe rumors."

I shoveled the eggs into my mouth. They were a bit cold, but to my surprise they were the most delicious eggs I had ever eaten. I was sad to see there was only a small portion. Though I finished the eggs, my stomach continued growling. It would be rude to not touch the grits, so I took in the smallest bite I could. My eyes grew wide. They looked like grits but tasted like nothing I had ever eaten. There was a mixture of flavors, mostly sweet. It was more like a dessert. I piled spoonful's into my mouth until my plate was empty. Surprisingly, that small breakfast filled my aching stomach.

"Thank you. That was amazing." I sat at the table reflecting on my satisfying meal. Normally servants would take away my plate. I glanced back at my messy pallet of blankets. The lady seemed to be watching me. Studying me even. I stood up, grabbed my plate, and walked to a bucket of dishes.

"Just leave it with the others, dear. I'll get to them eventually."

I had never put away blankets before but figured folding them would be an easy task. I was wrong. In the end, they looked like I had just rolled them up and piled them on top of each other. The lady grabbed the pile and headed toward her room. "Lovely," She chuckled.

"I will head out and wash." I said in a demanding voice. "I mean if that is okay?"

"Of course. Just take a left and where the trees become thicker, you'll see the stream of water. It's quite fresh and shouldn't be too chilly."

I began to head toward the door.

I found the stream easily enough. It didn't have the privacy I was used to, but there seemed to be no one nearby. Still, I didn't want to be caught…vulnerable. I could still wash in my trousers. It wouldn't take too long to dry if I walked around a bit. Although, saggy wet britches are never comfortable. I undressed, leaving my clothes piled messily on the ground next to my boots. My feet hurt from wearying boots two sizes too small.

I imagined cool water as I entered. It only waist deep but had been warming with the sun. My body slowly adjusted. My mind flashed back to my large washroom with a sizable tub and running hot water. I missed the oils and soaps I had become accustomed to. As much as I thought I would enjoy this privacy, it felt foreign to me. I lost track of time in that stream. The water held a small current but was so unnoticed that the water seemed to still around me.

Eventually, I felt something slither against my foot. That was it. I was done. When I emerged, I longed for new clothes and something to dry myself. Had I really been that accustomed to privilege? I dressed, trousers still dripping.

I peered down at the nearly still water and saw my reflection. I was too easily recognized. We would have to find out if it was safe to make it back to the castle. I still had no idea if my parents were okay, if the soldiers had seized the castle, or if word of my fleeing had hit the surrounding towns. I shouldn't have left.

"Did you fall in somewhere?"

I turned to see Amira. She looked radiant, messy, but lovely. This look suited her. Any look did. "Just washed up."

"Good, you can keep watch while I wash."

My eyes grew wide as I stretched my hands behind my head.

"I'm not going to undress, silly. Stop acting so nervous."

"Nervous?"

"Yeah, you know. The stretching behind your head and messing with your hair."

"I don't do that." I snapped immediately placing my arms by his side.

She began to remove her dress and I gulped loudly then turned around.

"What a gentleman, but I'm keeping my undercoats on. Stop being so shy. We grew up together."

"Yes, but that's different."

"How is it different?'

"You're... Well, you're a woman now."

"Oh, you noticed, huh?" She said chuckling again. "Alright, just don't run off with my dress. I'd hate to walk back in this state."

"I would never."

"No," She laughed. "But I would."

"That's vile."

"But amusing."

"Right, well, how much longer?"

"I'm getting out now."

"That was quick."

"Yeah, I'm not as needy as you I suppose."

"Not funny."

I turned around as she was getting dressed. She had washed off the horrors of the night before. Her hair was dripping wet. She glanced into my eyes and I could see the hurt she was attempting to hide. I knew it was best to not bring it up, but there were some things we just had to discuss.

"Mer. We have to get back."

"We don't know if it's safe yet. First, we need to go into town and see what rumors are going around. That way, we have an idea of what to expect."

"We need to get back quickly… My parents—"

"And my brother!" Her voice broke. I knew she was trying to stay strong. Maybe she was right. Rumors must have spread by now. If we could find out what the people knew about the night before, we would know when and how to make it back.

"How do we find out?" I asked.

"The celebration tonight."

CHAPTER EIGHTEEN

All Work, No Play

Aryn

The couple, Edwin and Margret, were busy the whole day. They said nothing about the day before, no matter how many times Amira brought up T\the Coin festival. Maybe news hadn't spread this far yet.

Edwin had worked in the field all day and Margret in the kitchen. Amira had experience in the kitchen so she helped the lady. She seemed genuinely fascinated by what Margret could do. It was hard to tell if Amira was acting. She'd make a good actor. I just felt I was only in the way.

"Maybe I can go help Edwin."

"Sure. I bet he would love the help."

Amira just looked at me with amusement in her eyes. I wanted to stick my tongue out at her the way she always did to me, but I would've felt too childish.

Their land wasn't large, but I was surprised to see how much work went into running the place. I wasn't sure if the old man had slept at all. As I approached I noticed the dark circles under his eyes, the lines of darkened skin that were exposed to the sun, and the roughness of his hands.

"Could you use any help?"

"Ah! You're finally awake. Thought you'd sleep forever." He threw his head back laughing and his big straw hat fell on the dusty ground, creating a dust cloud. I bent over to pick up the hat. "Well… Let's see. I've fed the animals, manned the field, and fixed a few pieces of fence. Ah! I know. You can muck the pig sty."

I raised my eyebrow "Crap?"

The old man handed me a shovel and pointed toward a gated circle of pigs. "Even the dirtiest of jobs can be important. You have to clear out the crap to make room for the good."

"I see."

"Won't be a problem will it?"

"Of course not. I'll just have to wash in the creek again." I took the shovel and made my way to the pig sty.

Manning the shovel was more difficult than I had imagined. Even training with a sword didn't work the muscles I was using now. I grew hot as the day pressed forward. I removed my shirt and allowed the breeze to cool my bare chest. My hands cramped and bled, but this was such a simple chore. One I would not give up on. Even if it did STINK. My hair dripped with sweat, regardless of how many times I pushed it out of my face. I stopped to look at the ground. The longer I shoveled, the more the pigs added to the pile. It seemed as though hours had passed before most of the mess was removed.

I glanced at my arm while reaching for my shirt. I had gotten dark that day. Just one day in the sun had really tanned my skin. I was unsure of what time it was, but I thought it would be time to clean up and get ready to head for town. Especially if I wanted to have enough time to let my clothes dry.

The creek was warmer this time, yet I longed for the coolness of the morning to refresh my aching skin. I took my time walking back to the cottage. The heat of the day dried me quicker than I expected.

When I entered the house, Amira stood near the door, finishing her hair. She was braiding it in a way I had never seen before and lacing her hair with flowers. She looked like a princess. A princess that had been lost in the woods, but still…she was beautiful.

"Ready?" She asked before turning to see me. "Wow."

"Wow? Wow, what?"

"Nothing. You just look…different."

What did she mean by different? I had washed the best I could. Did I look bad?

"Well, you've finally finished. Great, it's time to head out." The old man said.

I just nodded.

"I'll help too," Amira added.

I looked to the kitchen, the smells were overwhelming. There was every kind of vegetable and fruit, a myriad of colors filling the room. That wasn't all. She had baked pies and pastries that looked better than anything I had seen. Maybe I was just hungry.

We loaded the cart and began walking toward town. Of course, we were walking. They wouldn't have had to pull a cart if they had a wagon. Thankfully the walk was nice. The woman went on and on about every topic you could imagine. With the old man's hands free, he walked hand and hand with his wife as they traveled. Again, I could see the young couple they must have been and still were inside their aging bodies. It was strange that they never mentioned having kids. I didn't want to pry. They seemed truly happy.

They soon arrived at a large barn. It had been emptied out and decorated with flowers and tables. People were gathered in groups, food was left out to be taken freely, and a small group of men formed a band with any materials they could find. The sun had begun to set and lanterns hung from ropes, filling the barn with a golden glow.

I looked to Amira whose eyes seemed to drink up everything in sight. She had been to palace banquets. Why did this seem to impress her so much?

"Well go on you two. There's plenty of food and stuff to do."

"What about the cart?" I asked.

"It's for the people. We all share here. Especially in hard times. We're all family. Like I said…this is a celebration. Go. Have fun."

Amira took my hand and ran toward the music. She let go of me as she began swaying and clapping. She was horribly off beat, but so was the band.

Shouts came from further in the barn, which of course piqued my interest. She took off leaving me behind. I decided to follow her to see what the commotion was. Groups of people, mostly men, crowded inside the rear of the barn. It was noisy and stuffy. Not somewhere I liked to be.

"I call next round!" Amira shouted. I frantically searched for her. She was laughing and holding something strange. "You. Me. Darts. Now."

"What?"

"You heard me. I challenge you to a game of darts."

"Games, we don't have time for games." I whispered, standing closer to her. We need information.

"Game, then interrogate." She said with a grin.

"Fine. One game." She handed me three small sticks that looked like arrows and pointed me to a wall with circles drawn around each other. It reminded me of shooting arrows, but there was no bow and these things couldn't be used for hunting. She threw one at the target and hit the smallest circle and shouted. She threw two more, both hitting near the same spot. Obviously, she had played this before and probably not in the castle. "What is the point of this?"

"Point? It's to have fun."

I looked at her then back at the board. I threw one but it landed on the ground. I felt ashamed. I strained my back and threw again. This time I hit the wall…but nowhere near the target. I was good at hunting, fighting, and sports. And yet, I couldn't figure this game out. I took a breath and threw one more. It hit inside the largest circle. I looked to Amira, trying to hide my disappointment.

"Here," Amira said while handing me the dart. She stood next to me with my hand in hers and guided it. I was angry she was trying to help, but at the same time her touch felt exciting. I let go of the dart and it hit the target. Right in the middle. I turned to Amira and we embraced. It was a quick embrace, she soon stepped back looking embarrassed.

"Right. I'm going to go talk to some of the women here. If anyone knows anything, it's them."

"Absolutely. I'll see what I can find as well."

Within minutes of splitting up, I saw Amira talking with some girls that must have been around our age. She made it look so effortless talking to them. She could talk the truth out of anyone before they knew she was even trying.

"Ouch." I bumped into someone.

"Are you okay sweetie?" It was the older woman, Margret.

"Oh, yes, of course. I was just—"

"Not used to life outside the palace?" She questioned.

"What? Oh…right! I scribe."

"Right…you scribe…" She repeated with her eyebrow raised.

"You know?"

"Honey. I may be old, but I'm not dumb."

"But how?"

"You mean other than you rumored good looks and odd behavior? Rumors of the prince fleeing have spread pretty quickly."

My jaw dropped. "But you—"

"Treated you like any other guest? Yes. If you wanted to pretend to be a commoner, we would gladly treat you as such." She grabbed my hand. "I will not ask why you fled, but I am sure glad to have met you. And you're lovely lover."

"She's not..."

"For whatever reason, you left. I just want you to know that the two of you are safe here in our town." She padded my hand again and her expression changed. "But, now that I know for sure who you are..." She trailed off then looked me in the eyes. A tear formed and slid down her face. "Honey. Although we are in the midst of celebrating a marriage that apparently won't happen, not everyone here knows, but there's something I heard." I just looked at her, waiting for her to finish. "Not all rumors are true. Edwin heard from a fellow seller that the castle was under attack." I nodded. "So, it's true."

"The castle, what news?"

She held my hand tighter and bit her lip. "The attack failed to come to completion. Most of the rebels were caught or killed. Rumor has it they kidnapped the prince. Although, that part doesn't seem to be true."

"Kidnapped?"

"What else. What are you not telling me? You've been keeping something from me."

"I didn't find out until later today." For the first time, she bowed her dead discretely. "The king is dead."

Those words hit like a knife. The king dead. My own father. I stood up and ran out of the barn doors. I made my way into the dark near the edge of the clearing and punched the nearest tree I could find. I didn't feel any pain, only blood running down to my fingertips. Everything went quiet. There was no more laughing. No more music. No more children running around. It was dark. Silence.

Someone shook me and turned me around. It took a second for my vision to focus again. Amira was standing right in front of me. She was yelling but I couldn't hear her. Suddenly I could make out what she was saying. All the noise began to return.

"Aryn... I don't. I don't know what to say. I heard... I assume you heard..."

My eyes burned. "I shouldn't have left. I could have... I should have—"

"No! You would have been killed too!"

I stepped away from Amira.

"Don't you walk away from me! Talk to me!" Amira pleaded.

"Don't talk to me like that! I'm the Prince!"

Amira stepped back. "You're the King." She whispered in a shaky voice.

King... I felt dizzy. I leaned against a tree and slid down. Amira leaped toward me and held me in her arms. I barely felt her embrace. I just sat in the darkness in front of her. Kings don't show weakness. I stood and turned away. Thoughts flooded my mind. There was one thing I knew for sure, I had to get back to the castle...to MY castle.

CHAPTER NINETEEN

Familiar places

Amira

Aryn stormed off into the woods. Dark, ominous clouds rolled in and thunder shook the sky.

"Ren!" Rain fell from the skies above. Puddles muddied the bottom of my dress as I ran toward Aryn. "Stop!"

"No! I have to get back."

Grabbing Aryn's arm, I pulled him toward me. Raindrops fell from my face and my hair stuck to my neck. "We can't just go back. Not yet. We can't even see anything." He pulled away harshly and kept trudging forward, as if the cold didn't faze him. I followed silently behind him. He just needed some time. As long as he stayed far from the castle, he would be safe.

The moon began to fade behind a cloud. The temperature had dropped since leaving the festivities. Bumps rose across my arms and steam came from my mouth as I breathed heavily. Aryn kept moving steadily forward. The rain came down harder than before. I couldn't even see two inches, in front of my face. My legs burned from keeping pace with Aryn. I was careful to watch my step and avoid slipping in the mud.

My foot caught on a fallen branch, sending me tumbling to the ground. Aryn turned immediately. "Mer!"

"I'm fine." I said standing up and feeling my way around the large branch. Surely, I had managed a few bruises from the fall, but nothing for Aryn to worry about.

Aryn reached out to me, finding my cold arm. How was he so warm?

"I'm sorry. I shouldn't have let you follow me. You're freezing."

"I'm fine. I'm not a little lady. I wasn't going to let you wander the forest alone. Especially when people are after you."

The rain slowed to a mist and the clouds drifted away. The light of the moon reflected off of a nearby lake of water. Crickets chirped and the hoot of an owl sent a shiver down my spine. I gazed at the lake, a sense of familiarity washed over me. "Is that?"

The low light of the moon allowed me to see Aryn's face as he squinted at the water. The lake was surrounded by rocks, a familiar waterfall near the middle that I knew I recognized.

"It can't be. Can it?"

We both walked closer to the water's edge. The air felt warmer here. Steam rose from the water's surface creating a magical, glowing mist. The same light bugs from before danced in the air.

"That's our cave." I insisted.

"No. We're nowhere near that spot."

"No... But it looks exactly the same."

"Coincidence."

I slipped off a shoe and dipped my toe in the water. My entire body relaxed from the warmth of the smooth water. It must have been a hot spring. I slipped off my other shoe and glanced around.

"I wonder..." I hesitated.

"What?"

"That waterfall. Maybe there's a cave behind it."

"I doubt it."

I slipped my shoes back on, hating the cold soggy feeling as I walked.

"Maybe there's another way in."

"In where?"

"The Cave."

"Amira... There's no—"

I disappeared behind a collection of fallen boulders.

"Mer!"

"Aryn!"

I heard him coming up behind me.

Darkness shrouded my view.

"Mer?"

"Here. There's a…it's like a trail." I slipped through a narrow breakaway of rocks.

"Amira. This isn't safe. Its pitch black. The rocks could cave in on us."

I placed my hand on the cold smooth rock as it led me deeper. The light bugs began to flutter in front of my face, tickling my nose. They provided short bursts of blue luminescence. The glow was hardly enough to see the step directly in front of me, but I had an urge to follow these tiny mysterious creatures. I imagined them as tiny fairies from old bedtime stories.

Footsteps echoed behind me assuring me that Aryn was close by. He must have felt the same silence resonating in him because he had stopped calling out. Finally, I felt warmth radiating from behind me and could hear the whisper of his breathing in sync with mine. Knowing the darkness was too heavy to see his face, I reached my hand out and found his. Although he must have thought I was mad, he continued to follow me.

Trickling water echoed ahead. A cool glow lit the edges of the rock, reflecting the damp walls. I was right. It was a tunnel. It led somewhere. Aryn's grip tightened around my hand sending warmth throughout my body. My damp clothes made the cavern seem cold.

The sound of crashing water grew louder. The wall of the tight tunnel led into a large open space. It was a cave. One that looked strangely similar to the one we had seen before, and yet it was different. Above us was an opening in the ceiling of the cave which let in the light of a full moon, allowing its radiant glow to reflect throughout the cave. There were small pools of steaming water which filled the cave with heat.

I let go of Aryn's hand and stepped toward a warm pool of water. I reached my hands out and felt the heat melt away the numbing cold. At least, the hand that wasn't holding on to Aryn's earlier.

Where had Aryn gone? He had slipped away from me. My eyes scanned across the cavern to find him slumped against a far wall with his head hanging low.

Unsure of what to do, for maybe the first time, I walked toward him slowly. There had to be something I could say to make this better, to ease the pain. I wasn't the talker, he was. I remembered how he comforted me after the loss of both of my parents. I knew their deaths had been hard on him as well, yet he had remained so strong. At least, in front of me.

I wouldn't have made it without Aryn and Lorin. I thought back to the words he had spoken to me, but nothing felt right. Honestly, what had mattered most to me was his strong presence.

I shrunk down on my knees across from Aryn. Although we had always been close, it wasn't custom for us to touch often. Or hardly at all. I felt comfortable around him but reaching for his arm somehow felt strange. In the past couple of days, I touched him more than I had in my entire life. I was even scolded as a child for catching him at a game of chase.

"Perhaps we should get some rest." That was all I could manage to say.

He kept his head bowed, just starring at the ground beneath him. His tangled hair blocked his expression, but I didn't need to see his face. I sat with him a moment longer before I stood.

This wasn't the palace. That was for sure. The crashing water was quiet and soothing, rather than harsh. I found a flat piece of ground near a hot spring of water and removed my cloak. I draped it across a bolder near the wall to dry. The heat from the pool would be enough to keep me warm. My clothes had somewhat dried from our time inside the cave. Dry enough to sleep in, I supposed. It hurt to leave Aryn against the wall. I would have sat with him all night if he needed, but this was something he needed to deal with. I understood that more than most.

I laid on my side facing the water. The steam warmed my face. I began to drift away to sleep, but somewhere between awake and sleep, I felt him near me. With sleepy eyes, I rolled over. Aryn laid on his back looking toward me. He was only inches away. He had removed his shirt. I gulped. His newly tanned muscles flexed as his arm reached behind his head for a makeshift pillow. He turned slowly on his side, our faces mere inches apart. He stared at me with an intensity I had never seen in him before. His jaw clenched showing the masculine lines of his face. I could no longer see the boy I grew up with. In front of me laid the face of a King.

I could not pry my eyes away from him. His gaze never left my face. The light of the moon reflected in his eyes. I grew weak. What was wrong with me? This was Aryn.

He raised himself on his elbow, slightly towering over me. My breathing grew heavy, no matter how hard I tried to steady it. I could feel my heart pounding in every inch of my body. I felt as though I were trembling, but not from the cold.

His face grew closer to mine and instantly my lips parted. He stopped just before our lips met. Was he asking permission? All I could think was yes. His breath caressed my lips. I could feel the nervous tremors move through my body, hoping Aryn couldn't sense them. I had been kissed before, but it felt nothing like this.

He finally leaned in and his lips gently met mine. My stomach churned, my fingers and toes tingled. It was gentle. Tender. He leaned in closer and kissed me harder. The kiss was filled with passion. Still leaning on his side, he pressed down closer to me. We were so close I could feel his pounding heartbeat. I caught my breath while kissing him, but still felt breathless. I parted my lips further letting him explore inside my mouth with his velvety, smooth tongue. I could feel the emotions coming from him. Passion. Anger. Fear. Yet in this moment, he had let his guard down. He let everything out.

His hand gently caressed my face. The kiss became soft again. He slowly pulled himself away and stared into my eyes. He was shaking too, or was I imagining it? His hand traced my face like a feather, brushing a strand of stray hair away from my eyes. He clenched his jaw again. The pain returned to his face. I wanted to hold him in my arms. He pulled away, laid back down, and closed his eyes.

"Good night Amira." He said in a deep voice.

I didn't know what to do. My throat felt dry and my heart was still pounding. What had just happened?

I rolled to my side, facing the opposite direction. I didn't trust myself to face him right now.

Sleep did not come easily. My mind raced. Soon I heard his steady breathing. He was finally asleep. I turned to face him. He had turned on his side facing me. His eyes closed, I watched his chest rise and fall. I closed my eyes tightly and laid on my back looking toward the sky. The stars shined incredibly bright that night. I became lost in the sky until my eyes grew heavy and drifted shut.

CHAPTER TWENTY

Long live the Queen

Amira

Footsteps startled me from my slumber. I jumped to my feet, blinking sleep from my eyes.

Orange light showered in by the falls. Morning had come. The sunset peaked through the falling water. Aryn stood near the tunnel which we had entered. His boots untied as he slipped his shirt over his head.

"Where are you going?"

His expression was full of guilt. "I didn't mean to wake you."

"You can't go back alone."

"I can't hide forever. I'll retrieve my sword and head to the castle for whatever awaits me. I'm the King."

I grabbed my cloak and began to braid my hair behind my back.

Aryn turned from me. "You should head back to the village. It's safer there. You can be free."

"Free?" I walked up to him, face to face. "So I'm just your servant then. You're what? Springing my contract and setting me free? I'm worth nothing?"

"I didn't… This is what you wanted."

"You obviously don't know anything about what I want."

Aryn turned to walk through the tunnel. It was now lit with the bright glow of daylight, making it easier to navigate. I followed behind. All feeling from the night before had vanished in flames. Aryn abruptly stopped and faced me. If I hadn't been paying attention, I would have run into him.

"What are you doing?"

'What do you think?"

"You're not coming with me."

'Like Hell I'm not."

We stood facing each other. Anger filled both our eyes.

Aryn turned to keep walking, not looking back.

"It's safer to go back to the village." His walk was stiff and his muscled tensed.

"I will not leave my brother behind."

We exited the cave.

He turned to the left.

"Wrong way," I called out.

He paused. I could tell he wanted to argue. I had told the truth. I was going back for my brother.

"I'm not returning without my sword."

"Still the wrong way."

He stood, unmoving as I made my way forward. Moments later he turned to follow me. He passed in front as if he were the one leading. I didn't feel like competing right now so I followed behind.

We walked in silence. Every crunch the dry of leaves or snap of a fallen branch kept me alert. I was glad I grabbed my dagger from my brother's cabin and was able to conceal it beneath my cloak.

A branch snapped from across the way. I quickly grabbed for my dagger but kept it concealed among my cloak. A dagger was only effective at close range. If only I had my bow and arrow I kept hidden under the mattress in my room. My father had given it to me, despite my mother's disapproval. But it was Lorin who had taught me to use it. Although, I had never used it against a person before. I knew if I had to now, I wouldn't hesitate.

"Amira?" A familiar voice called out. As he came to the light I searched to see if he was alone. With the woods being so thick, there was no telling if someone was hiding behind a nearby tree. Except, there would be no reason for him to be out here alone and I couldn't be sure of whose side he was on.

Aryn stepped in front of me like a shield, but I pushed him aside and approached the man with caution.

"Tauren—" I held my grip on my dagger, "What are you doing in the woods?"

His eyes darted between the two of us. "I could ask you the same question." He held his sword low to the ground, but as Aryn stepped forward I noticed his grip tighten around the hilt. I studied his every move. Eventually, his shoulders relaxed and he sheathed his sword.

He bowed his head slightly. "Prince Aryn."

Aryn took another step forward.

Suddenly I noticed how pale Tauren looked. He smelled of fire and his clothes were torn. Had he been on the run too? Perhaps he didn't know of the Kings death. Something didn't feel right. Tauren Gulped loudly. His face appeared ghostly.

"I'm so sorry." He managed to get out. But he wasn't looking at Aryn. He was looking at me.

"Tauren?" My hand was still gripping my dagger.

"The village." He choked on his words.

I looked back at Aryn then took off running toward the village. Aryn yelled out at Tauren, but I couldn't make out what he said. As I kept running I heard the footsteps chasing after me. I didn't have to turn around to know it was Aryn and Tauren.

My feet ached from running and branches tore at my clothes.

I smelled it. Smoke.

Even from afar I could see the smoke and flames. I slowed as I came closer. Tauren caught up with me and grabbed me by the arm. "Amira. Don't. There's nothing you can do." Aryn pushed his hand off of me and punched Tauren in the face. Tauren barely flinched, just backed up and rubbed his jaw. I could tell it had hurt him, and honestly didn't know why he wasn't charging back.

I didn't care. I knew where the fire was…it was at the barn where the festival was held. As I approached my stomach dropped. The fire slowed to nearly a smolder. Townspeople were running around with buckets of water, frantically emptying them to stop the flames from spreading. People were crying and shouting. From the clearing I could see smoke from afar on all sides. It wasn't just the barn.

I took a deep breath and instinct kicked in. I ran toward the flames and threw off my cloak.

Someone I met the night before was throwing water on the flames. Sweat dripped from his entire body. Men were carrying women and children away to a clearing. Women were crying and holding their children tightly in their arms. There were bodies lying motionless on the ground. This must have happened hours ago. A man lay on the ground near the fire. His clothes burnt. He wasn't moving. I heard a small cough. He was still alive.

I ran to him. He began to ramble, but I couldn't tell what it was that he was saying. I lifted his head and shoulders. He needed to get away from the smoke. I tried to drag him, but he was too heavy. "Help!"

Aryn came running when he heard me call. "Mer."

"Help. I can't carry him alone."

"Mer… I don't think…"

"Aryn. Help!"

He pushed me aside and lifted the man's head. He looped his arms under his heavy body. "Grab his feet."

They carried him to a clear spot, where the smoke did not heavily fill the air. Despite the chaos surrounding me, I couldn't hear anything. The man was trying to talk, but his words were hard to understand. "Thank you." He managed to cough out looking at Amira and reached toward my face. He looked to Aryn, "Long with the King." A tear slid off his face. His eyes seemed to glaze over. All life… Just gone. There were burns all over his body. I ripped at his clothes to see if his chest was moving. I listened for a heartbeat. Nothing.

Aryn grabbed me, but I pushed him away.

"Mer. He's gone."

I blinked tears from my eyes. Although the smoke made it hard to see, I still watched the chaos surrounding me. My mouth dropped. "Edwin. Margret." I could barely make out.

"We will find them."

I couldn't leave this man behind. I didn't even know him. Did he have a wife? Kids?

Aryn stood to his feet and held out his hand. I reached down to close the man's eyes then hesitantly took Aryn's hand to rise.

Everything seemed to be dying down. The flames had quieted. People were slowing down. Families held each other and cried. Women cried over their loved ones.

As my mind finally cleared I began to wonder where Tauren was. How did he know what happened here? Better yet, how had he known that we were here previously? Anger filled me entirely. Aryn had already seemed to have picked up on what I was just now putting together. I trusted Tauren. Maybe not completely, but I thought I knew him better than this. But if he was a rebel, why had he let us escape? Nothing was adding up.

"Edwin." I heard Aryn shout. He grabbed my hand and pulled me along with him.

He finally came into focus. Edwin just stood there…staring at the barn. His clothes were burned. His eyes were staring blankly into the smoke and what little of the barn that remained. As I grew closer, I could see every line and wrinkle on the old man's face. Although his old age was obvious, something about him earlier seemed so youthful. His rosy-cheeks were pale but blackened by the smoke. His frame was withered. He looked as if he would fall to the ground any moment, he used all his strength to remain standing.

"Edwin," Aryn said again as he slowly approached the tired man. Aryn put both of his hands on Edwin's shoulders and stood face to face with him. Edwin barely acknowledged him. Aryn looked pained for words. "Please. Come sit down." He helped the old man to the ground. And knelt beside him. His hands never left Edwin. This struck me as odd. As Prince, he was rarely allowed to touch people and be hands-on. No matter how uncomfortable Aryn must have been being so close to someone, he knelt side by side with this frail man that had given us shelter.

I was frozen. Not with fear. But with Anger.

"Edwin. Edwin. Look at me. Where's Margret?"

He still stared out with almost no expression. He almost didn't need to say it.

"Edwin. Are you hurt?"

"She's gone." He let out in a soft whisper. I didn't need to hear him, I saw it on his face and could read his lips as he spoke. I fell to my knees and wrapped my arms around the kind man.

"You!" A voice yelled out from behind. I pulled away and saw Aryn getting pushed to the ground. Aryn's face remained still and he merely stood back up and shook himself off. The man pushed him again, but this time Aryn regained his balance. Still, he didn't fight back.

A couple of men ran up to hold the man back. I couldn't quite make out what they were saying but I jumped up to defend Aryn.

"He is why this happened! He's the reason for all of this! That coward!"

"Excuse me?" I yelled.

"Oh... Like you didn't think we knew? The palace was attacked and the so-called Prince fled. Looks like he abandoned the kingdom to come have a holiday with the townspeople and a pretty woman. Did you enjoy yourself?"

Aryn didn't respond. The men were all shouting and holding him back.

"Yeah. Long live the Queen!" He yelled out with hatred in his voice.

"That horrible joke of a king is dead now and this coward ran away from home. Now the Queen is burning down villages until she finds and rescues her little prince." He spat at Aryn's feet.

"That's enough." Edwin stood and barked at the man.

"You're one to talk. It's because of his spoiled ass that your wife is dead."

"I said that's enough. You will not talk to our King that way."

Everyone had stopped to stare at them.

"He's no King!"

I went up to the man and punched him as hard as I could in the face. It hurt...but I would never let him know that.

"And you've got a woman protecting you." He spat blood from his mouth, which made me happy. At least I did some damage.

Shouting erupted from all over.

"He's right." Aryn's voice filled the air and everyone went silent. "He's right."

"No! It wasn't him." I turned to see Tauren walk up slowly.

A group of men flocked to him. "He's a soldier. He did this! Let's kill him." People began shouting different methods of how they should kill him. People were arguing about Aryn. It was complete madness.

"Stop!" I yelled. "I made Aryn leave! He was protecting me. He wanted to double back, but I wouldn't let him. He was on the way to the castle last night when I stopped him. He's no coward. And Tauren... I don't know... Explain."

His bruised face painfully met mine. "I...I had nothing to do with this. Not the town anyway. But I'm not blameless."

Aryn grabbed Tauren's sword from his sheath and held it to his throat. "The lady said to explain."

"And I am. There was an ambush on the castle... One that I was a part of." My eyes widened. "The mission was to kill the King and kidnap the Prince. I had you in your chambers."

"They why didn't you take me then? I hardly had a weapon to fight with." Aryn questioned.

"Amira was there. I don't know. I've always been told that you were a spoiled coward, but then I saw how you offered your life for that of a girl. Just a servant. And, to be honest, Amira would have put up a fight...and I would never harm her. I know how the Queen feels about her. So long as she was in the castle, she wouldn't be safe. I've seen the way you look at her. I knew you'd get her out."

"Wait. The Queen? What does she have to do with anything?" I stepped forward.

"She has everything to do with it."

Aryn dug his sword deeper into his neck, the sharp blade drawing a drop of blood that trickled down to his color bone.

"It was her. It was meant to look like the rebels. And, honestly, I guess we were. Just not the ones you know of."

"Why would the Queen want to kill her husband and kidnap her only son?" I questioned.

Tauren gulped. "Why wouldn't she? Power."

Aryn drew closer. "We can't trust him."

I looked at Aryn, "I'm not so sure."

"I know they weren't close but she wouldn't have killed my dad. And what would the purpose of kidnapping me be?"

"It would make you look weak." I pointed out.

"That's not the only thing," Tauren admitted. "The order was to capture...or kill."

"Now we know he's lying. Why would my own mother want me dead?"

"You'd be out of the way." Amira said under her breath.

"So…you believe him? You believe that my own mother sent people to kill me?"

"Without your dad… Without you… There's no one in her way."

"Why now then. Tell me that."

"Your father was stepping down. You were stepping up. The coin festival. It would bring people from all over. Easy to look like rebels had snuck in. If she had waited until after you became king, a kidnapping would be harder." It was hard for me to say the next part. "And if you had married, then she would no longer be Queen."

Aryn's face grew pale. He turned his attention back to Tauren. "Fiona. Where is she?"

Those words hit me like a knife.

"She's safe…for now. The Queen chose her for a reason."

"Chose?"

"The festival… You really thought it was some sort of magic. Surely you knew those kinds of things are setups, right?"

"So, you are a rebel?"

"She's a Kuval. Her family has money."

"But she's just a palace maiden."

"Yeah…deliberately put there under your nose."

"So. You say she's in on this whole conspiracy you and your people have cooked up? I know Fiona. She is good."

"Her? I'm not sure. Maybe. Maybe not. But, I'm not lying."

"You're the one that burned this town and killed these people."

"No! We were told you escaped. Those of us who were loyal to her were told to hunt you down and bring you back. That was all. She told the others that you had been kidnapped and perhaps there were rebels in the town. This was a rescue mission. At least to the other soldiers. To us, it was a retrieval. At least… that was what I had thought. The others…the loyalist. They convinced the soldiers that the town was filled with rebels. That you were celebrating the death of the king. Since Aryn wasn't here, they must have killed him or hidden him."

"But you still killed these people."

"No. I fought back. I was taken, held down as they burned the town.

Two officers were meant to take me back to the palace for punishment...
But I got away."

"And we're supposed to believe you?"

"I believe him," Edwin spoke. "I saw him being held back. I saw him
fighting his own men just before... Before..." His eyes went back to the
barn.

Aryn still held his sword to Tauren's neck.

I stepped forward and lowered Aryn's sword. I looked him in the face,
searching for answers.

"Then they are right. This is my fault."

"No! It's the Queen's fault. She was behind all of this."

"Let him go," Aryn ordered. The men hesitated, then finally let him go.

Aryn kept the sword at his side and began walking off.

"Where are you going?" I called after him.

"See, he's a coward." The man yelled.

Aryn turned to me. "I'm going to kill the Queen."

CHAPTER TWENTY-ONE

From Fire to Furry

Aryn

I couldn't believe the words which had just sprung from my mouth. The queen, my own mother. I had never actually killed anyone before. Animals while hunting, yes, but never a person with a soul, let alone my own mother. If what was said was true, something had to be done. I wasn't planning on going back on my word. I was King now or at least I would be when I took the castle. The question was how? Amira was right, even if I hated to admit it. I couldn't just walk in there and demand the crown. There was no telling where loyalties lay. Was this why she kept me hidden away so long?

Ten men had offered to aid in the journey, if men were what you called them. Two of them were young boys between the ages of twelve to sixteen. Four of them were easily in their late forties or older. Many stayed behind to tend to the farms and families who had lost everything. Many lost wives and children. I didn't blame them for not volunteering. In fact, I wanted to refuse the help all together. It was their look of desperation, their burned clothes, and smoke smudged faces which touched me. Who was I to keep them from their revenge? No one stood up to stop the young boys. That led me to believe that they had no one here. Not anymore.

"We must form a plan. We should gather what supplies we can. Travel light." Amira said. Her appearance shocked me. She no longer held a smooth clean face or wore nice fabrics adorned with jewels. Her tussled hair and smudged face gave her the appearance of a warrior. This is what she had always wanted, I knew that. But seeing her like this, it wasn't what I wanted for her. Could I handle her getting hurt in this siege? Could I handle one of the boys not making it home? I had often studied battle in theory and practiced with swords. That now felt like child's play. This…this was real.

"There's a man." Edwin's voice cracked above the noise. "He has wealth. Men. I knew him once as young lad. He was always…resourceful. I have heard stories of his accomplishments. Go to him. Plead for his help and his men. I gotta warn you not to tell him who you are. Not at first." He scratched his head. "Heain't a fan. And to speak truth, pleading your cause won't help any. Fer all I know he will delight in the Queen's reign. It's coin he's after."

I glanced toward Amira. I could see her mind tinkering.

Coin? I had nothing but a borrowed cloak and a royal sword. A sword I had recently buried.

"He's a powerful man. In trade with Picies."

"A pirate?" I shouted.

"A…tradesman. But yes, a pirate."

"Never."

"He's not a bad man. I knew his father. He's just…ambitious. Once he likes you, he's loyal."

"Loyal until someone pays a higher price."

Amira walked close to me. I was glad she didn't confront me in front of the others. Instead, she whispered behind my ear. "It sounds like we need him. We need an army. Aryn, this could work. It could be a start at least."

I turned to face her. "And the coin? What would you suggest we do about that?"

Amira bit her lip. I hated how cute she looked when she did that. Cute wasn't the right word. I had tasted those lips. The yearning for another taste hit me hard. I pressed my lips together closely until my jaw hurt. A sly grin filled her face. This couldn't be good. Even as a child that look always meant something bad.

"I have a plan. It's risky." She looked at Tauren. Was that concern in her eyes? The thought infuriated me. "We need Tauren."

"Me? But what for?"

"We can't trust him." I spit out. "Not yet."

"He's all we have. If he can make it back, he can retrieve the coin I have hidden away and get intel and weapons. And…" I knew what she meant. Lorin. If he could get about the castle to gather weapons and intel, he might be able to find and free Lorin.

"But they know I was disloyal."

"Do they? You said yourself that you killed those who took you captive."

"But wouldn't it look suspicious if I make it back after the rest of my men had already made it?"

"Not if you play your cards right." Amira walked closer to him and touched his arm. I clenched my fists and took a step forward without meaning to.

"I'll be called a coward. They will think I ran." He whispered. Had he really cared so much about what people thought of him?

"Or that you were injured. You will be an asset. A sitting soldier. Do this for your king." She said in a softer voice. "Do it for me."

He exhaled. "I'll do it."

"So be it." I said stiffly. I turned toward the others, "Believe me. This will not be an easy task. You have all lost much this day. I'm giving you the opportunity to change your mind now. No one will think less of you. Your town needs you, as does your king. I will not force anyone to be my soldier. Take your time and choose wisely."

Almost instantly Edwin bent to his knees, although he seemed to struggle. The two young boys followed, then the eight other men who claimed to follow me. The entire town bowed down to me. I looked left. Amira gracefully bowed to a curtsy and remained there. Lastly, Tauren bowed. I was at a loss for words. I nodded to my people and they all stood and cheered.

Edwin approached me. "Although I will not be going with you. I follow you. Your majesty." As he bowed again.

"Long live the King." Amira shouted, followed by the echoes of the people. This had all been Amira and Edwin. The people had hated me merely an hour prior, now I was being praised as King.

I turned and began walking.

"Where are you going?" Amira caught up to my pace.

"I'm no King yet."

I turned back toward my people, "Quickly tend to your wounded, burry your dead, and gather your supplies. I have something I must first retrieve."

It had been nearly impossible to convince Amira to stay behind and help the people. Of course, she insisted on coming with me. Once I made it clear that the people needed someone to stay behind, she suggested I take Tauren and his sword with me. One of the men, who appeared to be in his twenties, offered to accompany me on my short journey to find what I had left behind.

We didn't just need men and coin, we needed weapons. Amira's stash, no matter how much she managed to save, wouldn't be nearly enough to feed our small band of men, nor pay the pirate. Yet, I had to go back to the castle. I had to see for myself. Besides, it was my fault Lorin was being held prisoner. If he was still alive. I would personally see to his escape. One thing I knew was that I wanted Amira far from Lorin at the castle. It could be a trap, but a trap I would try to out maneuver.

The man accompanying me spoke very little on the walk toward our destination. I learned that his name was Benjamin. I sensed an uneasiness in him and decided to question him no further.

We had finally made it to the familiar spot. The soil still fresh from resent disturbance. I had nothing to dig with but my hands. My hands had changed so much in recent days. My fingernails black with dirt, palms thick with fresh blisters and new formed callus. Benjamin knelt by me and began to dig as well, although he had no idea what we were looking for. That was until his eyes caught the jeweled handle of my sword.

She needed a fresh cleaning. There was a stream close enough. I handed the old sword to Benjamin, carefully examining the way he held it. It was obviously he hadn't held many swords before.

While Ben washed his dirty hands in the stream I noticed his coin. Farmer, of course.

"Have you always been a farmer? I mean, before the coin ceremony?"

"Just as my father and his father before him." He looked furiously toward me. "Our destiny is picked for us when we are born. Nothing changes with the coin."

"So, you're not a believer?"

"Are you?"

That was a question I had never had to ask myself before. At least, not until recently.

CHAPTER TWENTY-TWO

Planning the Game

Amira

Smoke began to clear, but the devastation lingered. Aryn's journey would be short, I knew what he went in search of. I remained hopeful that he would return with the sword, but the pit of my stomach churned at the thought of him leaving to infiltrate the castle alone. I had hoped to follow him, or at least send Tauren. Ultimately, a lad named Benjamin offered to accompany him. Although it wouldn't be hard for Aryn to elude his companion, I hoped Benjamin would make him think twice about doing anything rash.

My heart broke for this small community. They had lost so much, yet they kept going. They said their goodbyes, buried their loved ones, and started to rebuild. Neighbors took in neighbors and supplies were dispersed to those in need. Even in these hard times, I had never seen so much strength.

The night was cold, yet sweat poured from my face and chest, plastering strands of my hair that had fallen from my braid to my face and neck. The soles of my shoes were worn and my feet swollen. I had hardly known these people, but to me they felt like family. Something I had not had in a while. The thought created a longing in my heart for my brother. There was no way to tell if he was safe. The castle was but a day away. While the others carried out their tasks I would find a way to get to Lorin.

While helping shift debris with my now bleeding hands, I saw people stop and look toward the hill. What was quiet, now fell completely silent. I dropped the bit of debris I held and looked to the horizon. Aryn had returned. He had cleaned himself up and as the wind blew his cloak behind him his sword shone in all its brilliance. He looked like a king returning from battle. Something about that sword seemed so…majestic, even from afar.

His return meant it was time to leave this place behind. To leave the lives we knew behind. As we packed to leave, plans were hashed out. Tauren's job would be to apprehend weapons and coin. Aryn desired information above all. His face would be too easily recognized but with the new men, it wouldn't be hard for them to gather information.

"If we can find a way to insert them in the castle, maybe they can find ways to question the guards. At the very least, maybe they can retrieve some information from some of the women at court who carry loose lips." Aryn suggested.

"First, sweet talking the girls at court is a good idea but unless you are rich or royal they won't give you the time of day." I glanced at the men apologetically, "Besides, we don't need information from inside the castle. You were right about loose lips." I searched the eyes of the men around me, "Does anyone here gamble?"

I was greeted with confused looks. That was until a stern looking man cleared his throat. This was the first time he had even attempted to speak. "I…uh…have been known to venture into taverns…from time to time."

"Are you any good?"

"Good enough. But if what you are looking for is information, I don't need to be good. I just need to play the cards right." I could sense the mysteriousness about him, which would make him a perfect candidate for the mission. Yet, I sensed hesitation. One I knew better than to question. There seemed to be a battle raging inside of him. One he has tried to suppress for some time. I got a feeling this was what he had been holding back, that partaking in tavern pleasures might awaken something he had been hiding deep within him.

"What's your name?"

"Orin."

"Orin, are you sure about this?" I had seen men who had been consumed by drink and game until they were empty, purse and heart. He appeared strong and tan with the coin of a farmer. A drunk farmer in town gambling at a tavern shortly after the festival would turn no heads. He was perfect, yet I hesitated to use him. Aryn seemed to have no reservations. I nodded my head. "I know the perfect place."

They continued to make plans, Orin would bring friends along. They could play the part of drunken tavern men cheering on their friend in nonsense games. Another group would pass along the outside of the castle. I knew the inner workings of the castle and how things were brought in and out. Aryn's idea of loose lips sparked had given me an idea. The royal and wealthy women seemed to know it all. That is, who was sneaking around with who, who's expecting a child, and so on. The real women with knowledge were the ones who went around the castle unseen and unheard. Not even the jewels of the castle, something I had been just days ago. A maid. They held the highest secrets.

The second group of men would appear to be delivering supplies to the kitchen maids. Their real goal was, and I hated to use them like that, to flirt with the staff. No one knew the secrets of the castle better than the ones who truly ran it. That was why I spent so much time in the kitchen and doing the other messier chores.

There were three men left. I looked toward Aryn. "There is something I need to ask."

"I encourage you to stay behind, but since I know you better than to mind me, You, I, and the three remaining men will find our way to the dungeons. Lorin is a great asset and we will not leave without him."

I breathed a deep sigh of relief. I would have gone to my brother with or without help, but help was always better. It was less than a day's journey to the castle. If we left now then made camp for some rest, I could hold my brother in my arms the following night.

CHAPTER TWENTY-THREE

Night Falls

Aryn

I knew Amira was pleased to know we would be rescuing her brother. The truth was, he was like a brother to me too. All of this had been my fault. After packing what food, weapons, and clothing we could we set off on our mission. We were going home, but it wouldn't be that simple. It wasn't too late in the morning light. If we could find a place to get some rest and travel the rest of the day, we could make it to the castle by the cover of night.

I could tell Amira and I were thinking the same thing. Our safe spot. The cave.

I wasn't prepared to give a speech, but I was willing to do the best I could. "We have all suffered much on this night. As much as I want to storm the castle right away, we need rest. Even if only for a couple of hours. I know many of you had no sleep last night. I know of a place, hidden, not too far from here." I glanced at Amira. She nodded in agreement. It felt strange to share our special place, but patrols would be out looking. "We will go there, rest, and eat what we can find, then we sneak through the woods to the castle under the cover of night. We all know the plans." I looked around seeing heads nod. "Good. Finish your goodbyes. I will not lie, this will be a dangerous journey. It could be your last goodbye." Saying those words hurt. They weren't inspiring, but they were true.

The men gathered what they could carry, makeshift weapons, jerky, canteens of water, and a few blankets. We needed to travel light.

I searched the horizon. The smoke had cleared, but the smell remained. There seemed to be no sign of a nearby patrol. If we stuck to the woods and not the road, we might be hidden by the cover of trees. I saw the way from which we had come. The cave was not far from here. I headed toward the path, men following behind. Amira made her way to the front with me. She said nothing, which was unusual for her. She still suffered the pain of watching these people die, and the loss of her friend.

We made the journey in a short time. The waterfall and surrounding area appeared the same as it had the previous night, yet the sunlight made it look less mysterious. Still, it would be impossible to find your way into the cave unless you already knew the way. Or if you had Amira's sense of curiosity. It was more than that with her. She had a knack for finding hidden paths. Especially for bringing out those hidden paths in people around her.

The men didn't seem to believe there was anything beyond the falls. I let Amira lead the way. The heat of the day beat down on my face but as we made our way further into the cave, a warm breeze brushed my face and traveled down my back. The view was breathtaking. Had I really not noticed it last night? Light shown through the falls, dancing along the glistening walls. It appeared as if the walls were made of diamonds. It was clear that the men were as amazed as I. Probably even more. This was magical.

We made camp. I offered to keep watch as the men rested. I couldn't sleep if I wanted to. As the men found spots to lay down, I found the cozy familiar spot from the previous night. Sitting there made a smile come to my face.

"Lovely spot. Care to share?" Amira knelt beside me. The color had returned to her face. She apparently wasn't really asking because she made herself comfortable.

"Someone I know found this spot and shared it with me when I was going through a tough time." I leaned into her, brushing her shoulder.

"I see. So, you bring all the girls here." I tried to hold in a deep laugh, but it spilled from my lips with no control.

"Yes Amira. All the girls. In fact, it often gets quite crowded." I said raising my brow expecting a snarky response.

"Will you bring Fiona here? Would make an interesting honeymoon." The air around us became still and heavy. I hadn't known Fiona long, but I cared about her. I was more than willing to go through with marrying her. But if this had all been a part of my mother's plan, would I still want to marry her? Perhaps she was innocent in all this. One thing haunted my mind. The dream of Amira. Not only that but the stirring feelings I've had every time she grew near. I had lost myself in her, almost losing restraint. I'm not sure how I felt about her, I just knew that my feelings had obviously changed.

"You should get some rest." I said breaking the silence.

"And trust you to stay awake and get all these men up and moving on time. No thanks." She had a way with lightening the mood. A frown grew on her face.

"What's wrong? Your face is making an ugly scrunching thing." I laughed. I should have known better to joke like that to her. She replied with a stern punch to my shoulder. How did such a little woman pack such a harsh punch? But then she began to laugh.

"I was just wishing for some playing cards. We haven't played in so long. And without your precious body guards I can beat you like the little girl you are."

"Little girl huh?" I said flexing my chest and arms, giving a little kiss to my muscular bicep.

"Oh my stars. I wish I had something to throw at you!" Instead, she tackled me. Straddling me to the ground. I could feel her body pressed against mine. The urge to fight back was lost. Suppressed by other urges I fought to contain. She was smiling a wicked grin as her hair cascaded around her shoulders creating a barrier between us and the world. Her scent drove me crazy. It had changed. Her once spicy scent now held an air of smoke. It reminded me of smoked meat. I fought to keep my primal instincts hidden.

"Uhh. Uumm." I heard a clearing of someone's throat. Amira jumped off of me laughing until she looked up and saw Tauren eyeing her. Was that guilt in her eyes? She didn't belong to him. Then again…she didn't belong to me either. That was just Amira. She belonged to no one but herself.

"Maybe it's time to wake everyone and get moving… Before we get too distracted." Tauren's voice remained stern.

It hadn't felt like much time had passed, but he was right. It was time to get moving. I'm not sure how much rest any of the men had gotten, but we passed around jerky and drank from the water. We would need our strength. Even though this wasn't an all-out war, it was a stealth mission. We needed speed and clarity.

At least five hours after leaving the cave, the castle was in sight. We still hid among the trees as the sun retreated to its night of rest. Tauren had remained close the entire time. Something that comforted me and aggravated me. If he was close to me, he was also close to Amira.

"Tauren. You're up. You will distract the guards while the others sneak in. Amira and I know the way through the secret tunnels so that will give us cover." I hoped the secret tunnels would not be trapped, but it was our best option. "Tauren, you are to gather intel, weapons, and coin. If you cannot make it out with everything leave it all at the place we discussed earlier." He nodded. "Amira, you and I will make our way to your room. There are a few things we need to grab before rescuing Lorin." She simply nodded. "The rest of you are on a different mission. We need information and you know how to get it." It remained silent, everyone nodding just once. They were focused. "One more thing." I hated to ask in front of everyone, but now was my only chance. "Tauren, find Fiona. Make sure she is well." Tauren's gaze darted from mine to Amira's, but her face showed no emotion. Maybe I had imagined things between us. "Good luck." We all separated, except for Amira and me. I wasn't going to leave her side.

CHAPTER TWENTY-FOUR

Double Tricked

Amira

There were a few things I wanted from my room. My bow and arrows would come in handy, as well as the money I saved up, but it wasn't nearly enough to live on let alone start a war with. Aryn was up to something, but I couldn't figure out what. With Tauren's distraction we made it near the castle. The sound of footsteps approached. We needed cover. There was nothing but a small hole in the wall that lead to who knows where.

"Get in." I said.

"What. I can't fit in that he whispered." I crouched down and slid into the unknown. I waited for a second. I was about to jump back out and come to Aryn's rescue for being dumb, but he awkwardly slid in. The hole lead nowhere and was hardly big enough for the two of us. He pressed against me, attempting to conceal his entire body. His face but an inch from mine.

"We have to quit meeting like this Prince Charming." I whispered into his ear. He shivered as if a cold wind had blown up his back but his face remained focused. Intense, actually. As the clanging footsteps grew louder I tried to hold my breath, but Aryn kept breathing heavily. His hot breath kissing my face. I closed my eyes. Being this close to him made it hard to focus. If I hadn't noticed it before, I sure had now. He had grown into a man.

The footsteps grew silent and I breathed freely. Aryn pressed against me, motionless. I scrunched my face and he shook his head in question. "I wasn't sure if the guards would kill me or your breath." I giggled aloud.

His face turned bright red. I hadn't meant to embarrass him. In fact. His breath smelled wonderful. I had only mean to break the silence. He scooted out of the cramped hole and did the awkward, yet cute thing he always does when he's nervous. His arm shot up, brushing his hair away. Stars. Did he know how sexy that made him look? I could see the sculpting of his muscles and the dimples on his cheeks as his face remained red. I stood on the tips of my toes and kissed his burning hot cheek. My eyes grew wide as I stepped back. I hadn't meant to do that. It just happened.

"I was kidding by the way. About your breath." I faked a laugh and searched around us to see if the coast was clear. We made our way in and to one of the secret tunnels. Unfortunately, we had no lantern. Our steps were filled with caution. I unsheathed my dagger and reached for his hand. He paused and turned toward me. I felt his breath on my shoulder. "We shouldn't get separated." I whispered.

He didn't say anything. I could tell he was lost down here. Me on the other hand, I knew the way to and from my room, even in the dark. I pulled him along beside me. When we made it to the exit closest to my door I stopped and listened. I gulped, knowing this might be a trap. "I'll go in alone. See if the coast is clear. You wait here, I'll be right back." I expected a rebuttal or some type of argument, instead he agreed. That was strange. Maybe he knew it was for the better if I was caught and not him.

I slipped out of the tunnel into the hall way. It was nearly empty, but I heard footsteps. I grabbed a nearby vase filled with flowers and proceeded to walk with it covering my face, just like any other maid servant would do. My plan must have worked because I made my way to my room, with no one following me. I quickly shut the door behind me.

It felt so strange being back here, yet I hadn't been gone long at all. Memories of Haddy slipping into my room to discuss gossip or do each other's hair flooded my mind. It hurt but I didn't have time to reminisce. I had to save my brother. I didn't want to light a lantern and alert anyone of my presence. Luckily, the light from the moon shining through a small window was plenty. I knew this room like the back of my hand.

I slid my hand under my lumpy mattress in search of my bow. It was still there. I was surprised my room wasn't searched. But then again, how would searching my room help find the prince. I was of no concern. For all they knew I had run off with some eligible bachelor. I made my way to my desk and found the hole with my buried treasures. All there. I slipped it into a couple of coin purses, but shoved pieces of paper and fabric in them to quite the noise of jingling coins. I glanced around my room. There wasn't much here. Nothing calling out to be taken with me. I attached my bow and arrows, concealed under my dark cloak with my dagger still sheathed by my side. Both hidden, but easily within reach. I heard something at my door and quickly hid. I knelt crouched by my bed, dagger raised, until I was sure the noise had disappeared.

I slowly made my way to the door to listening intently.

Nothing.

I slowly attempted to open my door and slip out, but it was stuck. I tried harder. Nothing. One more time, as hard as I could, but still no movement. I was locked in.

Aryn…

I wasn't going to let him go on a suicide mission alone. If he thought I couldn't maneuver out of my room, he was mistaken.

The doors locked from the outside. A prison. The locks were added after rumors of certain maids roaming the night. I should have been more careful, but I didn't care. Over the years I had learned to pick locks, this one I could do with my eyes closed. I quickly snuck out of my room but passing Hadassah's door set my heart beating hard. My feet became heavy. I wanted more than anything to open the door and see her there. That would never happen again. The thought sent a lump into my throat that I could not swallow. I couldn't breathe. My eyes became clouded with tears. Just breathe.

I used the secret passage ways to get to the dungeon, but I wasn't sure which way to go. I wasn't the 'goodest' girl in court, but I also hadn't spent much time in the dungeons. That is except for the couple of times I was talked into switching chores and ended up feeding the prisoners instead of setting the grand tables. I knew how they treated prisoners. The thought made my feet quicken. I had to get to Lorin.

Suddenly, I felt a slight burning on my chest. I looked down, my necklace. It was glowing. Was I seeing things? It was the sea glass necklace I had gotten at the festival. Nothing special about it, I just hadn't taken it off. My hand went to touch it. It wasn't hot but there seemed to be a radiating warmth pulsing from the dangling pendent. Not only that, but it seemed to possess luminescent qualities. As I stopped, so did the warmth. When I took another step a small amount of heat surged though to my fingertips. I stopped again and turned the opposite direction. I took one step, the glass stone had become as cold as before. One more time, I turned and walked in the previous direction. It became warmer as I neared a door.

This was it. The dungeon.

I quickly tucked the necklace under my dress to conceal it. Now wasn't time to question how it worked. I obviously haven't slept well.

I held my dagger firmly in my hand. There was no sneaking in. Who knows what lay on the other side of the door? I braced myself and slowly cracked the door open.

CHAPTER TWENTY-FIVE

Heat of the Moment

Amira

The cool air nipped my cheeks. It was a stale cold, not crisp or fresh. I instantly covered my nose. The smell was almost too much to take in. It had been like this before, but not quite as bad. This time I was deeper in the dungeon. I couldn't place the smell. Rot and decay, musk and body odor, dried blood? This place was dark, just as the tunnels had been, my eyes didn't take long to adjust. Few lanterns gave off a warm glow, but just barely. Their flames flickered their last few breaths.

I searched for the guards and noticed one slouching against the wall as if he were taking a nap. I flung myself against the wall, hoping to avoid waking him. I worked to control my breathing and step lightly along the wall to get a closer look, under the cover of shadow. I was close. Almost close enough to attack. I swiftly pressed closer, holding my dagger to his neck. He didn't flinch. I poked him with the dagger and he fell to the ground.

He was dead. Surely Aryn hadn't done this himself. But, who else would have? My heart ached for Aryn. He had never killed anyone before. Neither have I, but I imagine this would be tough for him. My thoughts instantly changed. He was down here. Was he hurt? Worry swept over me, clouding the anger I had earlier felt.

The loud thud of the body had awoken something in the corner. Someone was there, behind the bars. A prisoner. He was of no harm to me, but curiosity grabbed hold of me. I slowly closed in.

"If you are here for your brother, you haven't much time." Came an old and frail voice. I couldn't make out a face, just the thin wrinkled hand that reached out to hold the bars. My hand reached out to his. Cold. Almost ice cold.

"How did you…? Can I do something to help you? Surely you don't belong in here?"

"Sweet Amira, don't worry about me. My time is coming to an end. A new beginning is on the horizon. Save the prince. Have faith in him. More importantly, have faith in yourself. You are destined for greatness."

"What? How?" Who was this man?

"Mer?" I heard Aryn's worried voice racing toward me in a loud whisper. "How?" He looked me over to see if I was okay. I couldn't help but grab him and hold him close. He was okay. For now.

"Aryn, we have to…" I gestured to the prison cell, but it was now empty. I stood motionless, squinting my eyes to see if there was anything hidden in the shadow. Nothing. I looked back at Aryn. His eyes grew darker. Heavier. "The guard…did you…?"

He looked away and nodded. "I didn't know who he was. I couldn't take the chance. Mer… What if…?"

"Shh…" I placed my finger over his mouth. Then held him in a tight embrace. He laid his chin on top of my head. Everything seemed to melt away.

"My brother?" I suddenly shot back in question.

"I haven't gotten to him yet. I heard a noise. A part of me knew it had to have been you." He placed his hand on my shoulder. "Mer. I'm sorry, I shouldn't have…"

I stepped back and punched his shoulder. "No, you shouldn't have. You owe me."

He smiled and nodded. He drew his sword and gestured for me to follow him along the wall, concealed in darkness. I suppressed a giggle, his shiny blond hair seemed to illuminate as the last of the dying flames danced away.

Loud cheering echoed through the walls and the smell of cheap brew filled my nostrils. I stopped to listen. There were at least three guards, but it was difficult to know for sure. I looked down to see an empty pitcher near my feet.

"I have an idea." I whispered in Aryn's ear. His look of disapproval had no effect on me. I hid my dagger behind my back, knelt down, and grabbed the pitcher. Aryn grabbed my arm, but I maneuvered away swinging my hips as I walked away slowly.

"Refill anyone?" I bat my eyes and held the pitcher high in hopes no one would notice its empty contents.

"Well, well, well. Looks like it's time for a snack gentlemen." The largest guard said and by large, I wasn't talking about his muscles. I was wrong, there were four men. Four drunken, slow men. But I was still highly outnumbered. I hoped Aryn would figure out the plan.

I heard a gasp to my right and caught a small glimpse of Lorin. Don't look at him. Don't give yourself away. I also hoped he wouldn't give me away before I made my move.

I slowly walked toward the large man still sitting in a chair and sat on his lap. This wasn't too uncommon for him. Men like him expected women to treat him this way. Often, the lower-class servants would flirt for spare change. I told myself I would never sink so low, this was only for show. I giggled and played with my long hair, studying the men. Glancing toward the corner where Aryn stood, I gave a slight signal with my hand, hoping he would notice.

I still held my dagger firmly behind my back with one hand. My heart raced. This is something I had never done before. I knew what to do but wasn't sure if I would be able to go through with it. Glancing back toward my brother, I knew this was the only way. I moved my leg a bit, causing my dress to slide up, slightly exposing some skin. As all eyes darted down, I drew my dagger and plunged it into the man's neck, slicing him open as I pulled it through. As I removed my dagger, blood spilled out. His eyes grew wide as he tried to stand grasping for his throat. I swallowed hard, knowing I had only seconds.

I spun on my heels as my dagger was met by a broad sword. His strength was greater than mine. I put everything I had into holding the sword off. The other two men were slower to act, gasping and taking in the horrific scene. I should have used my bow and arrows, but I only had a few. I needed to save them for a moment where close range combat was not an option. No, I was rethinking my decision. He removed his sword and prepared to strike again, the other two reaching for their swords. I spun to grab the sword of the man whose throat I just slit. My soberness gave me small advantage over these drunken men.

My dagger in one hand, and sword in the other, I charged the man who was closest, the one who attacked first. I tried to keep my eyes on the other two, but three against one wasn't an easy task. I heard a loud grunt and the slicing of a sword to my left. Whatever it was distracted the man for long enough for me to plunge my new sword deep into his belly. It was harder than I expected. I had sliced through hay and flour sacks, but a human body was different. I pulled my sword and he fell to the ground making the most awful gurgling sound, I cringed. I spun on my heels to meet my next opponent, sword drawn.

"Aryn!" I almost killed you.

"Amira. That was dangerous. If I hadn't been here…" The look in his eyes became distant. Blood dripped from his sword as I noticed two more bodies lying lifeless on the floor in my peripheral vision.

"What the Hell do you two think you are doing? Mer? What have you done?" Lorin screamed.

"Saving your butt." I spat out. "You thought I'd leave you in here?" I searched for the keys. They were in the pocket of the fat man. I hated going through his pocket, but I had no choice. I saw the bulge of the keys and went for them.

I unlocked the cell door and threw my arms around my brother. His face had been bloodied and his nose obviously broken. The way he winced when I grabbed him made me assume he had at least one broken or bruised rib. What had they done to him?

Aryn came up behind us and patted Lorin on the back. "Good to see you brother." Lorin clenched his teeth. He was in obvious pain. "But we need to get going."

"I'm not leaving without Rachel."

"When we get out of here we can find her."

Suddenly the dungeon doors flew open and light chased away the darkness. A swarm of guards were headed our way. "Run!" I yelled, tossing Lorin a sword from one of the fallen guards. He seemed to pause and take in the scene.

"No. Go. I'll distract them. You two need to get out of here."

"No!" I yelled. Before I could reach out to him, he took off running toward the guards. I started to chase him but Aryn held me back. I stood and watched. There were five guards. Five against one. How could we leave him? While fighting off one of the guards, another came behind and stabbed him through the back. I screamed and their attention turned toward me and Aryn. Aryn pulled my arm. I tried to break free but couldn't. I saw Lorin fall to his knees. I saw the guards shouting. Everything happened in slow motion. I couldn't hear a thing, just a ringing in my ears from the blood curdling scream that escaped my lips.

Aryn pulled me harder.

They were coming.

CHAPTER TWENTY-SIX

Raging Fire

Aryn

I couldn't believe the sight before my eyes. Lorin. He was like my brother. Every ounce of me wanted to either drop to the floor or run after him. One thing held me back. Amira. I knew what she was going through. Even though I wasn't as close to Isaac, memories of his last days flooded my mind. Memories I thought I buried. Now they came crashing back, but this time I had lost another brother.

Amira.

I pulled on her, but she resisted. It took all of my might to grab her and run. The door leading to the tunnels was hidden. I only hoped that I had remembered exactly where it was. I had no time to bang on the walls looking for a trap door. I heard the footsteps charging toward us but had no time to turn and look. With any luck they were far enough behind to not see us disappear through the door.

Instantaneously all of the lanterns fell from the walls and a fire erupted. Smoke filled the air making it impossible to see. The strange part was that it almost formed a wall, beyond the smoke was clear as day. I still held Amira close by my side in case she decided to run off. She almost seemed lifeless.

The door. There was a small crack, a small amount of smoke trickled to the door as if it were leading us. I fearfully let go of Amira, but she stood still watching the smoke and flames grow taller, it was as if the dungeon wasn't being burned. So close to the fire and I could barely feel the heat or smell the heavy smoke.

"Come on!" I got the door open and pleaded for Amira to follow me. She just stood there. Suddenly, she let out a small screech, grasping at her chest as if it were on fire. It seemed as if she had awoken. She looked toward me then back at the fire. She grabbed at her chest and held something in her hands. She nodded toward me and jumped through the door. I slammed it behind her before the guards had a chance to notice it.

I heard shouting and footsteps. "This way." A loud voice rose and the footsteps fled away from the door. Apparently, the fire had died down, but it caused just enough distraction to let us escape. We were lucky.

Amira knelt on the cold stone ground, hands gripping at the rubble and head turned down. Her long hair cascaded around her face hiding her soft tears. I knelt across from her. She looked into my eyes. Tears streaming down. I took her in my arms and rocked her, just as her mother had me when I lost Isaac.

I held her tightly, feeling her beating heart thumping against mine, despite the layers of fabric that separated us. I knew her heart was breaking into a thousand pieces. If I could give her mine I would. I would do anything to take this pain from her. After several long moments and quiet sobs, I pulled away. My fingertips gently lifted her chin. Her face blotched in white and pink. Still beautiful.

"Mer... We have to go."

She didn't respond.

"Amira. Please."

She cleared her throat and wiped away her tears. "Then let's go." She stood and began to walk away.

Everything was a blur after that. We had few conflicts leaving the castle. Although the sun was clearly soon to rise, we still had the shelter of darkness for at least another hour. We made our way out and past the cover of trees. Before we could keep going to meet back at the location we all agreed on, she fell to the ground. This time her sobs were louder and uncontrolled.

I could do nothing but kneel and cry with her.

As the sun rose we both stood and headed toward our cave. It was a long and silent journey. I kept my eyes and ears open for anyone who might be following, but I was confident of our escape. Soon word would be out. As we made it to the safety of our cave Amira began to undress to the under clothes she had worn the night we found the other cave. I turned away, giving her some privacy to wash up. I needed a good washing too but first I would check the perimeter.

We were the first to arrive. Everything seemed safe. As I made my way into the cavern I saw that Amira had emerged from the water. She was now rinsing her dress and laying it out to dry. It made me uncomfortable to know that she was still unclothed and the other men should be arriving soon. Instead of saying anything I followed her lead. My clothes had been blood covered and sweat soaked. I stripped to my under drawers and immersed myself into the cool water. I held my breath as I slid under the surface. Opening my eyes, I watched the blood and dirt drift away. I rose above the water again, it was about belly button deep. I ran my hands through my tangled curly hair and stared at the blurry image in the water.

Looking back to check on Amira, I saw she had curled up on the floor with a blanket left from the night before. Best not to wake her. She needed sleep. I continued to wash my clothes. Still, I couldn't get the image of the curly blond-haired boy that looked back at me. My mother often scolded me because of my young boyish hair, but she never let me cut it shorter. It always confused me. Now I knew why. She didn't want anyone to see me as a man. As a king. I grabbed my sharp bladed sword and began to cut away at my curly, blond locks.

It wasn't my best work.

As I set down my sword Amira rolled over to look at me. A silly smile rose upon her lips. "Ren. What have you done?" She studied me seriously, then stood and walked closer. "Sit" She pointed to the rock.

I did as she asked. She grabbed her blade and began working on my hair. She kept it long. Maybe an inch or two in length, but I assumed it was more even now. I took a deep breath inhaling her scent. Still sweet, with a hint of spice. Even without a proper bath or soap she smelled amazing. I closed my eyes, lost in her scent.

"Done." She said and clapped. I rose and looked out into the water. The face looking back at me looked so different. Older. I could more easily see the definition of my jaw and eyebrows. At this length, my hair looked dark and so did my skin after my time away from the castle. The man starring back at me certainly wasn't a prince. In truth…I didn't know who he was.

I turned to face Amira. I was still shirtless and she was still in her underclothes, now more of a brown than a white. As she inhaled I could see the top of her cleavage rise and fall, I looked away and cleared my throat. She must have known I was uncomfortable because she sat back down, wrapping herself in the blanket. I grabbed another blanket and sat next to her. I struggled to find something to say. Instead I wrapped my arm around her and we sat in silence.

CHAPTER TWENTY-SEVEN

Treasure

Amira

Warmth encompassed me. I woke to the sound of heavy breathing. My head on his chest as it rose and fell steadily. His arms wrapped around me. Both of us in little to no clothes, still wrapped in blankets separating our skin. I'm not sure when we fell asleep or what time of day it was. I sat up and looked around. A pair of eyes set on me and he cleared his throat. I blinked and reached for my dagger. Before I stood to my feet I recognized him. It was Orin. Him, the two younger boys, and one other man.

I looked down, still barley clothed. Heat rose to my cheeks and I held the blanket tighter. "Sorry..." I stammered. "I washed my dress." I waked over to see if it had dried yet. It hadn't but it was close enough. A damp dress was better than embarrassment anyway. As happy as I was to see them, I sure wish it had been at a different time. As I dressed myself I saw Aryn start to wake.

"Mer?" He cleared his throat, rubbing the sleep from his eyes. Even without his nearly shoulder length hair, he looked adorable. I coughed and gestured toward our guest. He stood quickly, trying to cover himself. His face turned bright red and I couldn't help but laugh. I knew what it had looked like, but I never cared what anyone thought of me anyway. He and I both knew that nothing happened and that was enough.

Aryn quickly got up and dressed. I could tell his clothes were still wet as well. He shivered as he put them back on and they stuck to his skin. We readied ourselves for the debrief. Aryn quickly explained that our mission didn't go as planned and left it at that. No one asked any questions.

Orin smelled of brew and it made me nervous, but he seemed steady. More steady than the two younger boys which made me giggle briefly. I'm glad they enjoyed themselves, but I hoped they had come back with something useful.

"We met with the others. Everyone made it out good en'uf. They went to the location Lauren gave 'em to collect what they could. They should be here shortly."

Both Aryn and I nodded. "Anything else. Did you learn anything?"

"A few things. Yeah."

I questioned him with my eyes, the way my father would me when I was in trouble.

"It seems." He looked at Aryn. "The King is dead that part is true." There was something in his eyes. Pity maybe?

"And?" Aryn questioned further.

"Rumor is you did it." Pointing to Aryn. It was silent for a minute before he continued. "Apparently you murdered your father after the festival and took off with a..." He lowered his voice, "Whore."

I gasped. "Excuse me."

"I apologize miss, it's thems words not mine."

I studied Aryn's face but could hardly get a read on his emotions.

"The Queen. She has declared you a treasoner and sentenced you to death."

"So it's true. This was all her ploy to get rid of me?"

No one spoke.

"What do you want to do Ren?" I asked under my breath.

He stood studying the wall in front of him, of course it wasn't the wall. He was inside of himself. Formulating a plan.

"We sail to Picis. We meet this Captain Cassius."

"Actually..." Orin interrupted. "We won't gotta to sail anywhere."

"What do you mean?"

"Prince Cassius, Captain Cassius, whatever he is. He's here."

It didn't take long for them to give us the details. Apparently, the Captain-- who is rumored to be after the throne of Picis-- is here under business.

That's it. We would need to find a way to arrange a meeting with this guy. If the men brought back enough coin and weapons we might have a chance to convince him to fight with us. Maybe we could use his desire for the throne of Picis to our advantage. That is, if he wasn't already working for Queen B.

Our conversation was interrupted by shuffling sounds outside the cave. We stayed quiet and readied our swords. Someone was coming in through the path that lead to our cavern. Perhaps we had used it too often and made it more noticeable. It was definitely more than one someone. I heard gruffs and grunts of men shuffling closer.

I readied my bow.

"Hey, hey now. It's us. Don't kill the only few men you got." One of the guys blurted out. They had been drinking too. Hopefully for a cause. The few men that followed after carried chests. It took two men per chest. They set both on the ground and we grew closer. The men were cheering and hugging each other. Aryn bent down and opened the first chest. Swords, arrows, spears. Not many, but more than we needed.

The second chest was opened. My eyes grew wide, taking in what I saw. Gold, coins, and jewels. A lot of it. Surely this much would be missed easily.

"Tauren?" I hated to ask for fear of what the answer would be. Everyone looked blank.

"He wasn't there."

My breath caught in my throat.

"Which means he wasn't caught. At least not yet." Aryn reassured me. Why he was being so nice, I wasn't sure. He hated Tauren. "Are you sure you weren't followed? This could be a trap."

"We're farmers, sure. But we're also hunters. We know how to cover our tracks."

I curiously looked toward Orin.

"What we're supposed to live with one purpose? I say the more skills you got the better."

"I agree." And smiled.

"So now we find this Prince Cass."

"Captain." Someone corrected.

"Pirate." Aryn spat out.

CHAPTER TWENTY-EIGHT

Waiting Game

Aryn

I didn't like her plan one bit. We spent most of the night in the cave arguing about how we would get to the pirate. The men had heard rumors of his impending departure. No one knew when he was leaving, but the sooner we acted the better. I wanted to go with her. At least Orin volunteered to accompany her. He had earned my trust easily enough, fighting for a king he didn't know, with no army to support him.

Amira freshened up the best she could with fresh water from the cavern. She fixed her hair in a simple braid, leaving enough aside to frame her face from wondering eyes. With her filthy dress and old cloak, she was unrecognizable as a lady. To the unfamiliar eye, she was just a girl. She gathered her coin purse and filled it until it was nearly bursting. Hopefully it would be enough.

"Well…here I go." She said, raising her cloak above her head and smiling. I expected her to be nervous, but even I couldn't get a read on her. Where her confidence came from, I had no idea.

"Mer. Wait." I grabbed her arm. I'm not sure what I was trying to say. "Be careful." She just smiled at me and nodded. Before she walked through the exit, she looked back once more and narrowed her eyes on me. The same way she did while playing a game when we were children. This isn't a game Mer.

There was nothing to do now but wait.

A few of the men offered to go out and hunt for food. No one would question a group of men hunting. I on the other hand, was cooped up in this cave. An older guy named Stephan decided to stay back with me in case I was found. I was just glad to have the company. Who knew? A few days ago, I had longed for peace and quiet, but now I didn't know how to comprehend the thought of being alone. I felt more alone now than I ever have. Stephan kept the conversation simple, although he did seem to inquire about my relationship with Amira. I insisted we were just close friends. He simply nodded.

"Did you lose anyone? In the fires I mean?" I finally got the courage to ask.

A distant look rose upon his face. A few seconds later he gave a half smile. "No. No, I didn't lose anyone in the fire."

"So...no family?" I thought it strange that he was alone at his age.

"Not anymore." A sad smile lingered and he scribbled nonsense into the dirt with a stick.

I nodded, not wanting to upset him by continuing the conversation.

"I had a wife. Young and beautiful, far too beautiful for me. She had just given birth to my daughter." His throat caught, but he kept going. "Beautiful blond hair and fair blue eyes, like her mother. She was so tiny. I could almost hold her in hand." He looked down at his large hands with a distant gaze. Then he dropped his hands and looked up, obviously forcing a smile. "Then the plague came. They were both just too weak. It was over shortly. For that, I was thankful. My wife was too sick to even know we lost our baby. They both passed in their sleep." I noticed a single tear leave his face. I didn't know what to say to comfort him.

We sat in silence for a while. "I'm going to gather sticks for a fire tonight. If we hide it in the corner no one will be able to see it from the front of the falls. I won't be far away. Shout if anything goes wrong." He said. Actually, it was more like asking. I nodded my head and he made a slight bow as he left. I should have been accustomed to it, but it felt strange here. Here I was no prince, no king. Here I was Aryn.

CHAPTER TWENTY-NINE

Pirate Prince

Amira

I impatiently waited at the location I was given, Orin not too far away. There was a ship here, the crew busy loading and unloading supplies. No captain in sight. I could wait. I stared out into the water, letting my mind wander. The water reminded me of Lorin. Growing up, I was never afraid of much. That was until I got in the water. It was Lorin who taught me to be brave. He taught me how to swim. Now, the water felt natural.

I neared the edge of the dock and slipped my boot off. Slowly, I slid the tips of my toes into the water. It was cool and crisp, sending a chill through my spin, reminding me of the changing seasons. Everything within me felt cold. Even the salt filled air smelled different. Birds fluttered in the sky, finding places of refuge as winter became nearer. Astrean had one of the warmest and most stable climates of the seven kingdoms. Come winter, the birds always flocked to the woods, making hunting for the lower class easier. No one grew too hungry in Astrean, even if some had pigeon while others feasted on roast pork and a buffet of beef, fish, chicken, Pastas, and desserts.

"Somethin' I can do to help ye' miss?" A low and deep voice slid slowly from behind me. I turned to face him. The sun shone brightly behind him, his face a mere shadow in front of me. It took a moment for my eyes to adjust.

He was tall and muscular. Although clothed from head to toe, his shirt was fully unbuttoned and tucked into his tight trousers, exposing his chiseled chest. Raven dark hair fell messily upon his shoulders, braided in some parts, yet hidden by a large hat. I couldn't make out his eyes until he raised his head slightly. Dark, brooding eyes glared back at me intensely while a crooked, sly smile braced his lips.

I sucked in a deep breath. Something about him seemed so familiar, but men like this didn't roam the streets of Astrean. He was a man of the sea. Judging by his hat, a captain. This must be him.

He made a flaunty attempt at a bow, waving his arms around at random then reaching for my hand. "And you may be?" He said tilting his head just enough so that I could no longer see his eyes, only his deviously handsome smile. A shock pulsed through me as I reached out with my hand. He took my hand and gently kissed it…as if he were meeting a lady, yet I was dressed as a mere peasant girl.

He was charming. Playing at a game. One I could play too.

I raised my chin high and lowered the hood of my cloak. This far out, it was unlikely anyone would recognize me. "I'm a potential friend."

"A friend? Why, is that all?" He stood, his eyes narrowing as if they would burn through my skin.

"A client."

"Ey'. I see. Well let's go on to my office then." He gestured toward the ship. I knew Orin would not be happy about me going aboard a ship with a stranger, but this was my one chance. "After ye'"

He led me aboard, his arm behind my back, barely touching me. I could feel the heat radiating from his hand. The deck was wet and men scurried from place to place, all stopping to stare at the captain. I wondered if some of the men even fancied him. Respected possibly, feared…likely. There was a fierceness about him. Just being in his midst made me fear trespassing him.

I boarded the ship, eyes turned to me as I walked past with my head held high. I knew what they would think of me. There were too many reasons a young peasant woman would want to be along with such a devastatingly handsome Sea Captain. I just hoped that wasn't what he was expecting. I lightly brushed my arm against my side as I walked, reassuring myself that my handy dagger remained hidden, just out of sight.

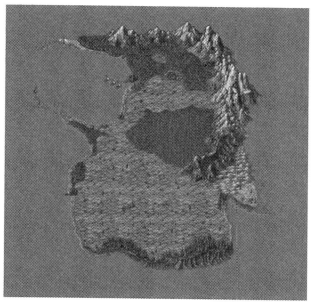

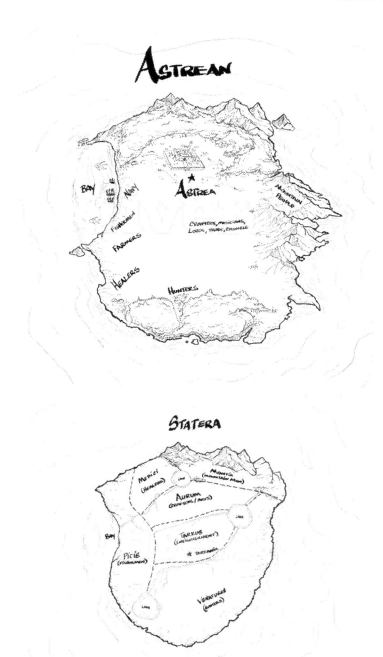

A shorter, plump man raced forward to open a door in front of us. His 'office' I assumed.

It was a terrible mess. Papers and maps were scattered in every direction. Plates and cups piled up in corners. The only pleasant things here were the artwork that hung upon the walls and a cabinet of treasures against the left wall. It was cozy. The books stacked along the opposite side of the room reminded me of Aryn's study. A large lounge area, complete with a table covered in half empty bottles, lay against the porthole. The center piece of the entire room was a grand desk and chair fit for royalty.

The only comfortable place to sit was a large hammock that hung beneath the porthole. I took a tall stance in the middle of the room and faced him. He walked to the table and grabbed two glasses, wiping one out with his unbuttoned shirt in an attempt to clean it I assumed. The Captain moved to the large desk and bent out of view, returning with a dusty bottle. After pouring the dark liquid from the once hidden container into both glasses, he handed me the one he had wiped out. I slowly accepted, not knowing what had once been in the glass I now held. This was no ordinary brew. The fragrant smell caressed my nose, it was a fine wine fit for a king. He took a long swig and looked back at me with his empty glass in hand.

I took a large gulp. It was much stronger than I anticipated but I fought off a grimace. He smiled, letting out a deep laugh, then poured himself another glass. He offered me another. Honestly, I wasn't even sure when this glass had last been cleaned and I despised another taste of the drink. I politely declined.

"I'm here on business."

"Right. Well go on. What's this business ye' speak of?' He said taking one last gulp. Setting his glass on the edge of his desk, he leaned against the top and crossed his feet. His sculpted torso still peaked from beneath his unbuttoned shirt and although it was quite cool in the room, beads of sweat glistened on his bare chest.

"You have something I need. I wish to make an agreement with you."

"Ey' and what be that?" He narrowed his eyes as he spoke in a slow deep voice. He rose from his desk and walked closer to me. Now only inches away, I had to tilt my head back to meet his gaze.

"You must know of the King's death and the Prince's treason?" I raised my eye brows.

"Ey'. That. Not sure if it's my place to say, but seems like the queen is turning out quite lucky in all this aye?"

"Quite lucky in deed." He didn't say as much, but I sensed he was wiser than the common passerby. "I plan to make many transactions with you, so long as we can stay on the same page." I was careful to not give too much away.

He remained mere inches from me, his black eyes starring mysteriously back at me. His poker face was strong, that was for sure.

"First, a few friends and I seek safe passage to Picis. I hear you are headed that way."

"Ey'?" Was all he said. "What would ye' be paying?"

I pulled the coin purse from my cloak and shoved it toward him.

"And why would ye' be wanting to go to Picis when you live in the wonderful Astrean, my lady?" He said bowing again. Lady? How did he know? The festival. That was where I remembered seeing him. I had bumped into him. I'm surprised I hadn't recognized him until now. He narrowed his eyes further, questioning me.

"My business is of no concern to you...yet."

"Yet?"

"I will be traveling with at least five other men."

"That's a lot of men." He said glancing back at his handful of coins.

"I have a lot more coin where that came from. But you will only receive it upon our arrival back to Astrean."

"Well, that is curious. Ye' want me to smuggle you and five other men out of paradise, and then back in?"

"That's only the beginning."

"I'm intrigued." He said leaning closer, as if that were possible. I could feel his warmth, as if he was pressed against me...he wasn't far from it.

"Come with me and you may find out the rest."

"Alone?" He said grinning mysteriously.

"I have men waiting for me. You may bring two of your men with you if it would make you feel more comfortable. I will pay for yours silence as well as theirs."

He stepped back and rubbed his beard.

"What are we waiting for? I'm always ready for an adventure."

"And have you chosen your two men? They must be trust worthy."

"Ey' but if I go alone I get three times the coin."

"You would follow me alone?" I narrowed my eyes.

"Ye' u can't be too harmful can ye'?"

"I may be small, but I am fierce." I stepped closer, breathing heavily. So, there was more space between us…it did not seem that way. I could smell his musky aroma as it burnt my nose. It was intoxicating. Much like the drink he offered me, strong yet alluring. I held my stand, gripping my hands into tiny fists.

"Well then, my fierce lady. Where we be headed?"

"I hope you don't mind blind folds." I teased, knowing Orin was standing ready to escort us.

"I like this game." He leaned closer, grabbing a small piece of my hair and twisting it between his fingers, sniffing it before releasing it back to my face.

This man was trouble. Or maybe it was me who was in trouble.

CHAPTER THIRTY

Dirty Deal

Aryn

The sky grew dark, beckoning my fear of Amira not returning. The men had all settled on dusty blankets along the cavern walls, few of them slept. Others tossed and turned, fighting the nightmares that invaded their slumber. The cave, although spacious, felt stuffy and cramped. I lingered near the rock by which Amira had recently slept, stoking a fire which remained alive, despite the damp cool air.

My limbs ached with stiffness from lack of movement so I stretched out on my back, facing the waterfall. I stared at it as if it were a window, even though the water was too heavy to see through. My eyes heavily drifted shut.

Footsteps echoed through the cavern. Someone was coming. The fire had died, the only remaining light was that of the moon and stars slipping through cracked ceiling of the cave... I fumbled in the dark, frantically reaching for my sword. I prayed my eyes would adjust to the darkness that now surrounded me. I could see the flickering glow of flames growing brighter from the entry tunnel. A few men stirred, waking from the growing brightness and increasing sound of footsteps. They quietly woke the men who yet slumbered. Each man rose to his feet, sleepy eyed and confused.

Some of the older men stood before me, as if attempting to shield me. Instead, I stepped forward. I would meet whoever was coming. No matter their intention.

A bird like whistle echoed through the cavern...the signal. "Lower your weapons." I whispered to the men. The men lowered their weapons obediently but remained on guard. I stood anxiously, waiting and hoping she would come through the tunnel entrance.

Amira entered the cavern first, lantern held high illuminating her face. I briskly walked toward her and placed my hand on her cheek. I was elated to see her unharmed. She smiled up at me and I fought the urge to hold her in my arms. I was so lost in her smile that I hadn't noticed the man following her. The pungent odor of alcohol and sea air now surrounded us, making my stomach turn.

I grabbed Amira's hand and pulled her beside me. He had come alone? No guards?

"You must be the Pirate." I snarled, drawing closer to him. He had at least two inches on me and looked as wide as door frame. I clenched my fists thinking of Amira nearly alone with this man. I thanked the stars Orin had accompanied her.

"These must be your men." He scuffed, eyes searching the faces gathered behind me. "And woman, of course." He said smiling wickedly toward Amira.

I clenched my jaw to refrain from saying anything I'd regret. "Amira has discussed our agreement with you?"

"Ey' she has."

"And you came alone? How do I know you are who you say you are?"

"I never said who I was, have I?" He arrogantly walked past me inspecting our humble hideaway.

"Are you or are you not the pirate Cassius?"

He stopped but did not turn. He simply stood silently staring at the ceiling.

"Are you—" Before I could finish, he cut me off. Something that angered me greatly.   "And who are you exactly?" He back still facing me. Why did he refuse to look at me? This wasn't an intelligent conversation. Did he not know who he was talking to? Right. Apparently, he didn't.

"Edwin. Edwin sent me to you. He said you could help us."

The man turned when he heard 'Edwin', a genuine smile appeared on his face.

"Old Edwin, huh? Still kicking around I see. And how's his ever so lovely bride doing these days?" It was as if he turned into a different person. Still arrogant, yet chipper and charming. One more reason not to trust him.

I heard a loud gulp behind me. Amira placed her hand on my arm and stepped forward.

"Margret...we lost Margret." Her voice caught in her throat and her gaze drifted down. The man stepped closer to her and placed his hand on her shoulder. I am standing right here. How dare he! Although, genuine sorrow seemed to spread across his face.

"I'm sorry to hear that," He paused, "May I ask what happened?"

"The queen." Was all I could mutter. He seemed confused.

"Queen Beatrice ordered a village to be burned. For no reason at all, she was but one of the many casualties."

"I see." He replied in his thick accent as he stepped away and turned around.

There was no reply from anyone. Was this conversation, if you'd call it that, going anywhere?

"And ye're after the Queen, is that right?"

No one knew how to respond.

"We demand justice." Amira stepped up.

"And who will serve this justice?"

"Me. If I have to." Amira said with confidence.

A small chuckle escaped the man's lips.

"Deal." He held out his hand for me to shake but kept his eyes on Amira.

"What exactly are you agreeing to Pirate?" I said, hands still at my side.

"Name's Cass. Prince Cassius."

"Prince? Prince of what?"

He waved his hand around like a drunken lunatic and preformed a sloppy half bow. "Prince of the Sea of course. Future King of Picis, and anything else I set my sight on."

I tasted a bit of blood from biting my cheek so harshly, something that I learned to do in the presence of my parents. What made me mad was the look he kept giving Amira. He was setting his sight on her. Her and who knows what else.

"And how do you plan on taking Picis? As far as I've heard King Malik still stands on the throne."

"Leans on it is more like it. Let's just say, plans are being put in motion." How could anyone trust the wicked grin that filled his face?

"We have the coin, as we agreed earlier. Half now, half when we return with more men." Amira explained.

"Am I to carry it back all by me lonesome?"

Amira glanced at me. "I'll send some men to help. But heed my warning, they had better return unharmed."

"Aye'." He held out his hand once more. I took it, reluctantly.

Before he left, we hashed out plans for meeting at the dock just before sunrise, which was merely a few hours from now. We would travel in groups to avoid drawing attention to ourselves.

In the morning, we would set sail to Picis.

CHAPTER THIRTY-ONE

Open Seas

Amira

The cool, salty breeze of morning bit at my bare face. My hair, although tied back in a braid, swung wildly in the wind loosening stray strands. Sleep had not been easy the night before. I laid awake watching Aryn toss and turn. He kept his distance. He only spoke of our plans yet seemed to keep a close eye on every move I made.

After maybe an hour of sleep, I woke to rustling feet and soft whispers. There were still a couple of hours until dawn. This was the perfect time to head out. We left in smaller groups, as discussed. We had little trouble making our way through the woods. We crept through the quite town to the spot we had decided on. The patrol was easy to sneak past in the cover of night but would be heavy come morning.

The ships were more guarded than we anticipated. Perhaps the Queen had expected us to run. Luckily, Cass had anticipated that outcome. There were large barrels at the back of an old street pub. Tauren and the men could get on board easily enough without being questioned. It seems Cass had a few fisher coins lying around, but I dared not to ask how. It was Aryn and I that were being hunted.

Hiding in the barrels made my body stiff and I smelled like dried jerky when the wind blew in the right direction. Although, the thought Aryn hiding in a barrel of dried meats, getting tossed around, sent a tickle to my stomach. Quickly covering my mouth, I held back my laughter. I wished I could have seen his face. Especially when his barrel seemed to receive a few extra kicks along the way. Cass didn't know who he was dealing with but if he had, I doubt he would behave any differently. Something told me Cassius wasn't one to bow down or follow rules.

I wasn't fond of hiding below deck as they prepared to set sail. Aryn still insisted on remaining silent, which made time almost come to a dreadful stop.

Finally, we set sail.

Although Astrean was a day's sail away from Picis, I was told it would take nearly three days until we arrived at Picis…depending on the weather.

I now stood on deck starring into the vast sea. Had all the lands really been connected at one point? No need to sail across the sea? Where was the adventure in that?

All the men were hard at work. I finally spotted Aryn standing near the rear of the boat with a bucket in one hand and a rag in the other.

"And what exactly are you trying to do?" I laughed.

"Scrubbing the deck." Aryn replied with a scowl on his face.

"What? Not the grand sea adventure you had hoped for?"

"I'm blending in, just like the others."

"I wouldn't call that blending in. Here, move over." I replied and bent down grabbing a salty wet rag and began brushing it against the deck.

"I don't need your help."

"And I don't intend on hiding under the deck, fearing for my completion, for the next three days. I need to keep my hands busy."

"Very well then."

"Oh. Thank you, your majesty, for the permission." I leaned in bumping him, trying to release his playful side. He only grabbed a second rag and followed my motion.

Hours had passed, men bustling around doing this and that. Not an idol hand on the entire ship. The rough sound of men singing helped pass the time. Although, I would hardly call their songs gentlemanly. I swear I saw Aryn blush once or twice at the mention of women in the songs. Shy, these men were not. I caught Orin giving me a few subtle apoplectic glances. True, I was a lady but I had also spent much of my time in the pubs. Their songs only brought a smile to my face. It was refreshing to see people so carefree. Working the large ship almost seemed like a dance. A dance all the men knew well. All men except the new ones aboard the crew. Even they seemed to fall into place in their own time. It was Aryn and I that stuck out like a sore thumb.

I envied these men. They lived for adventure, free at sea. Unending possibilities.

"Amira." The smooth deep voice startled me. I must've fallen under a trance with the steady movement of song and sea. I looked up, shielding my eyes from the blazing sun. It must be nearly noon. The dark silhouette of a man came into view.

"Why, if it isn't Prince Cassius himself, gracing us mere workers with his lovely presence."

"Anything for my adoring fans." He grinned with his sexy, crooked smile.

Aryn started coughing as if he were choking. I slapped him hard on the back but he just glared at me.

"What can I do for you Captain?" I stood, wiping my sweaty brow with the wet sleeve of my dress. I'm sure I was a sight for sore eyes at that moment.

"Actually, it's what I can do for ye'." His eyes darted to Aryn's then back at mine. "Take a walk?" He said, holding out his arm like a gentleman. Although, gentleman wasn't the word I would use. His sleeves were ripped, exposing bits of his dark arms, and his shirt remained unbuttoned nearly to his belly button. Puffs of dark hair encircled his chest. I swallowed loudly, glad the sound of sea and song easily drown out simple noises. My hand touched his forearm. His skin was hot to the touch. Sun kissed. Lucky Sun.

"I thought ye' might like to discuss your sleeping arrangements."

"Oh." I stopped, suddenly nervous. What was he suggesting?

"I'm sure ye' be uncomfortable in the bunker with the rest of the men"

"It's fine. I can protect myself…and I find hammocks quite comfortable. Even with the swaying of the sea."

"I was wonderin' if ye' be more comfortable in my cabin?" He said with a sharp eyebrow cocked. A scar ran across it making him seem more rugged.

"Uhh." For once, I wasn't sure how to respond.

"Not with me of course, I prefer my captain's quarters anyways. I've spent many a night sleepin' at my desk."

"Oh, no. You don't have to give up your cabin." I couldn't help but bite my lip. Why was I acting so nervous?

"I promise it's nothing special, ye' just have some more privacy is all."

"Oh, um…thank you. That would be nice I suppose." I said backing away and crossing my arms.

"Ye' know it's mighty bad luck to bring a woman aboard a ship."

"Well, then think of me as another man of the crew."

"That would be impossible." He said, almost a whisper. It was strange, sometimes he had this cocky arrogance and thick accent but others, he could almost pass as a gentleman. It made me wonder which Cass was the real Cassius.

CHAPTER THIRTY-TWO

Fish of Plenty

Amira

The gentle swaying of the ship easily rocked me to sleep, as if I were in my mother's arms. This is where I belong. Free.

The captain's cabin was quaint. It reminded me quite a bit of my room in the castle, but this was different. Setting out to sea made me feel like a bird finally leaving the nest she was always meant to.

Sleep overcame me, even in a stranger's bed.

Two long days had gone by. Cass had insisted I did not have to work for my keep but I was never one for idle hands. If the men had to work for food, so would I.

The journey was taking longer than expected. Dead wind. We were at a halt. The men were getting anxious and we were steadily going through the storage of mead and food. I chose to use my time wisely. I desired to learn every trade I could get my hands on. Speaking of hands, mine were now covered in blisters and cuts. The art of rope tying was simple enough but the sheer weight of the ropes were hard to manage with my small hands.

I picked up on the mens' language easily enough. The men took to fishing to pass time. That was a bit more difficult for me. It seemed like a waiting game. Was it normal to have such bad luck with fish? But it wasn't just me...there were no fish.

We were now on day five…out of three. It wasn't supposed to take this long. I knew voyages sometimes took longer than expected but we hadn't moved a bit. There simply was no wind…day or night. A slight breeze might pick up, cooling my sweat soaked dress, but that was it. I hated to admit how much I wanted a bath.

On day six, I noticed Cass' frustrated expression. He hadn't laughed the same in two days and his persistent flirting had nearly ceased. That was when whispers of curses began spreading among the crew. Most of the men started giving me ugly looks. Do they think it was me causing the dead wind? Am I the curse? Was Cassius right about it being bad luck to bring a woman aboard?

I ate dinner with Cass most nights. He was surprisingly gentlemen-like when we were alone. I hounded him with questions. He would speak of travel and adventure but never of family. I chose not to dig further. He listened intently whenever I spoke, but never asked questions. I'm guessing he understands the importance of keeping some things to yourself.

Tonight, was different. Instead of the lavish meals he always tried to impress me with, we were down to the dried meats and stale bread that the rest of the crew ate. I didn't mind. My stomach growled heavily, especially with the slow passing days. The odd part was that Cass didn't eat. He said he had work to attend to and his mead would be plenty.

That night I snuck out of my cabin, well Cass' cabin. I made my way to the storage room. That's when I realized…there was no more food. And why would there be? They had packed plenty for four or five days, which was longer than they were expecting. But they had also taken on twelve new crewmen. It was a miracle they made it this far.

That night, I had a dream. I told the men to cast their nets off the other side of the ship. They did…and they caught fish. Plenty of fish. So much fish that the length of our journey would not matter, we would have food for months.

The dream felt real. The next day, I told the men to do just that. When I mentioned it, the crew simply laughed at me. They had already tried that side. There was nothing. Finally, Aryn, Orin, and the others followed my advice. As soon as they cast the net the ship rocked and leaned in that direction, knocking the sailors off guard. They pulled on the nets but they wouldn't rise. The other men seemed confused but came to help. I could hardly believe my eyes. Just as the dream, the net was overflowing with fish. Men scrambled to help out.

I felt overjoyed...that is until I felt a presence beside me. Cass remained stern. Finally, he spoke. "Never in my days..." Then he looked at me with question in his eyes. I thought I could sense something else...fear, maybe?

The men were delighted. They sang, ate, and drank. All the men had gotten drunk. Even Aryn seemed lighter than usual. I headed back to the cabin.

"Mer." The heavy stench of cheap mead filled my nose.

"Aryn," I whispered, almost giggling. I had never seen him like this. So relaxed. He wasn't the same poised prince I knew. His hair was disheveled, the ends seemed even more blond that before. The sun had changed him. His skin even more tan now. His shirt was ripped and unbuttoned. He leaned against the wall as I watched his chest rise and fall. The boat rocked, knocking us both off balance. He leaned into me with his arm steading him on the wall behind me. He was close. Close enough that I could feel his breath on my ear as he looked down at me.

"You're drunk." I wasn't scolding him. In fact, I was teasing him.

"I am no such thing."

"Of course." I giggled.

With his other hand, he caressed my face.

"Why do you do this to me?" He questioned. His eyes narrowed on me.

"Wha...what do you mean?"

He placed his finger on my lips. The taste of salt lingered. "For once, just don't talk."

I wasn't sure I could at that moment. Before I realized what was happening, I was pushed against the wall, his lips pressed against mine. I didn't hesitate, my arms wrapped around him, breathing him in. The taste of salt and the smell of must filled my senses. Most women would hate that smell. I found it enticing. I wanted more. My lips parted slightly, letting him in. He didn't even ask permission, his velvet tongue took my mouth, exploring every hidden place that had never been explored before. My hand reached under his shirt, gliding up and down his back. I was lost...but it was exciting.

"Uht… hmm…" The sound of someone clearing their throat woke us both from our trance.

"Cass… Uh…"

"I came to wish ye' a good night. Seems as though someone beat me to it. Ren, I hope ye' not too drunk to find your way back to your hammock."

Aryn smiled at me one last time before stumbling back to the other men. Cass' face was impossible to read.

"Well then, Goodnight me' lady."

"Goodnight." The awkward silence filled the room as I stood alone.

The harsh rocking of the ship had awoken me, the room still dark as I searched blindly for the lantern. I struggled to steady my wobbly legs. Shouts echoed from above. Thunderous waves crashed against the sides of the ship, knocking me to the floor. I crawled toward the wall and felt for the door. As soon as I managed to open the door chaos surrounded me. Men, soaked to the bone, were running back and forth shouting things I could hardly understand.

"Aryn!" I cried out, completely forgetting to keep his name a secret.

"Ren!" A large man bumped into me knocking me into the wall. It was still night. I followed the commotion to the stairwell leading to the deck. Water came rushing in, making it hard to climb. It was especially difficult in my nightgown, which I embarrassingly realized might be near see-through once completely soaked. There was no time to run back to the cabin. Where was Aryn?

I finally reached the deck. The storm roared and lightning brightened the sky around me. I reached for the man nearest me and tugged his arm tightly. "Where is the Captain?" The crashing waves were so loud that I could barely hear my own thoughts as the rain poured down my face, blurring my vision.

"Er. He be at the helm."

"What happened?"

"He switched course, set out to Aurum. But it led straight into the monster of the sea. She's a bad beast, this one. Best get to safety or ye' be tossed overboard." He shouted over the rain and released himself from my grip.

I looked toward the helm and saw a faint outline of Cass at the wheel. The rain drenched my night clothes and continued to make it difficult to see. I could barely see what was right in front of me. I weaved my way through the men, grabbing them when needed to stay upright. What had he meant 'switched course'?

"Cass! What in the seven kingdoms are you doing?" I shouted.

He hardly took his eyes off of the sea. There was a look in his eyes…a deadly, determined look.

"Where are we going?" I shouted this time pulling on his arm. He was so stern, I felt like a small child tugging on him.

He finally broke his gaze and looked at me. His expression changed as he looked me up and down. That familiar crooked smile filled his face. I peered down. My suspicions were correct…my night dress had been soaked and now only a sheer layer of sopping wet cloth covered me. I crossed my arms to hide myself from his lustful eyes. He took his hands off the wheel for only a moment and handed me his coat. The wheel began to shake and spin wildly. I took his coat and quickly wrapped it around myself, hoping to hide my embarrassment. It was warm from his body heat, but quickly turned chilled as the rain slid between me and this coat. It that was several sizes too big and no matter how tight I wrapped it around me, it seemed the rain found its way in and dripped down my shivering body. At least it covered me. He grabbed the wheel and held it sternly, eyes focused on the sea ahead.

"We need to get out of this storm!" I yelled.

"What do ye' think I'm doing girl?" His brow furrowed in frustration. "It's as if she's followin' me!"

"Are we headed to Picis or not?" I demanded.

"Ah… We were, I just changed course a bit. Pit stop is all."

"Well turn us around!" The ship rocked and I nearly fell. Someone had come behind me and held me up.

"My lady." I turned to see Orin. His scruffy beard had grown even longer in the past few days. He easily fit in with the men aboard this ship. It was no wonder I had not been able to pick him out from the crew as they worked.

"Where's..." I paused, "Ren?"

"He's below deck lookin' for you."

If he was below deck he was safe. I hoped...

A horrible sound came from behind me and I ducked. Orin leaned over, shielding me.

"Straps! Take the wheel." I heard Cass yell, he took off toward where the sound had come from. It was raining hard, too hard to see anything.

"Turn us towards Picis now!" I demanded to the man called Straps.

"Ye' aint the cap'in girl."

I stormed off to talk some sense into Cassius.

Just as I ran to him a massive wave crashed into the ship. I fell back and hit my head on something, not before seeing a dreadful sight. He was there one moment...and gone the next. Just as waves come and go, that wave came, taking something with it.

Cass.

It happened in the blink of an eye. I screamed out, struggling to get to my feet. I ran to the side, leaning over the ship and called out to the black water raging around us. What just happened? It was as if the sea took him. I struggled to jump in after him, Orin had run up behind me and held him back.

"We have to save him. We need him!"

Familiar arms wrapped around me, pulling me down and holding me close. When I finally stopped struggling, I cuddled deeper into his arms. The winds began to slow and the storm ceased, followed by a calm breeze and pink halo signaling the break of dawn. I looked into Aryn's eyes. "What do we do now?"

CHAPTER THIRTY-THREE

Curses

Aryn

I held Amira in my arms for only a few brief moments before she composed herself. She stood so mightily, despite her small stature.

"We will send a boat to search for the captain!" She demanded. It was then that I noticed she wore only her nightgown and the Captain's coat. She had said she was staying in his cabin. I protested, but she promised that she would be alone. Safe. Now I wasn't so sure.

The men were silent, taking off hats and bandanas, they stood in a solemn solute.

"What are you doing?" She demanded, turning to look at the men.

A man, whose name I did not know, stepped forward.

"This is y'er fault. He soulda never allowed no girl on this ship." He yelled, pointing his water-logged finger at Amira. Men shouted in agreement others protested. Fights broke out. It was like watching wild animals. The sea may now be calm, but the raging fear and anger remained aboard the ship.

"He's still out there. We can find him." Amira shouted.

"The cap has gone down, we all saw it. We solute him and will drink in remembrance of 'em, but I'm the cap now. Unless anyone of ye' opposes." He said holding a sword out in front of him, searching the eyes of the men around him. "All agreed say ey'." Rounds of men shouted 'ey'.

"Then where are you taking us?" She asked directly, walking so close to his sword that it nearly stuck in her belly. Not even the ship's crew were brave enough to stand so close to the new Captain.

"I don't know what kind of deal ye' had with Cassius, but I'm dropping ye' off at the nearest dock…or island." He said narrowing his eyes.

"Our deal was Picis!" She demanded again.

"Be glad I'm not throwin' ye' to the sea." He smirked at Aryn. "We head back to Astrean. Seems we have a hefty bounty aboard, and I tend to collect."

Arms grabbed hold of me. I struggled but couldn't get loose. I heard Amira screaming behind me. I gave everything I could but something came crashing down on my head and everything went black.

The ground was hard and my clothes wet, pasted to my skin. It was dark. A lantern in the corner lit the area just enough for me to realize where I was.

The Brig. The ship's dungeon. Locked behind bars. My first thought… Where's Amira?

My men were eventually thrown in with me. No word on Amira. I faintly remembered the night before. My lips on hers. Had I really done that? With all of the celebration of fish, all I could think about was hunger. But not for food, for her. What surprised me the most was how she responded. She wanted me too. I could feel it. I've become so jealous, seeing the way Cassius looks at her and the way she looks back at him. Last night, she was mine…and now she was gone.

At least a day had passed. We shouted and tested the strength of the iron bars keeping us. Nothing.

"Well, that's no way for my guests to be treated. Especially not a prince." A familiar voice came from the stairs. I knew who it was but, how was that possible?

CHAPTER THIRTY-FOUR

Belly of the Whale

Cassius

I awoke in darkness and stench. Liquid was slushing all around me, but no higher than a foot or two. I stood to examine my surroundings. I wasn't on an island. The ground beneath me wasn't made of sand or stone. Instead, it was wet. It felt like flesh.

This was it. I was in the Deep. Not everyone believed in the Deep. People believed in many things, mostly the stars…where the Great Sorcerer emerged. When a good man died, he was burned and his ashes rose to the sky to become another shining star. Fishermen and pirates didn't get this curtesy, most died at sea. We believed in being swallowed up by the sea and becoming forever one with the water. The salt of the water was said to be the last tears of men fighting for breath.

I searched for an escape, my time couldn't be up. I still had so much to accomplish. My plans… I never believed in the Great Source from the stars. Maybe as a child, but I learned early on that a man makes his own way. If I had to fight my way out of the Deep, I would.

The echoing sound of growling surrounded me. Maybe this was all a dream. A mystery girl showed up, a siren more likely. A deal to take her to Picis that I had turned my back on that sent me to my death. I had easily learned who her mystery 'friend' was. I wasn't stupid. Still, I'd abide in their little plan. They could be of use to me. The girl was nothing like I had ever seen before. Such fierceness, such passion.

The men spoke of curses. Something I didn't believe in, that is until the wind died. One day would have been nothing extraordinary but so many days with not even the slightest breeze at all... Maybe I was the only one who notice, but there seemed to always be the slightest breeze as Amira passed by. Not enough to move the ship, but enough to caress her soft dark hair.

Everyone had heard the rumors of darkness...the shadow. Legend says that when light was created, something else was ripped away. A shadow. That darkness has slipped across the lands, lurking in the shadows. Again, something I didn't believe in. The men spread hearsay of Amira bringing the shadow aboard the ship. No wind and soon no food. The thoughts injected themselves into my mind but were soon cast away as I saw her perform a miracle. By her words, the fish were back. So much so, the ship nearly sank from the weight. She wasn't a shadow, she was light.

Something changed in me that night. I saw her with him, the run-away prince. Jealousy raged within me. How could I have been so blind? She didn't want me, she was using me. I changed course to Aurum. There was business there I needed to attend to, then I'd take care of the prince. His head would fetch a hefty price with the Queen. And with him out of the way, things would be easier.

I reached for my sword, but it had been taken by the sea. Luckily, I still had a dagger hidden away in my belt. I waited for my eyes to adjust, but the darkness never seemed to fade. I stabbed my dagger into the flesh that surrounded me. A great groan filled my ears and immense pain rushed through me. It was as if I had been stabbed in return. I reacted quickly and dug my dagger back into the flesh, the pain followed immediately. What was this magic? Once more, I thrust my dagger into the flesh wall. Again, searing pain shot through me.

I had to rethink my way out.

It was hard to tell time here, but it seemed as if days had passed. Hunger ate away at my stomach. My body still ached, yet no flesh seemed to be torn. The thirst is what took me first, my throat dry as leather. Even breathing brought with it excruciating pain. I prayed for death. No one deserved this torture. Especially not a Prince... even if I had yet to officially claim the title.

All strength was drained from me. I laid on the strange, wet ground. My flesh now soft. The water lapped around me, washing over my face. I felt my last breaths coming. Suddenly a flash of light appeared above me.

Everything white. I was still unable to move. The light was blinding. Just as in the darkness, I could see nothing. With the thirst that had stretched for an unknown amount of time, my throat like sandpaper, I was unable to speak. Just then I heard a voice.

"Cassius. Although you do not see me, I see you. You are meant for greatness. Don't let darkness lead you down the wrong path." The strange voice continued to speak to me. I've lost my mind. I took one more deep breath, as I released it I felt free.

Suddenly everything around me began jerking. A quake maybe? The water around me vibrated. I found strength to open my eyes one last time. Light. It was coming from somewhere. Water came flooding in. I fought to stay afloat, to catch one more breath. Eventually, I was completely submerged in the water. A great gushing pushed at me, the heat I had felt was replaced with cold. The darkness replaced by light. I was surrounded with the color blue. I floated with the waves until I saw a small boat floating toward me. I found strength I was unaware that I possessed. I pulled myself into the boat and laid there looking at the night. Stars shown brighter than ever before and the moon was blinding. A great whale surfaced, spraying water into the air as it took breath. I simply watched as it splashed away, never to be seen again.

What a strange thing. Maybe a dream? This small raft was filled with jugs of water and fresh food. At that moment, I did not care if this were a dream or death. I indulged every sense. The food and water were like nothing I had tasted before. The water tasted almost sweet. The food was fresh. Fruits so lush, the juices ran down my neck. Meat so savory, the spices lingered on my fingers until I licked them clean.

The raft floated for a short time before I began hearing shouts. Familiar voices filled the air as the sun took to the sky.

CHAPTER THIRTY-FIVE

New Captain

Amira

Here I sat in Cass' cabin…well, not Cass' anymore. Everything had gone wrong. They knew who Aryn was. Me..? I was a witch, they said. Aryn and I were kept separately, I remained locked here while unsure of where they were keeping him. The most likely location he was, the brig. I hope Aryn is alright. The only one who came to visit was Captain Judas. He certainly wasn't the gentleman Cassius was. Judas was older with skin like leather and missing teeth. He was still a big guy, which might be why no one fought against him.

He tried to have his way with me… Since according to him, I had been easy with Cass and my men…he didn't take it well when I fought back. He eventually gave up, saying something was wrong with me. I spent my time planning a revolt. I could escape the room easily enough, but it would mean nothing if I couldn't get Aryn and the others off of the ship with me. The best thing to do was wait. Wait and hope Aryn was okay.

Harsh shouts of the crew had awoken me. Things have been tense lately. The wind was still gone and the men had grown tired of old fish. I also suspected a lack of respect for this so called new Captain. The men were always loud…but something was different. It sounded as if fighting had broken out on deck. Although, with pirates, that didn't seem too out of the ordinary. Still, I readied myself. This could be the opportunity I had been waiting for. I had no weapon save a dinner knife I hid away.

Suddenly, there was a banging on the door. I hid in the corner of the room, shrouding myself within the shadows. Once the door opened I would attack and slip out. Maybe with the ship preoccupied, I could get to Aryn and use the lifeboat to escape in the dark of night.

More banging, then the door burst open. I slowed my breath, readying myself. I held the knife in my hands and slipped behind the dark figure. Knife to his neck.

"You never cease to amaze me, me lady." The deep throaty voice spoke without fear. He stood tall, unwavering. It couldn't be.

I slowly slipped around him. My breath was sucked away, as if someone had punched me deep in the gut. "… Cassius?"

"In the flesh." He bowed, even though I still held the knife out. I could hear the smile in his voice. He pushed the knife away gently, his hand lingering on mine.

"I don't understand."

"If I'm speaking truth, neither do I." I heard a mad chuckle escape his lips.

"Anything I should know about?" I said, gesturing beyond the door.

"We've got a lot to catch up on."

"…And Aryn?" I bit my lip, trying to hide a nervous tone from escaping my lips.

"Ah. Yes. The boyfriend." He said slowly and somehow still flirtatiously.

"He's not—"

"He'll be fine. In fact, it's probably time to go rescue him. Would you like to do the honors, or shall I?"

Making our way to the top deck, I noticed a few slain bodies lying around. No one I honestly cared for, but still…I grimaced at the blood, still something I wasn't used to. I've seen death, but not this close. I saw Judas tied up with ropes. I returned the glare he gave me as I walked past. Few men were injured, but it didn't seem like anything serious. Bloody noses and cuts.

I was hesitant to follow Cassius, but wasn't this the moment I had prayed for?

We walked down the dark stairwell to the brig. It was then that I realized just how fowl Cass smelled but that wasn't important at the moment.

"Well, that's no way for my guests to be treated. Especially not a prince."

I found a couple of lanterns to light. I was suspicious because Cass didn't release Aryn. Not right away. Instead, it seemed like he toyed with him for a few moments.

"Mer. Are you okay? What happened? How did he get back on board? Where's Judas? Did they do anything to you?"

I grabbed the keys dangling form Cass' coat pocket and walked toward the small jail. Cass didn't stop me. He just leaned against the back wall, arms folded and legs crossed, watching us. I ran into Aryn's arms. "Are you okay?" I stepped back looking at each of the men. "Are you all okay?"

"All right, all right. We've got work to do if we're going to make it Picis." Cass said, heading to the deck.

"Picis?" I ran after him.

"That was our deal, was it not?" He turned to me with his eyebrow raised. This man was mad, but not in an angry way.

"So, you've changed your mind?"

"Ey" He said as he continued toward the helm. "There be much to say, but first we start with…does anyone here hold any objections to my being cap'in?" His language always seemed so different with the crew.

No one opposed. "Then so be." Shouts erupted from the men. "Now, you be wonderin' what happened to ye' ole' cap'in, huh?" Heads nodded. "It be hard to explain. In the depths I awoken, in the belly of a whale-" Men shouted. I was confused but listened none the less. "Visions I had. A voice spoke to me. All is clear now what we must do."

And that's all, he didn't explain anything else.

I made sure the men got plenty of food and water and saw to any wounds I could. My sewing skills had finally come in handy.

'So… How long have you known?" I crept up behind Cass.

"Soon as I saw him. Hard to hide a life time of playing Princess."

"Prince." I corrected sternly. He just smiled.

"Why do they call you Prince?" I asked.

"Ay', yes. My dad, Xerxes,-"

"Xerxes?"

"Let me finish?" I shut my mouth and nodded. "Well…I'm a bastard, but still heir to the throne. More so than Malic, if you ask me. Rumors state he's a bastard too, that the queen had an affair. If the rumors are true, then you're looking at a prince."

"But Xerxes is dead…"

"Ey'."

"That would make you a king."

He smiled down at me. "Clever lady."

"It seems as though you need my assistance. Men, you said. I might be able to help with that."

"But?"

"But I be needin' your help as well."

That was it, a deal.

CHAPTER THIRTY-SIX

Masks

Aryn

Finally, the wind had picked up. So much so that we seemed to skirt across the sea. The strange part was, the water remained relatively smooth despite the heavy wind. The sun shone brightly but clouds added a nice shade and comfortable temperature. This trip had taken longer than expected and certainly had its ups and downs. At least now I knew Amira was safe.

Now that all of the men knew who I was, they looked at me differently. Although, I was still treated the same, like a cabin boy. They were from Picis, anyway, I wasn't their king. I wasn't anyone's king. Not until I took my throne back. I was basically a no one. Amira had earned the respect of the crew. Rumors had spread of a power she wielded. Strangely, I had started to believe it myself. Maybe it was the long days at sea messing with my mind.

We were maybe a few hours from port. It had been years since traveling to Picis with my father. I wasn't quite sure how they knew how far out we were. All I saw was water and sky. Amira had been below deck with Cassius. I tried not to let it bother me but couldn't stop thinking about them alone together. Soon they asked me below as well. Something was going on.

They shared their plan with me. I felt angered that I had not been asked to join their little meeting from the beginning, but I was learning I had no power here. They explained everything in detail. Infiltrate the castle. Attend a Mascaraed ball with Amira, that part I did not object to, and then leave. There was obviously something they weren't telling me. They said it was the only way to secure the men we needed.

There was something hidden on Amira's face. I still didn't trust Cassius.

There was one problem with the plan… How would he get in? I was the one to suggest using the barrels. Cassius wasn't fond of the idea, but it was the best we had.

We docked the ship, in a discrete area I pointed out. There was a path leading to an extravagant lodging within the woods. Cassius sent for a tailor and we went to work. It felt strange wearing such fine clothes after the past couple of weeks. A nice shave was welcomed too. Cass had taken care of the invitation. We were meant to arrive days before hand to prepare, but instead we had hours. That didn't seem like enough time to scrub myself of the lingering fish smell. The clothes were foreign to me. They were his, altared to fit me. I swallowed my pride. More like choked on it.

There were people running all around me preparing what they could. It reminded me a bit of home. I took to memorizing the names of the invitation and any other detail that might put us in any kind of danger.

I heard a sharp whistle and turned. My heart stopped. Amira. She looked like a princess…or maybe not a princess. Something…more magical. She was clothed in black and silver from head to toe. She wore a figure hugging dress with a lower neckline than I had ever seen her in. My throat grew dry and my ears burned. She wore dark makeup on her face and her black hair cascaded down her back in waves with jewels weaved throughout. She held her mask to her face. Black and silver, matching her dress. She looked like a raven. A beautiful creature of the night.

"Well?" she said turning slowly. I was speechless.

Behind her, a slow clap started. "Breathtaking. If I do say so me'self." I bit my tongue and narrowed my eyes toward him. He stood awfully close to her, too close for my liking. I stepped forward. Two could play this game.

"You look ravishing Mer." She blushed, giving Cassius an awkward glance.

"You look handsome as well, Ren."

"You mean Phillip. Phillip and Mary Conroe that is."

"Of course." She replied.

"Ah. But one more thing. A wealthy couple as yourselves, a lady isn't complete without her jewelry." He held out a diamond ring. Amira awkwardly glanced between us before finally holding her hand out toward him. He reached for her hand and slipped the ring on...ever so slowly. He held her hand in his and his eyes lingered on hers. Hers lingered back on him...

"So, we should probably get going right?"

"Of course, Aryn." Cassius said, pausing before using my name.

We took a carriage to the castle. It wasn't quite as grand as Astrean. The roads were mostly dirt rather than stone. It hadn't changed much since my last visit, except this time there was no royal welcome. We were greeted, of course. I showed our invitation... Holding my breath. I knew very well this could be a setup or that we could be recognized, our plan discovered. The masks helped. Amira seemed to keep her cool the entire time. Our ride had been silent but I planned on asking questions at some point tonight.

The ball wasn't that different to ones we had thrown back home. Except, here I was an attendee. It felt nice actually. No pressure. Here, I was Aryn. Well...Phillip. But maybe I preferred being Phillip. Phillip with my wife Marry. I smiled at the thought, but a small sting of guilt pained me. Aryn, Prince Aryn, was still betrothed to another. But here and now, I was with Amira. And I didn't want anything else.

We danced, ate, and tried to make small talk with others. It was easier to remain silent, avoid as many questions as possible.

Dancing with Amira was magical. The way she moved in my arms...it was entrancing. Maybe she was magical after all. She had cast a spell upon me. Maybe she had long ago...

I noticed her glancing around the entire night. She knew something. Something I didn't. I knew Cassius was here. He snuck in by hiding in barrels of wheat, I hoped it stuck to him and caused him to itch. I'm sure saying that made me sound like a child, but I didn't care. The question was, what was he doing here?

All were seated in a dining hall with rows upon rows of fish, seafood, and desserts offered. To be honest, I had grown tired of fish. Was this all they ate? King Malik stood to make a toast. Rumors had spread of his sickness and now I could see it in his face, no matter how hard he tried to hide it. Even from where I stood, I was able to tell he wore make-up. He sounded breathless as he spoke. He kept it short, then was escorted out of the main hall. Scattered whispers filled the air, but no one dared speak loud enough for anyone to hear.

The feasting began. I ate all the fish I could manage. Amira seemed to enjoy it more than I had.

Suddenly, the doors burst open and guards ran around like ants.

They found us.

CHAPTER THIRTY-SEVEN

Home

Amira

We were held at the castle until late in the night. The plan must have worked. Guards and officials scurried about. Aryn didn't have a clue as to what had happened…but I knew. King Malik was dead. After the craziness, we were all dismissed. Given very little information.

We waited at the lodging Cass provided. He was still yet to join us. I worried. Aryn demanded answers, so finally I gave them. Most of them, anyway. I explained how Cassius was the son of Xerxes. With King Malik dead, Cass was headed toward the throne…if all went well. I didn't know much about what happened to Malik, just that he had been sickly for a long time. I was against killing in cold blood, especially to get a throne…but how was that any different than what we were planning? I swore to myself that if we captured the queen, we would do things by the law. Which was more than she deserved.

Days went by before a carriage and guards finally arrived at the house. The men had taken turns guarding the outside of the lodging. I listened but heard no fighting. Perhaps it was good news.

A knock came at the door, John- one of our men- answered. Standing before us was a polished Cassius. Clothed in fine blue velvet and gold buttons. He had shaved, or at least trimmed, his beard and hair. Where his captain's hat once stood, a small golden crown with jewels of sapphire now glimmered in the light. He still held his crooked smile and his gaze bore into me.

"So…" I said.

"I would like to cordially invite you, personally, to my crowning tomorrow."

"Seems as if you already have a crown." I joked

"Ah, yes. This old thing. No this is for show, temporary." He winked at me, "If this impresses you, my lady, you should see the one I'm getting tomorrow."

His speech had completely changed. Even his posture. It was as if he were a different person. Except he wasn't. No one else looked at me the way he did. The way that sent heat down my spine. Well...maybe Aryn did. But I couldn't focus on that now. I had to stick to the plan. For Aryn and for our people.

Cass... Prince? King...? Cassius, didn't stay long. Too much to do, he said. Aryn didn't say much. I couldn't tell what he was thinking.

The next day we readied ourselves. What do you wear for a coronation of...a friend? It didn't matter. His servants had dropped off our outfits. It was strange seeing people without coins or brands. I often wondered how other kingdoms worked without the coin system. Were they free to choose? I envied their freedom to choose.

The coronation was beautiful. Cass was beautiful. Aryn was beautiful. I apparently was too according to a lot of people. I wasn't used to such compliments. Even at the castle, I found ways to avoid men. I would have to get used to dressing glamorously and to Picis soon...

Just as Cass had promised, he gave us men. One hundred men to take back Aryn's castle. With Aryn as king, an alliance would be formed. Astrean and Picis have always had a strong alliance. He would give us men, we would give him wealth and power beyond that of any of the other six kingdoms. The agreement would remain, we would come to their aid if ever need be. Also, they would remain 'Pirates of the Sea' controlling the trade. I didn't like that. I wanted things to be fair...but you can't have everything.

We set sail the very next day. Now it all felt so sudden. We had a few ships and one hundred men. We wouldn't attack right away. Instead, few would come to land with us, the others sailing and waiting. Slowing spilling in little by little to not arouse suspicion.

It was my idea to build our own army from our own soil, not just our group of ten men. People will follow Aryn. I knew it, I always had.

As they expected. It only took a day to sail to Astrean. It was a vastly different experience from the first trip. I didn't know what happened to Judas, but I wasn't sure I wanted to know.

It felt strange to be back on Astrean soil. As much as I wanted to travel the world, a part of me never wanted to leave again. I knew that wasn't possible though. I thought back to my father, how hard it must have been to leave us behind every time he left. Except…I had no one to leave behind. I was all alone.

Our mission began.

CHAPTER THIRTY-EIGHT

Promise

Aryn

We first arrived at a small hunting village far from the castle. It wasn't at all what I had imagined. These people were not well off. We clearly were not expected. They hardly believed I was back. They had questions, of course. The Queen had spread awful rumors of my cowardly actions and selfish love affair with my maid. She had also been burning more villages and raising taxes. From what we could gather, the wealthy were becoming wealthier and the poor were becoming poorer. This had to end.

Eventually, they offered to shelter us. Some of them were scared to rebel against the Queen. But these men were hunters, born warriors. It was a good place to start. Amira was wise beyond her years. She reminded me so much of her father.

Food was scarce. Children were hungry. The fires had scared away much of the wildlife. We had very little to eat. It would soon be time to leave these people and move to another village.

A small girl approached Amira, she offered her a meal of dried meat. I was tired of dried meat, even I knew how special that small gift was. She said it was all she had, but she wanted to offer it to the king. Me... King. This little girl wanted to give me her last meal. I didn't know how to respond.

Amira smiled. She broke a piece of the meat and offered it to me. All eyes were on me, what I would do next. As king, I could not deny a gift, I also didn't want to take this little girl's meal. Amira nodded and I took a bite. The meat tasted sweet. It was much better than I could have imagined. I found myself taking another bite and then another. This small piece of meat had filled me up. Amira broke off another piece and handed it to the girl. She began to eat. Amira began to walk around the camp breaking off small pieces of meat and handing it to the people. I didn't know what to think. Was this a trick? What she had held in her hand was barely enough for one person, yet I was left full. I walked up to her to observe.

"Care to help?" She broke off a piece and handed it to me. Surely, I couldn't do as she did...she was performing a miracle right before my eyes. Right before everyone.

I finally walked up to a family. I held a handful of meat. Who do I feed first? Who will eat and who will go hungry? The woman I stood in front of was clearly with child. I offered her a decent portion and planned to give the rest to the child that stood by her legs. Yet, when I broke off some for the child plenty seemed to remain in my hand. I broke off another piece and gave some to the father. I moved from family to family, others offering to help. All amazed at what was happening. By the end of the night, hundreds of bellies were full. That wasn't it... We had baskets of leftovers...all from the same small meal the little girl had offered me.

They lit a fire and celebrated with song and dance. All were praising Amira but she said it wasn't her. I'm not sure anyone believed her. She danced by the light of the fire. I was mesmerized. Finally, I pulled her aside.

"How?" I asked.

"How what?" She replied innocently.

"You know what." I shot back.

She stepped back and crossed her arms. "I...I don't know. I keep having these dreams. Visions maybe. Things just happen...before they happen. I've just been trusting them. I don't know how to explain it... it's like someone is guiding me and telling me what to do. How to help people." She avoided making eye contact with me.

"So that's what you have been keeping from me?"

It was dark but the nearby fire still illuminated her face, she tried to turn to the shadows.

"Mer?"

"Yes...and..."

"And what?" I demanded.

"Cass…"

I pulled her close so I could see her face clearly. "What about Cass?" My voice more than a whisper, but I didn't care.

"Aryn…don't look at me like that."

"Like what?"

"I'm engaged."

I didn't know what she meant.

"To be married…to Cassius."

"What?" I yelled.

She tried to quiet me. "The army, if I marry Cass, we get the army. That was the deal."

"You never told me. You can't. I won't allow it."

"It's too late. I've already accepted. We already have the army… More men, if we need it. If one hundred men can't take the castle, Cass plans on coming back with more men."

"He's going to take my castle?"

"No. No. We discussed. It. The throne is yours. Our marriage is sort of an alliance."

I turned around and began to storm off. I needed to be alone. How could she?

She grabbed my arm tightly, but I didn't turn to face her. I couldn't.

"Don't you see?" She pleaded, "I'm doing all of this for you!" I could hear her heavy breathing.

"I can't do this right now. We set out tomorrow. Gather more men."

There was no sleep that night…

The next morning, I was awoken by a townsman. He bowed and apologized for disturbing my slumber. There was nothing to disturb.

"There's word from the queen. She knows you're back. She knows you're here."

I jumped up and grabbed my coat. I dispatched a small group of men across the land to find answers. Before they left we had an unexpected visitor.

"So, you're back?"

"Tauren." I replied, "Still working for the queen?"

"Still spying." He said. I had little trust for anyone, especially Tauren.

"I came to give you a message from the queen..."

"And what is that message?"

"I've also come to tell you not to listen to her."

"Tauren," I demanded.

"She has sent word across the land... You surrender and the people will be free. No more villages will be harmed, taxes will decrease. Your army will be spared. So long as they pledge loyalty to her."

There was a long pause. I couldn't trust her, yet my mind went to Amira. If I surrendered, she was free of Cassius. Cassius, a man that would kill his own brother, a madman rambling about being swallowed by a whale. She would be free.

"There's one more thing..."

"Go on," I demanded.

"It's Lorin..."

"I know..."

"No...you don't. Since you've been gone...the queen. She can do things. She found Lorin, dying. Aryn, he's alive."

"That's impossible."

"I've seen him. He's being kept in the dungeon...everyone is terrified of the queen. She's been...doing things. I can't explain it."

The way he spoke, I knew what he meant. Amira had been...doing things too. How have I never noticed? Both of them? I didn't know either of them. Not really.

"I'll travel back right away. You stay here. Take care of Amira."

"No, you shouldn't. Do you know what she will do to you?"

"It doesn't matter. My people come first."

"If you cared about your people, you would be the king Amira sees you to be."

"I'm no king..." I muttered under my breath. "Fine. I won't leave until morning. I'm sure you're dying to see Amira. I have things to attend to, we will talk about this later."

Except, that wasn't true. I grabbed my cloak and slipped out.

Chapter Thirty-Nine

Confessions

Amira

As soon as I saw Tauren I ran into his arms. I hadn't realized how much I missed him.

"Amira..." He stepped back to look at me. "You've changed." I wore my hair in a braid down the side and had switched to simple clothes and trousers, easier to travel and fight in. I had also been training some men in my spare time. They insisted on not learning from a woman but Aryn insisted they listen to me. I enjoyed watching the men, like children, play along. We didn't have much time. They were hunters after all but hunting deer and hunting men were completely different.

Tauren quickly explained things that have been going on around the castle and Astrean. He explained odd things the queen had been able to do. He also questioned a few rumors he heard about me, but I didn't know how to respond. I didn't know what was happening to me any more than anyone else did.

Then he explained the queen's request. Before he could finish, I ran to Aryn's tent.

Although, I knew he wouldn't be there.

I gathered supplies and went after Aryn.

Tauren stopped me. "Amira. Don't do this. You can go after him, you can stop him. But make sure he doesn't get to the castle. The queen expects me back. And I expect to arrive alone. You may go find him... but don't let him surrender. As much as I hate to admit it...the kingdom needs him." He scratched his head in a nervous response, the same way Aryn always had.

"Don't worry. Go. I'll make sure Aryn doesn't make it to the castle."

Hopefully, I wasn't too far behind him. I made sure to pack everything I needed for the trip. I had a plan. I needed it to work. I wouldn't catch up to him right away. I'd keep my distance at first.

As I expected, it only took a couple of hours to catch up, but I stayed far behind him, far enough behind so he could not see me but I could watch him. I knew how to get to the castle. I would catch up to him when the time was right. It wasn't hard to follow his tracks, I knew him too well. I prayed he would stop for camp come night. It would be nearly two more days before he reached the castle if Tauren's directions were accurate.

He did. If I were to stay close to him, I couldn't light a fire. I also couldn't sleep on the ground with wild animals and no fire. I climbed a tree and made myself as comfortable as I could. Hoping I wouldn't fall in the dead of sleep.

The bark poked at my back and my butt quickly grew sore. Even my hair got caught in the loose bark any time I attempted to move my head. This was not the most comfortable place to sleep. That was for sure. There was something peaceful about the night. The cool fresh air, the sound of owls hooting in the night. I shivered as the night grew longer. Even my cloak and extra blanket I packed weren't enough to keep the cold at bay. I longed to be close to Aryn, his warmth. I quickly threw that thought from my mind. I couldn't keep thinking about him in that manner.

The next day he was on his way again. It wouldn't be long until I could show my face. Finally, I recognized where we were. And right on time. The sun had nearly set. I had followed Aryn for nearly two days now... impressed with my stealth.

It was time. I slowly walked up behind him. He didn't even turn.

"You shouldn't have followed me." He said.

"How?"

"I've known you my whole life Mer...but you can't stop me."

"I've known you my whole life... I'm not here to stop you. I know you would never allow me. I just can't let you go alone."

"I have to."

I grabbed his arm and turned him close to me. "Aryn." I pleaded.

"One more night. It's all I ask."

He looked confused.

I gestured toward the cave I knew we had come close to. Even he had found his way to it.

"I don't know...just give me one night. One night to talk you out of it or one night to come up with a plan...or one night to say goodbye." He turned away from me. I grabbed him once more and stepped in front of him. Without hesitation, I placed my lips on his.

He pulled away, but just barely. I could still feel his breath on mine. "Mer?"

"Don't. Don't say anything..." I grabbed his hand and lead him through the narrow path. It was growing darker. We walked in silence hand in hand.

"We can stay here for the night...then I head out." He said, reaching for my pack and digging for supplies. There was still wood from when we stayed before. He readied a fire.

"Aryn...there's something I need to say."

"Don't." He stopped me.

"Aryn. I love you."

He looked at me with so much hurt in his eyes.

"Aren't you going to say anything?" I pleaded.

He turned away from me once more.

I stepped in front of him. There was barely any room between him and the wall of the cave, but I didn't mind the closeness. I looked into his eyes. My breathing became uncontrollable. My palms began to sweat and a fire grew inside of me. Suddenly he pushed me against the wall, forcefully yet gentle. His eyes narrowed at me. It wasn't anger, it was hunger that blazed in those beautiful eyes of his. He took me in his arms, pushing me harder against the wall, pressing his body against mine as his lips took control.

We were lost. Lost in each other. Fighting between the need for air and kisses. He lowered his head, kissing my neck. My legs grew weak and a soft moan escaped my lips. "I love you," I said breathlessly. "I love you."

He stopped and looked deep into my eyes. "I love you too." His voice deeper than I had ever heard before. It drove me crazy.

"Then marry me. Marry me and we can be together." I whispered.

"You're asking me?" He said in a throaty voice.

"I'm begging you."

He took me closer, kissing me with more passion than I thought possible.

"Here. Now. Marry me." I pleaded.

He stepped back the turned around adjusting his sloppy clothes.

"Mer...I can't."

"Why can't you?" I pleaded.

"Mer...this could be our last night."

"Then spend it with me..."

"I can't...I can't ruin you."

"Ruin me?"

He grabbed me by the shoulders. "Mer. Whatever happens tomorrow, you will go on. You won't be alone. You can marry, you can be happy." He paused, "Anyone would be lucky to have you. Tauren...even."

"What?"

"Mer..." He spoke as if he were hurt. "Just promise you won't go to Cassius."

"Aryn!" I yelled.

"I will."

"You will what?"

"Marry you..."

"What?"

"In every way...except physically. Amira. I'm yours. I always have been and always will. I'm yours until the day I die." I threw my arms around him, knocking him to the ground. I climbed on top of him, kissing him. Our bodies pressing against each other.

I greedily ran my hands through his hair and he moaned. He flipped me over, attacking me like an animal. We were both hungry for each other. I didn't want this to ever end. The flames of fire grew brighter, dancing in celebration. He kissed my neck again and my back rose, arching toward him. He breathed in my ear. The heat spread through my body. He nibbled it gently, making me lose what little control I had left.

I pulled myself up, sitting on his lap. He kissed me once more before pulling back.

"We should get some sleep..." He said, slowly getting up and reaching for the blanket to lay out.

It took me a moment to compose myself.

"Here, I brought some mead. I thought we could use some." I tossed it to him and watched him drink eagerly. He insisted I used the blanket, but eventually agreed to share. One more night in each other's arms.

"You're impossible to resist, Amira. You know that right?"

"Apparently not that impossible. I giggled." He kissed my forehead and quickly drifted into a deep slumber.

It was time. He wouldn't wake for nearly a day if I dosed him right. I left most of my supplies with him. He needed them more than I. I wasn't far from the castle… From the Queen.

It was time.

CHAPTER FORTY

Illusions

Amira

He drank the mead, just as I had hoped. My plan was to distract him, get him to let his guard down. Maybe I went too far. It was I who let my walls come crumbling down. I was glad things didn't go too far last night. His resistance made me love him even more. He's a good man. That's why he deserves the throne. The people need him. He was strong and wise…but most importantly, he was kind.

There was no telling what I was walking into, but I knew the chances of me walking back out were slim. Maybe I should have given in to desire last night. One night, maybe the last.

I could have found a way to sneak into the castle, but that wasn't my plan. I would walk through the front gates…or maybe ride. My legs ached for a horse. I had some remaining coin. I could stop at a nearby village and buy a horse. Maybe that would make a better impression.

I strode into the nearest village, not far out of the way. I wasn't in too much of a hurry anyway. Brave. That's what Aryn often called me. He was wrong, I was anything but brave. Sweat poured from every inch of me, from places I wasn't aware it could. That was my plan. Just walk right up to the enemy. Sometimes there's a fine line between bravery and stupidity. What would my father say?

I found a nice family, they were healers. It was true. The queen was branding people. It wasn't just the coin they wore, it was embedded on their skin for everyone to see. Their children remained unbranded, they still had a chance to be whatever they wanted. Maybe they would choose to be healers. Perhaps, the coins were right occasionally. Some people seemed happy with their place.

I bartered for a horse but all they had was an old donkey. They had heard who I was and offered the donkey for free. I could see this was their only form of transportation. I couldn't just take it, but they insisted. I left some coin with them even after they refused to accept any. I wouldn't need it anyway.

Guess I was riding into the castle on a donkey... Not quite what I had expected, but why not?

Here I was, riding a donkey into town. Faces began to turn toward me as I road down the stone-paved road. My butt sore as I flopped back and forth. Still, I tried to sit upright and appear fierce. Whispers began to circulate amongst those who watched. My heart beat quickly and my hands began to shake. It was possible I would never even make it to the castle. I held the reign's firm.

A woman appeared before me. I stopped the donkey from running into her. Here I sat, on a donkey, in the middle of the road. She looked deep into my eyes. She held a bouquet of flowers in her hands. A beggar, selling wildflowers. I ached to do something for her. That was no life. She bowed down and slowly placed the flowers at the donkey's feet.

Why would she do that? Surely the profit she would make from the flowers would be scarce, but it was something. Now she had nothing.

"For King Aryn." She whispered, "And the good Lady Amira." She stepped away. I sat motionlessly. Others came forward, offering flowers or nice fabrics, laying them at the feet of the donkey. I nodded and continued forward.

Pray for me.

I passed through the capital of Astrea. Not one person stopped me. They watched me ride the donkey through the road, but never stopped me.

Finally, I arrived at the tall gates. I gulped loudly, holding the reins so tightly that my fingers grew numb. The guards seemed confused. They stepped forward, weapons facing me. I held up my hands in surrender and dismounted Maggie, the donkey. She deserved a name. They searched me and took my dagger. The one my brother had given me...

Here I was. Naked. I still wore my clothes sure, but I was as defenseless as a child. I knew this moment would come.

The guards escorted me away. Was it strange that I wondered what would happen to poor old Maggie?

I wasn't taken to the dungeons. I was escorted straight to the throne room. Directly to the Queen.

A long walk in silence. I stood before her. Queen Beatrice. Aryn's own mother.

"Will you not bow before your Queen?" She demanded.

"I bow before my King," I spoke strongly.

"I could have your head for that. First treason, planning an attack on the castle, killing the King, my husband, kidnapping the Prince. Everyone knows what you are. You've placed some sort of spell over my son. I have realized that none of this is his fault. Once we get rid of you, the curse will be lifted and he will be free to rule beside me."

She was crazy…or clever. Make me the evil one. Make the people believe this is all my doing.

"Where is he? My son? Is he well? I sent for him and yet here you stand." She stood, waving her hand toward me, "And don't think I haven't heard of your lovely engagement to the bastard King of Picis. What was your plan? Take Astrean and Picis for yourself? How selfish girl."

"I'm here to talk about your surrender," I said.

"Ha!" An unexpected laugh escaped her lips. She was tall and thin, her golden hair braided exquisitely under her crown. Her crown was anything but modest. There were seven, what looked like daggers, pointing to the sky…symbols of the Seven Kingdoms. She practically ruled them all. "Yes. Let us talk. Guards." She waved her hands. "Leave us be."

"But-" A guard tried to cut her off, the glare she gave him in response to his outburst made me pity him.

She would risk being alone with me?

"First, bring the prisoner."

We stood in silence, sizing each other up. Maybe I could take her with my bare hands. I wouldn't make it out of the castle alive…but at least she would be taken care of.

The doors were thrown open and a wicked smile crossed her lips. I kept my gaze on her.

"Mer?" A shout came from behind me. A voice I knew more than any other. I blinked. Frozen. I couldn't turn, afraid what I would see would confirm what I already knew.

"Bring him forward." The Queen demanded.

It was him…Lorin.

I ran to him, but the guards held their swords toward me. How was this possible? He couldn't be alive…I saw it happen…

"I saw him die!" I yelled, confused and angry.

"You might have seen him fall, my dear, but die he did not. You're not the only one to develop…a few skills. Yes…I've heard rumors of your marvelous works. I don't know where your help comes from, but I too have a friend who helps me."

"Mer…what are you doing here?" Lorin pleaded.

"Lorin…I had no idea… I would have…I would have come for you."

"No. Don't listen to her. Mer, don't worry about me. Please."

"Send him away…and leave us." She demanded.

"Wait no!" I ran after him, but the doors were shut before I could reach them. I turned to face my enemy. "What do you want?" I questioned, holding the tears in. I wouldn't give her the satisfaction. I could not show weakness now.

"Girl, I only want to talk. For now."

"Then go ahead."

"Hm…I never did like you." She said, almost under her breath.

"And what about your son? Do you love him?"

"My sons! Yes, I loved them. Loved them both and lost them both. You have no idea what that is like. To watch your first-born die and your last baby taken away."

"I didn't take him away! You drove him away. After you killed his father." I yelled.

"Wow, quite the accusation you've made there…but, no. I wasn't talking about Aryn." The way she said his name sent chills down my spine. What did she mean?

"Yes, well, I imagine I have some confessing to do. Just between us girls. You want the throne so bad, girl. There is much you don't know. A Queen never gets what she wants. The plague took Isaac, yes. It was your nasty mother's fault."

"You leave her out of this!" I yelled bawling up my fist. I didn't attack… she had something I could not risk losing…Lorin.

"But before that…I lost another son. You didn't know that did you?"

What is she talking about? What other son?

"It was at a time when the kingdom was beginning to appear weak. We needed a strong family. Boys to inherit the throne…but I suffered many miscarriages. We hid that from everyone. We couldn't give them a reason to think us unworthy of the throne. Of course, the King had many bastard children and I only had one. Finally, another was born. He was beautiful. So small. I hardly heard him cry. My second son. He looked just like Isaac."

She paused for a moment, "He was gone forever. I never got to say goodbye. Never got to feed him or kiss him. To watch him grow. Failure to thrive, they said. Born too soon, too frail. I screamed and screamed but was held down. Two days later, Ezra finally came in. He was holding a baby. My heart soared. My baby boy was okay. Except…It wasn't my baby boy. One of his whores had given birth shortly after me. Her's survived. Blond haired, blue eyed brat.

I wanted nothing to do with the child. I was given no choice. Either I claimed him as my own or lose my throne."

"Aryn… Aryn isn't yours?"

"No."

"And his mother?" I questioned.

"She was sent away. Bought. There could be no evidence of the child not being legitimate."

"So, she's alive?"

The queen chuckled. "No. I took care of that whore a few years later. Without Ezra knowing of course. He hadn't hidden her away as well as he thought. In fact, he often visited her. He grew terribly upset when he found that she had…run off."

"So, you never loved Aryn."

"That's not true!" She cried out. She had gone mad. "I grew to love that child. I still do…but not more than I love the throne. I deserve to be happy." She cried out again.

"I'll never let you have the throne!"

"You hurt me…you never see your brother again. Don't worry. I won't kill him. As it turns out, I need him alive. But in what state is up to you."

"What does that mean? 'You need him alive?"

"You see, when your dirty mother died and took my son with her I was beside myself. I nearly died myself. It was in those deep shadows I found my strength. The tradeoff was that I would be tethered to a life force- a bloodline, really." She smiled. "Yours."

What did she mean? 'My bloodline'?

"That's what killed your father, just so you know. I took too much too quickly. Lucky for me, he had two healthy children. Which means I only need one of you alive."

I rushed towards her losing my calm, but a force stopped me. It was as if I had hit an invisible wall. My feet could no longer move. I wanted to scream, but no words would come. Instead, I stared at her with daggers in my eyes. I didn't need words to tell her how I felt.

"Guards." She yelled out, this time in an eerily calm manner.

"Bring her to the dungeon. She will be executed in the morning."

I stood still. Speechless.

"Oh, don't worry girl. Aryn will be safe and so will your pathetic little army, so long as they pledge their loyalty to me."

The guards grabbed me by the arms forcefully, digging their fingers deeply into my tender skin. I would have bruises...or maybe I would be dead before they appeared.

"Don't even think about fighting back. I know you have a fight in you. Just think... your life for theirs. Aryn, those pathetic farmers, your brother...all spared if I can get rid of you."

I wanted to fight...but wasn't this why I had come? My life for theirs.

"Oh...and one more thing. Don't count on your precious Cassius to come to your rescue. He desires power. I have plans for him. And you... you'll be gone by evening tomorrow. Everything will be as it was."

"They will never follow you." I spat at her.

"They will have no other choice." She replied.

I was tossed in the cold, dark dungeon. Memories of the last time I was here flooded my mind. But it was okay. My brother was okay. Except...he wasn't here in the dungeon with me. Was what I witnessed an illusion? I wanted to believe he was alive...I had to.

I sat alone in the corner of my cell. I rubbed my arms to ease the chill in the air, but it didn't help. It didn't matter anyway. I was doing this for

Aryn. He was a good man. The people needed him. He is strong, he would fight back. They would all fight back. This was what I was meant for... my destiny.

Suddenly, I heard the shuffling of chains behind me. I quickly turned to see who or what accompanied me in this musty dungeon.

"Do not fear my child. I mean you know harm." Came the voice of a frail man. There was something so familiar about him, yet I could not place it. He came into the light and held his hand to my face. It was ice cold and felt like leather. His hands and feet had been bound by thick, rusty chains. How dangerous could this man have been? And how long had he been here?

As I looked upon him, I felt no danger at all.

"Do not fear. Just as the sun sets in the East and rises in the West, so will your day come to rise my child."

My heart ached. I knew he meant well. "I'm afraid that isn't so."

"And why is that?"

"I'm to be executed in the morning," I said falling to my knees.

"Things are not always as they seem, Amira."

"You know who I am?"

"I have always known you."

I slowly backed away, but there wasn't anywhere to go.

"Your time has not yet come... Mine, on the other hand, has long been overdue."

"I don't understand," I replied.

"When I first came I made light and life, I made myself flesh and blood. But with the light came darkness and with life came death. I've done all I can, now I must go. It is you. You were made for such a time as this."

He sounded like an old man rambling, but part of me believed him. "Me? I'm just a girl."

"You are so much more, Amira. Where I go, you will not yet follow. But where you go, I will always be with you."

"You're not making sense."

"It will, in time." He caressed my face as a father would a child. "I see so much in you. Others have come before you and failed. The darkness can be tempting. Remember that the smallest light can extinguish the dark." He touched the pendant I still wore around my neck. "Good. Keep this with you, you will need it." His brows furrowed like he was in pain. "When you feel empty, this will fill you. My power will be given to you, if only you receive it. Remember…my power brings life. Use it wisely."

I was too stunned to talk, my mouth gaped open wide. He was speaking as if he were…

"Tomorrow, my time will come. But you, child, you must leave. Now."

"But…how? The guards, the execution? My brother."

"I'm here to take your place."

"How?"

Just before my eyes, I saw his figure transform. I was looking into a mirror…or I wasn't? I couldn't breathe. I was staring at myself. Even his, her…clothes changed to match mine exactly. His chains were gone.

"You don't have much time." Came a voice sounding eerily similar to mine.

"I can't just walk out of here."

"You must trust me, the door is open, the path is clear. Do not stray. Run straight there. Don't look back."

I heard a noise like the dungeon door locking…or unlocking.

"Now!"

I backed into the door, feeling the cold bars chill against my back. Instead of bracing myself against the door, it swung wide open…and I fell with it, right on my butt." I heard a giggle from the cell. Really?

I didn't want to leave, it was as if I had no choice. I felt pulled to the woods. 'The path is clear do not stray.' So, I ran.

CHAPTER FORTY-ONE

The End

Aryn

I woke, my head throbbing. How much mead had I drunk?

"Amira?" I groaned. Wishing I would have kept quiet. It would be best to sneak out. We had said our goodbyes last night. It was the perfect time to sneak away…while she slept.

The cave was dark, it was still night. How is that possible? I felt like I had been asleep for a year. I rubbed my aching head. Amira was nowhere to be found. After finally managing to get to my feet, all I saw was some food and water laid out, everything else. Gone.

No!

It was still dark, she mustn't have been gone long. Had she planned this? Was any of last night real or was it only part of her plan?

I heard a noise up ahead. Good. I was close.

I followed the noise but lost it. My hair kept falling into my eyes and I kept trying to push it back.

Suddenly, a sharp point was at my back. "Turn around." I heard.

I knew that voice, even if I had barely heard it before. "Tauren?"

"Thank the stars." He almost seemed joyed to see me, "You haven't gone. And Amira? Where is she?"

I kicked the ground. "She must have headed out before me… While I slept…" I hated to admit it.

"Slept? But you left nearly two days ago?" His eyes grew wide.

"No… I…" Oh no…the mead. She hadn't drunk any.

"She dosed me!" I yelled in a fit and immediately took off running. I had to get to her.

I heard Tauren's loud footsteps crunching the dead leaves under his feet as he ran behind me.

"Aryn! You can't just run into the castle. Maybe she's not even there!" He yelled out as we got closer to the city of Astrea, "We need a plan."

I ignored him and kept running, pounding my feet one in front of the other, no matter how tired my legs grew. I was finally thankful for all my training and exercise...and a little proud that I could outrun a bull like Tauren.

I approached the city, the outskirts were empty...like a desert, but I heard commotion toward the inner city. I pulled the hood over my face; the shopping grounds were crowded today making it easier to slip through. Roars of cheering sounded me, the smell of cheap mead filled the streets while groups of people stood in mourning attire, weeping. A death, maybe? An important one. Perhaps they were all still mourning my father. Something I had avoided.

Tauren finally caught up. "You're even denser than I thought," He said.

"She's here somewhere," I said.

As we approached the center of the city, I saw it. The stage was set, a single guillotine standing proudly under the sun. The stone and dirt stained crimson.

"No," Tauren whispered breathlessly.

I knew what he was thinking...but it couldn't be true.

By now the crowds had scattered, only a few people stayed to clean up the 'mess'. A beheading...an unholy death. The body was most likely taken away to avoid burning. The ashes to never reach the stars.

I couldn't move. She couldn't be gone. It was someone else. It had to be someone else. She wouldn't let herself get caught.

I felt his hand on my shoulder. "Your majesty," It felt strange to hear him call me that, "we have to go...there's nothing else we can do." I shoved his hand away, my hood slipping only slightly. But it was enough.

"Cease him!" A voice called out.

"Run!" Taurren yelled, "I'll hold them off."

I didn't run. I just stood there, allowing them to take me. That was my plan anyway, to surrender. I'd see the Queen. Face to face.

Just as I had hoped, I was brought straight to the throne room. Only, it remained empty except a few politicians and guards. No maids, no servants, not court members. This was judgment.

"Where is she?" I demanded.

"What? The girl? Son…" She stood from her throne and walked toward me. My hands and feet were bound. She kissed my cheek softly. "She's gone. She will no longer be of influence to you." I spat at her. She had to have been lying. Her response wasn't what I expected. She turned and laughed…

"What did you do to her?" I yelled.

"I got rid of everyone standing in our way. Don't you see? We can have everything now."

Rage burned through me as I thrust around trying to free myself. "Amira!" I cried out, sinking to my knees. I continued to struggle, but I couldn't break the chains. Suddenly, tears slid from my eyes. She can't be gone…

"You always were a sensitive baby, weren't you?" She complained.

"How could you do this? To me? To my father?"

"I did nothing to you, you ran. And your 'father'…" She choked the words out, "He was planning on pushing back your coronation. But I took care of it. The same way I took care of your little whore."

"Don't you dare!" I yelled.

"What get rid of the wench, so you could marry Fiona, a well-born and beautiful woman?"

"Fiona?"

"What have you forgotten about your betrothed already? Don't worry. I've convinced her you were under a spell. She will forgive you. Or at least have you, none-the-less."

I had forgotten about Fiona. I had been unfaithful to her…but I hadn't chosen, her not really. I was just playing the part. Amira had always had my heart…and now she was gone. And the Queen was going to pay.

"Join me. Join me and you will regain your throne. So long as you know who is truly in charge."

"Never."

"Hmmm…" She honestly seemed like my answer shocked here, "Fine. Send him to the dungeon. I'll give you one more chance. Join me or die."

"You would kill your own son?" She laughed again. "Oh, Aryn. So clueless, so innocent."

She waved her hand and I was dragged to the dungeon.

I sat in the corner for the rest of the day and night. I didn't yell. I didn't try to escape, I didn't drink the water that was left for me. All I could think about was Amira. She was dead…because of me. She had believed in me. Why? I'm no one. She was the one who deserved the throne. The people loved her. She was strong, selfless, kind.

My head spun and tears fell silently until there were no more. The coins were a lie. I had known deep down all along. I wasn't chosen for this. I was born into it and manipulated to play the part. The people didn't need me. They needed her. She was smart. She was a warrior. She could have been a diplomat. Now she would never be anything. At least if she had stayed with Cassius, she would be alive.

The dungeon door opened, light spilling out. The sharp clicking of heels slowly walked toward me at a steady pace. I didn't even look up.

"Have you made your decision?" Her harsh words spoke.

"I'd rather die than rule beside you."

"I've given you every chance. You're a man now, you make your own decisions. So be it." I heard her heels clicking against the floor even more forcefully on the way out.

The door opened and at least four guards came in.

"On your feet." A guard demanded. I stood. Ready for whatever was next…at least, I thought I was.

A sharp knife sliced through my chest. I groaned as it entered deeper. As the guard pulled it back out, I stumbled to the ground, reaching for my wound. At least she kept her word.

The guards left, shutting the door and locking it behind them. I held myself up on my knees until I could do so no longer. I struggled to breathe, the taste of blood filled my mouth. I struggled to keep my eyes open. Why fight it? I chose to embrace death.

CHAPTER FORTY-TWO

Sleep

Amira

I ran as fast as I could, not looking back. I found the strength I was unaware I had. The woods swirled around me. The sun had grown dark this morning. Something I had never witnessed, but now it shown brighter than ever before. Beads of sweat dripped down my face as if they were racing one another. My clothes were torn by the branches I snagged along the way, but I never stopped.

Finally, I started to slow. I should have stopped by the cave to check on Aryn...but something led me here. I was back at the camp. My legs now ached and my throat dry as leather. I felt as if my chest would explode and my side would rip open. I stumbled into the campgrounds. Everyone quiet.

Heads slowly turned toward me. Fright filled the eyes that lingered on my sweat soaked body. No one came near me. I stumbled to the ground, not able to stand any longer. My eyes searched the crowd for Aryn. I'm not sure why I expected to see him here. I should have stopped back at the cave. Yet, something inside me told me he wasn't there.

"Amira?" Orin questioned, approaching me with caution. His eyes wide and face pale. "How?"

"I need..." I coughed, my throat almost too dry to talk, "To see Aryn. There something he needs to know."

He slumped down to the ground with me and placed his hand on my shoulder, almost shocked he could actually touch me.

"Amira... It's you..."

"What...?"

"We heard… We heard you were killed. It's all over the kingdom. We all thought."

"I'm here. It's…you wouldn't believe me anyway. But, Aryn…I need to speak to Aryn."

He paused, then slowly rose reaching his hand out to help me up. I grabbed it and got back on my feet. Something was wrong.

"Amira come with me…"

I followed.

We arrived at Aryn's tent. He just paused at the entry. I stood still. Waiting… For what? I didn't know.

"Amira…when we heard… He went after you."

Fear washed over me like a fierce tsunami. I pushed Orin as hard as I could. He backed away slowly. I hit him as hard as I could across the chest. "Tell me!"

"Amira… He's dead."

I felt numb, weightless like I was slipping away from the world. I'm not sure how long I stood there before coming back to. I pushed the tent doors aside and ran in.

There he was.

Laying on his bed. With a crown. Not one of gold…one of sticks and flowers. A handmade crown. Coins lay all around him and candles were lit on the stand near his bed. He was dressed in the clothes Cass had given him. His face was pale.

I slowly walked to his side. I reached my hand toward his face but paused pulling it back. I brushed his hair away from his face and kissed him. His lips were cold.

"Aryn." I cried. "Aryn. It's me." I shook him. "Aryn. Wake up." I cried louder.

I threw myself at him, weeping. I've seen death before…but this… this was too much.

'Brave', that's what everyone called me. I wasn't brave.

I pulled myself onto the bed with him. My best friend. The man I loved. I swore I'd never be one of those girls. I'd never make a man my whole life, but he was. He was my whole life.

I hadn't just lost him. His people had lost him. I couldn't do this. I was just a girl. I wasn't a warrior, a princess…I was a nobody. An orphan.

I wasn't chosen for this. If I was, someone had chosen wrong. Dead wrong. I could die right here with him. I should have died. I should have stayed in that dungeon. The man in the prison, Aryn, maybe even my brother... they would all be here if it wasn't for me.

I ran...like a coward. I ran.

I laid there. My head on his chest. There was no warmth, no soothing heartbeat, just cold.

"Amira." Orin stood near, holding a plate and a drink. "You need to eat."

"No," I replied hoarsely.

"You need your strength. Your people need you."

"They aren't my people, they were his."

"They were...but, it's you they follow..."

"Then they are blind!" I yelled throwing a handful of coins at him.

He set the plate down and turned toward the exit. Facing away he whispered, "We will have to do the ceremony soon. He deserved it."

I knew what he was talking about. Giving up his body as an offering to the stars so he will forever live in the sky...but I didn't want him to live in the sky. I wanted him to live with me. To be here, holding me in his arms. He could sing. I thought... Such a silly thought, but I longed to hear him sing now. He would always hum or sing when we were young. His voice was so much deeper now...was.

That's it. He would forever be a part of the darkness of the sky now...

...Darkness. I suddenly remembered the mad rambling of the man in the dungeon. My fingertips embraced the pendant he had mentioned. I grabbed it tightly, ripping it from my neck. I yanked it off of its chain and threw it to the floor. It cracked, letting a small amount of liquid pour from it. It was clear but luminescent. He had said his power could conquer death.

I jumped from the bed. It would give me power. I remembered.

I had already lost everything. There was nothing left to lose.

I inspected the glass pendant. The top that hooked it to the chain looked as if it could be unscrewed. My small fingers worked on the pendant until it finally opened. In my hands, I held a small warm vial. I held it up to the light of the candle, tipping my head back and drinking the warm liquid.

It tasted sweet.

I stood there. Nothing happened...

I turned back toward Aryn. I walked to him, slowly. It was time to say goodbye. I leaned down and placed one last kiss upon his cold lips. A wave of heat knocked me to the ground. The wind blew from outside, shaking the tent violently. Thunder sounded and lightning sparked in the sky. I could see it, even through the tent.

A light shown so bright, I thought I was left blind. I blinked but couldn't adjust my eyes. Everything went dark.

Cough... cough... "Amira?"

My sight began to return. That voice. I didn't need to see who it was to know...I knew.

I sat up looking toward the bed. His fingers moved, his hand grabbed at his chest as he gasped for breath. I ran to him.

"Aryn!" I yelled, jumping on top of him. He groaned. "Sorry, sorry," I mumbled.

"Amira?" His eyes finally opened and looked deep into my eyes. He tried to sit up, but I pushed him back down.

"Take it easy tiger." I couldn't believe what I was seeing. It was him. It was Aryn!

"What happened? I don't understand. I thought..." He looked so confused.

"You died." I blurted out, not thinking. Smooth, Amira. Real smooth. I didn't care. I leaned over and kissed him. I kissed and kissed him. If this was a dream, I didn't want to wake up.

"Amira, is everything okay?" Orin entered the tent. His jaw dropped and he backed up. He just stood there.

"Um... Aryn's back." I said. What else was I supposed to say?

After a while, he replied, "Sure...okay..." and scratched his head.

We all sat around in silence.

"Maybe we should...tell the people?" Orin's eyes squinted.

"He's right." Aryn grabbed my face and kissed me one more time, running his hands through my hair. "I think you have some explaining to do first, then I need to see the people."

The way he said 'the people' not 'my people' bothered me.

"How did Aryn...make it back to camp?" I asked, before explaining my adventure...if you'd call it that.

"A soldier. A friend of Tauren's. He snuck him out of the castle and brought his body here." Tauren...I wondered how he was.

I explained what had happened the best I could. I'm not sure they believed me.

The Sorcerer. The Original Sorcerer. That was the only explanation I had. But if I understood him correctly, he was gone now. He said it would make sense in time, but I felt more confused now than before. He said he would give his power to me?

After explaining, Aryn prepared himself. I helped him pick the flowers from his hair. He blushed. I told him he should have kept his flower crown, yet he refused. He kept grabbing his side. I stopped and looked into his eyes, slowly lifting his shirt. There was a scar. A scar that wasn't there before. I ran my fingers across the raised skin. He grabbed my hand with one hand and my face with the other. He leaned in, embracing my lips with his.

"Hmmhmm..." Orin cleared his throat. "Are we done...kissing?"

"Never." I smiled.

I tried to shove Aryn out of the tent, but he grabbed my arm. We walked out together. The crowd didn't believe what they were seeing. Two ghosts.

One by one, they dropped to their knees.

"Long live the King."

CHAPTER FORTY-THREE

As firm as Water

Amira

Days had passed since our return. Aryn and I slept in different tents, I was still engaged to Cassius and we still needed his army.

Rumors had spread across the land. Men and women were coming from all over to join us. Soon rumors would reach the queen…if they hadn't already. The time to strike was now. There was no time for hesitation.

We separated the men into training groups, but I still feared for them. They would be facing real soldiers soon. They took their orders from me and their deaths would be on my hands. If I could die for them, I would.

Tents were erected and scattered around the camp, but most people slept on the ground beneath the stars.

We had been standing around discussing strategies for days. In the morning, we finally march.

I lay awake in my tent. I couldn't eat or sleep. I was leading this army and I had never even fought in a battle before. Truth be told, neither had Aryn. I sat up, listening to the crackling embers of the fire and the chirping of bugs. Nature seemed so calm as if it was unaware of the impending doom looming over the land.

I quietly pulled on my shoes and cloak then slipped out of my tent.

"Aryn?" I whispered outside of his tent.

"Are you asking permission to come in?" He joked.

"You're awake?" I asked as I quietly pulled the door open and entered.

"Yeah…" He replied. He still lay in bed. The cold nipped at me and I crawled in beside him. He didn't argue, instead, he spread his blankets over me. I cuddled up to him. I could feel his warmth surround me and his hair tickled my face, I wish I could feel this way forever. With my head on his chest, I was finally lulled to sleep listening to the steady beating of his heart.

Before the golden morning light filled the sky, I snuck out of his bed. I readied myself in my tent, slowly braiding my hair back. I held a small mirror, cracked and hazy. The girl staring back at me looked nothing like the one who had worked at the palace so recently.

"Beautiful." I heard a voice from behind me. I didn't turn. I just set the mirror down and finished tying my shoes.

"If you're into soldiers, I know plenty." I joked.

"Just the one," Aryn replied. "Here, I brought something warm to drink. And some food. At least I think it's food." He laughed, scratching his head as he'd always done when he was nervous.

I grabbed the drink and took a big gulp. It burned my mouth. He did say a warm drink. I wanted to spit it out. It tasted bitter.

He smiled, holding in a laugh. "It's new. It's called coffee. Apparently, it helps keep you awake."

"Umm..." I took another sip trying to maintain a straight face. Whiskey, I could do. Coffee... I'd have to get used to.

"No flower crown today?" I joked.

He turned red. I loved embarrassing him.

We spent a few minutes eating together before joining the rest of the men. There wasn't much talking. There didn't seem to be anything to say. Everyone was on the edge, eyes filled with fear.

Aryn wanted me to speak to them, the army of assembled men...but they were his men. That, and he was the master of smooth talking. My mind wandered to Cass. He was also a smooth talker. Maybe they had more in common then they knew. Maybe...just maybe...everything would work out.

I stood behind him as he gave his speech. He was the smooth talker, not me.

He spoke of not having been in battle. What resonated with me the most was when he spoke of death. He said it was nothing to glorify. Life is what we must celebrate. Life and freedom.

"We should be free to make our own choices. Our own destinies." Was he speaking about the coin system? I had often wondered what life would be like without it. Other kingdoms worked just fine without it…but hadn't the Sorcerer himself set it up. It had to serve some type of good.

"The queen manipulated the system, she made me Prince when maybe…that wasn't what was meant for me. I promise to do everything I can to put the right ruler on that throne." He turned toward me. The whole army seemed silent. Then, clapping erupted. Shouting. Men began to fall to their knees. Aryn looked at me and smiled.

What just happened? I admit I wasn't listening to every word. Were they bowing…to me?

Aryn mounted his horse and I followed by mounting mine. Not everyone would have horses. The men gathered what weapons they could. Others were makeshift…it was all we had and we were running out of time. If we didn't strike first, she would.

The men joined together and sang songs as we rode toward the palace. It reminded me of being aboard Cassius' ship. All these men, coming together. We got word from Cassius' navy. They had landed and joined us in the days prior. That's one reason Aryn and I were being so careful, why I couldn't be seen sneaking from his tent. At least we were until he pulled that stunt during his speech. Did he not want this? This kingdom was his. Astrea was his. Once we took it. If…we took it.

We marched toward Astrea. The streets were empty. I was glad. It meant the women and children were out of harm's way. The castle gates were up and guards lined the towers, weapons raised high. They'd been expecting us. We kept our distance. Groups of men had been sent in ahead as scouts. We weren't just some random intruders, we knew this castle… tunnels and all. If our men could get in, we could get the gates to fall. Then we'd attack. For now, we waited.

Cassius' second navy had not shown up yet. But we couldn't wait for Cass and his army.

The enemy had shelter. Our advantage…we had the land and the people. They would soon run out of food. They were trapped. An army on one side and mountains blocking the ocean on the other.

A faint sound broke the silence and continued to grow louder. I listened intently. I knew that sound, the echoing footsteps of marching soldiers.

They wouldn't wait to starve. They were coming.

We readied ourselves…but no amount of training could have prepared us for what we saw next. There was no pretending we were brave. We all trembled, leaning on one another for strength.

An army marched toward us. A large army, much larger than our own but it was no ordinary army.

"Hold!" I yelled, despite how hard it was to speak at the moment.

The men marching toward us weren't men at all. Or at least, they weren't men anymore.

An army of bones and swords marched toward us.

Decaying bodies, dirty clothes torn and bloodied hung from their rotting bodies. Their rusted swords swung at their sides as they marched in line, a terrifying rhythmic tune sounding through the air. As if a deadly melody were being played, echoing for the entire kingdom to hear. I sensed the terror from the men behind me. Truth be told, I felt the same terror quaking in my own bones. I squeezed my hands closed to control the trembling. My hands seemed to always be what showed my nerves. Aryn must have known this because he quickly glanced from my face to my hands. I had practice at keeping my face calm and unyielding. Those card games must have paid off.

I raised my now steady hand, giving the command for the first group of men to charge. They hesitated. I commanded again. They rushed forward, battle cries surrounding the palace. The sound of their weapons against the rusty metal and decaying flesh was unmistakable. Then it happened…our men fell and the army of bones…didn't.

I watched as the men intertwined with the opposing army as if they were a deck of cards being shuffled. One-by-one they fell. Aryn was right. There was no beauty in death. I heard every shout of pain and cries for help. I've never felt so small or helpless, even as a child.

My throat went dry and the smell of blood became so overwhelming I could taste it. The iron taste lingered on my tongue, making me feel sick.

I watched as our swords struck at the bones of the undead like a child in training, whacking at a wooden figure that would never fall.

The screams faded into silence.

That's enough. I couldn't just sit on my high horse and watch. I drew my sword and galloped forward.

The winds blew, a small twister formed before me, sending my horse into chaos as I fell to the ground. I frantically reached for my sword. Aryn came galloping behind me. I only noticed when he jumped down to cover me. The wind howled as sand stung my eyes and invaded my mouth. Breathing felt impossible. A twirling wind of black began to take form. It was Queen Beatrice. Or…not really her But merely a shadow of her. Dirt and sand flying around made it almost impossible to see. She was there, but not physically. Her menacing laugh echoed around us as the sand cut like glass.

What are we to do?

"Aryn?"

He looked at me and shook his head. He helped me to my feet, trying to shield my face from the flying sand that cut like glass. My now lose braid whipped around like a weapon in the wind while loose strands stuck to the sweat on my face.

This was the one thing we hadn't prepared for.

"Fall back!" I yelled, other men repeating me so all could hear. We couldn't give up…but we couldn't win this way.

It was too late. We were surrounded. I kept signaling for us to back up…but now the army of dead faced us, our backs to the sea. The water would be our tomb.

As the wind blew, I heard a voice carried on the waves. "Trust." It was like I knew exactly what to do. My hands steadied and relaxed. I made my way to the back of the army, shoving men out of my way. Aryn followed yelling at me. I could see hopelessness on the men's faces. I hadn't given up yet…I wouldn't give up.

The dead army was at a standstill, awaiting command. My army now stuck between the sea and the dead. I now stood at the shore. The wind blowing my practically now loose hair behind my back.

"Mer?"

"Shhh."

I held my hands up, closing my eyes. This had better work. I called on all the power within me. The wind blew around me, swirling, raging. Waves erupted from the water in front of me. I willed the sea to move with everything in me. Slowly, the water began to separate. It formed two walls, a path down the middle. I didn't know what I was doing, not really. I knew it wasn't me. Or…not all me. It was as if I were asking.

The army behind me began shouting. I looked at Aryn. His face filled with shock.

"Shall we?" I gestured.

"Uh... Is it safe?" He asked.

"No idea," I replied.

"Go," I shouted to the men, but they wouldn't move.

I took a deep breath and began walking. The sand below my feet felt dry. I heard the crunch of dry sand under my boots. With every step I took, the wall made from water grew taller. I walked slowly, staring at the towering waves. I could see the fish, the plants. Everything. I reached out to touch the water. My hand went straight through. I could feel the sea. My hand was wet, but when I pulled it back it was dry. I repeated this a few times, slowly pushing my hand in and out of the water before the shrill screams of agony snapped me back to reality. The army was attacking.

"Run!" I commanded. The path spread nearly a half mile wide. The men ran into the sea, well...the dry sea. But that was it. We were trapped...

"They're coming." I heard the shout from around me. Come on. I had to do more.

I stretched out my hands and closed my eyes. Help. I thought.

Suddenly, a staircase of water formed before me. I placed my foot on the first step. It was solid. I didn't have time to marvel. "Climb!" I commanded. We climbed to the top of the sea, the army of the dead closing in at the bottom. They would follow us. Here we stood...on the water.

In all the chaos I had lost Aryn. Where was he? He was supposed to be at my side. Better yet. I was supposed to be at his. I was his protector.

After frantically looking around, I finally caught a glimpse of him. He was at the bottom of the sea helping others climb. The opposing army was seconds away from him. The walls had to come down.

Please, Aryn. Climb!

Time was out, "Aryn." I whispered, knowing he wouldn't hear me.

I held my hands in front of me and slapped them closed. The ocean rocked and I struggled to maintain balance. The water began to cascade down into a terrifying waterfall. The waves crashed upon the enemy army, completely wiping them out. Swords had done nothing to the rotting army, but the weight of the crushing waters tore them apart and scattered the pieces of their bodies on the ocean floor. I heard the scream of the Queen, despite how far away she really was.

We stood silently on the water, surprisingly steadily, all of us afraid to move...even me. I tipped my toe forward. The water still held me. I took a few more cautious steps. The hem of my clothes remained dry.

My entire army to toward me exhausted and confused. Only half of the men we came with stood on the strangely firm sea, and they were in bad shape. I watched as strong men held their broken and bleeding brothers. Even in the midst of devastation, Aryn was all I could think of. I had already lost him once. I couldn't do it again.

I stood motionless, trying to come up with the next step. Which card do I play next?

I heard a loud crashing sound. Part of the castle had fallen. Perhaps some of my army had made it in. It was the perfect play.

"Forward!" I yelled. Still atop the ocean platform. No one moved.

"Forward! She said!" Aryn yelled, coming up behind me. Little by little, the men began to move. I longed to throw my arms around him. Instead, I mounted a horse offered to me. Another offered to Aryn. Together we lead our men.

"Take the Castle!" I yelled.

I grabbed my sword tightly and charged into battle.

CHAPTER FORTY-FOUR

Strength and Honor

Tauren

Rumors circulated the castle for days. I hoped they were true. I had chosen the wrong side to be on…from the beginning. Everything I tried to do to make amends, failed. Amira was gone. There was nothing I could do to save her. Now I was a prisoner. A battle waged outside these walls and I was forbidden from fighting. On either side.

If the army was here though, that meant one thing…she was alive. But how? I saw her die. I saw her headless body being carried away. I still feel the ache in my heart. I couldn't protect her. Yet still, rumors spoke of her death along with Aryn's. They also spoke of their resurrections. Queen Beatrice had put a quick hush to those rumors, but they were all I had to hold on to. I was an orphan, just like Amira. Or at least, I was now. My mother had hidden the truth from me, from everyone. Before she died, she told me who my father was. Maybe that was why I had spared Aryn that night.

I had grown to hate him. He had everything, but I had nothing. I was the rightful heir to the throne, but that's not what I wanted. I've seen what power can do to someone. I just wanted… more. More than what I had. I had to lie my way into the guard. Then, I was stuck babysitting the brat gathering information for my superiors. Little did I know…the queen was behind the whole thing.

I would have killed my own brother that night if Amira hadn't been there. Half-brother, at least.

What killed me most was that we were in love with the same woman.

I saw the way she looked at him. He had everything, including her. Now I didn't care. As long as she was alive. I was a bastard. I'd die a bastard.

I wished desperately there was something I could do within this dungeon. I closed my eyes and prayed. If the Sorcerer was real, whether here or in the skies above…all I wanted was strength. Strength to take down this castle.

Winds blew within the dungeon, which was impossible. There were few slits in the walls to let in air and light, but none more than an inch wide and six inches long. What was even stranger was that the wind seemed to ignite the lamps rather than blow them out. The dungeon was ablaze. I felt a heat run through my body. I fell to the floor and screamed in pain. As soon as it started, it was gone. I rose, feeling strong. Stronger than ever, actually.

I walked to the dungeon gate and attempted to kick it down. To my surprise, the door flew off of the hinges, with hardly any effort. I cracked my knuckles. I could feel the strength flowing through me. I knew what to do. Take down the Queen.

There was one thing I had to take care of first. Lorin was down here too. I hadn't spent much time with him. In fact, I found myself avoiding him while posing as a guard. If he was half as smart as Amira, he would have seen right through me. Still, he was her brother. If that was all I could give her, then it was worth it. He wasn't being held in the same cell as me, but I knew these dungeons.

He was being held in the lowest cell, deep in the dungeon guarded by four soldiers. I still felt the strength coursing through my veins. That strength would come in handy right now. Still, four against one wasn't fair. I threw a rock down a dark hallway, letting its sound echo. The guards took the bait. They looked at each other, silently deciding who would stay and who would check it out.

Two of the guards, the small two, nodded and headed my way. The quieter I could take care of this, the better. I held myself against the wall, making myself as small as I could. As the first soldier came my way, I slipped behind him and held him in a choke. Snapping his neck was all too easy. Like snapping my fingers. I quickly held onto his body, letting it slowly slide to the floor to avoid a loud thud. I quickly took his sword. Within seconds the second guard appeared and looked down at the body.

Before he had a chance to yell out, I slipped behind him and quickly slit his throat lowering him slowly to the ground.

"Fredrick, you bastard. What are you two doing?" One of the guards yelled out while the other laughed. They would notice the lack of response, so I had no choice but to charge them.

Once all four guards were taken care of, I kicked the door down. Dirt rose from the ground and quickly filled my lungs. I bent over coughing.

"Traitor!" The prisoner yelled. He looked weak and broken, yet still charged at me. I admired his will. To take someone on as large as me, with no weapon. I merely stepped aside as he stumbled to the ground. I held out my hand, but he refused.

"Look. I'm here because of Amira."

"She made it out?" His eyes lit up with hope.

"Made it out? She was here?"

"A day ago. Two… maybe." He looked around. There was no window, no holes to bring any light. "I'm not sure when exactly." He looked back at me, still on the ground. "She just walked right up to the Queen."

"She did what?" He tried to stand, so I helped him. This time he took my arm.

"There's a battle going on out there. If I had to guess, your sister is the one leading it."

"I wouldn't doubt it." He chuckled.

"Go to her. Help her."

"What about you?" He asked.

"I have unfinished business." He nodded and took my arm once again. He looked me in the eye. There were no words, he just nodded again and limped away.

I didn't have a hard time slipping through the castle. I knew of a side door to the throne room. That was where she would be. There were only two guards by that door. I could take care of them easily…except I knew these men. I also knew who they were loyal to. I had no choice. I slipped up and took them out. As quickly and quietly as I could. They at least deserved that. I took care of their bodies, hiding them in a nearby hall. I hoped their bodies would be burned so they could join the stars.

Eventually, I found an opportunity to slip through to the throne room. I found myself hiding between two pillars. Maybe I could take down all of the guards inside… But there were more than twenty. I got as close to her as I could, then made my move.

I ran toward the Queen, but something hit me in the back of my head. Everything went dark.

I woke on the ground. I could feel cold marble floors beneath me. Was I still in the throne room? When my eyes opened, I saw her staring at me.

"You're awake. Good. You can enjoy the show…traitor." The Queen spoke with anger and fear in her voice.

I struggled to my feet, but something held me back. Chains. My hands were chained to the two pillars I stood between earlier. Close to the Queen…but not close enough to do anything.

"Why not just kill me?"

"Where's the fun in that?"

I struggled with the chains. I still felt the strength in me. I could easily bust out of these chains, but the guards would kill me before I could get to her. I wished I could bring this place down on her…

I looked at the pillars again, then the ceiling. Maybe… It seemed impossible. But then again, so did a lot of things these days.

I pulled with all of my strength. The soldier laughed at me. I gritted my teeth and pulled harder, wrapping the chains around my hands tighter. I wasn't trying to escape. The harder I pulled the more the ceiling cracked. Soon, chunks of the ceiling began to fall. The guards stood watching.

"Kill him." The Queen yelled.

With everything I had left, I pulled. The walls shook and the ceiling came down.

That was the end for me.

CHAPTER FORTY-FIVE

Falling Walls

Aryn

I followed her, just as I would follow her anywhere. Even to death. Even from death. Something had changed within me when I came back. I felt an emptiness. Not the same kind of empty I felt before. I had no memory of where I was while I was gone, but wherever it was called to me. Or maybe I called to it. Either way, death was not something I feared anymore. The only fear I had was losing her. And I was...soon. If not in battle, then in marriage.

I was struck from my strange trance when an arrow came slicing through the air, inches from my face. It struck my horse, merely grazing him. It was enough that he nearly threw me from the saddle. In the end, my steady balance saved me. I regained control and charged the gates. Yet, they still stood and the arrows continued flying toward us. I looked toward Amira. She had better have a plan. All I knew is she wasn't slowing down and neither was I.

She gave me a quick wink and tilted her head to signal a turn. Suddenly, her horse took a sharp right as she rode off. I didn't question her. Not with that smirk she gave me. I reared my horse to follow hers, the rest of the army ridding or running after us. She made a fast loop around the castle signaling a circle with her hands.

"We ride!" She yelled.

Again. I didn't question her.

"We ride!" I yelled to the men behind me, not truly knowing what was happening. Where was she headed? There was hardly anything behind the castle, mostly mountain. If we rode behind it we would be trapped... Except... The back would not be as heavily guarded. It would be insane to follow behind the castle, or insanely brilliant.

Perhaps she was planning an attack from behind.

But, no.

She kept going. Making a complete circle to the front of the castle. The more we rode, the faster we seemed to go. Inhumanly fast, even the men who were marching. The arrows never seemed to hit us, I could hear them whizz by but never hit their mark. We continued to ride in circles. The men began to sing, their voices lifted with the wind surrounded the castle, echoing against the stone walls. In all honesty, I couldn't make out the words. The louder they sang, the more the castle walls seemed to shake. As we marched, the sun seemed to remain stagnant and unchanging, showing no indication of time.

A sound like thunder rose, the gate cracked and the doors plummeted to the ground.

Guards charged us, clamoring over the debris as rocks still came crashing down, hitting the guards as they rushed towards us swords raised. Between the blood and debris, it was hard to imagine I was on the same beautiful piece of land that I grew up on. There were no birds soaring through the skies, nor fisherman casting their nets for a long day of work. No young boys training on the field. Instead, there was war.

I came upon my first guard, still having the advantage of my horse. I jolted my sword between the crevices in his armor. Lorin had taught me well and I knew the armor castle guards wore. Lorin even had me clean my own armor and weapons. I was as familiar with it as he was. I jerked my sword back, but it stuck. As I pulled harder it finally broke loose and the body fell to the ground. It shook me. I had probably trained with this man.

The horse under me let out a loud scream and we fell to the ground. An arrow dug deep into the beast's chest. I had no time to show any sympathy. I rolled to my feet. Quickly grabbing the sword that had been ripped from my grasp. As I tightened my grip around the hilt, a jolt shot through me, another sword met mine. I barely held my sword and my arm shook at the weight of the opposing sword against mine. I stepped back, repositioning my feet and regaining the grip. He came at me again. A man I had never seen or never noticed. His towering frame stood an entire foot taller than me. I watched his eyes as he swung. This was a dance and I could win. It was a game of footing.

His sword crashed down as I ducked and spun out of the way in just enough time to slip behind him as my blade met the front of his throat. My blade running easily through his soft flesh. Just like that, I had taken another life. A life that would never come back. I would never completely understand why I had come back, except to protect her.

Instinctively, I knew where she was. Just a few yards in front of me. She slipped her way through the army like an assassin. I had seen her train when we were young, but this…this was different. Almost scary, but beautiful. She reminded me of dancers we once had at court, twirling on their toes as if dancing on clouds. Amira, too, seemed to be carried by the clouds.

A lump caught in my throat as I watched her take the lives of many men around her. Surely, she was struggling as much as I was, if not more. You couldn't read it on her face, not unless you knew her like I did. She knew these men were real. They had families, loved ones. She also knew they stood in her way. And nothing could stand in her way. I made my way toward her. I wouldn't let her out of my sight.

I wasn't the only one watching her. The giant was coming. Him I knew well. Or, knew of. I had thought him to be a legend. Standing nearly nine-feet-tall and as wide as two well-built men, he was making his way toward her. His large strides carried him quickly. Only I stood in his way.

He swung a large weapon at me. It resembled a large hammer, too large for a normal man to wield. One blow could crush a soldier. Especially a small girl such as Amira, no matter how strong she was.

I whipped around him, quickly striking his legs. The giant howled, but it hardly slowed him. He swung again, missing me by an inch as I rolled across the ground, his hammer shaking the ground and creating a cloud of dust near my head. I coughed, thankful that I was able to roll away. My armor was restricting me. But there wasn't anything I could do about that now. I had to be quick on my feet.

From the corner of my eye, I saw Amira swing in and manage a blow to his arm, which hardly left a scratch. He was covered in small scars from battles won.

Another man charged Amira. "Amira! Behind you." I shouted. She turned, quickly dodging his swing. The giant continued toward her, but I wasn't going to allow it. He took another wide swing. Again, just missing me. Only this time I lost my grip on my sword as I fell to the ground. I scurried to my feet, no weapon in sight. I was quick, there was no time to panic. I could continue to dodge him. Keep him occupied as long as possible.

I heard Amira scream out behind me. As soon as I turned to look, a force came pounding into my back knocking me from my feet, flinging me yards away from Amira. I tried to stand but darkness clouded my mind as my body became too heavy to carry.

I coughed, my mouth dry and full of dirt, my vision blurred and my head pounded. As I drew a deep breath in it felt like knives stabbing into my ribs, but no one was there. I had broken something. Judging by the pain, more than one something.

A loud grunt escaped my lips as I tried to stand but couldn't. He was walking right toward me. The giant… This was it.

Suddenly, the giant stopped. He starred expressionless at me before falling to his knees. The rest of his lifeless body soon fell. The ground shook with immense force, but it wasn't the falling giant that caused it. Looking up through the dust-filled air I saw it… Winds picked up. It was her again. This time she was much larger and let out a wretched scream. There was a fire in her eyes. Then she began to chuckle again.

"You're a tough one to stomp out girl." She continued to laugh. "But then again, that's a good thing… for me. I thought it was strange when I began feeling more and more powerful. All that power coming from such a small girl. Looks like I'll be keeping you around. As for your army, you can say goodbye. As she towered over the land, winds swirling, she raised her hand. Thunder and lightning struck, turning the skies dark. The lightning obeyed her commands, striking my men down one by one. There screams echoed beyond the thunder.

I looked down at the sword in my hand. I thrust it deep into the ground and began to take off my armor.

"What are you doing?" I faintly heard Aryn scream through the storm.

"I love you," I whispered to him, hoping he understood. I wanted to face Beatrice during this moment, but it was Aryn I wanted to keep my eyes on. It was his face that gave me courage. I reached down to grab my sword. I held it so tightly in my hand. My eyes were so dry from the dirt and sand, but even then I couldn't keep the tears from escaping. I nodded at Aryn to let him know it was okay. "It's up to you," I yelled loud enough for him to hear, or so I hoped.

I took in a deep breath and upon releasing it, I plunged the sword into my chest.

I remained standing as long as I could. Aryn instantly wrapped his arms around me, cradling me and lowering me to the ground. I kept my eyes on him. I couldn't hear what he was saying. The screams were too loud. Had I been wrong? No. It wasn't my men screaming. It was her. The storm was dying… but so was I.

CHAPTER FORTY-SIX

To the Stars

Aryn

The storm was over. The skies were still black. The landscape was lit only by the surrounding fire. As the dust cleared, Beatrice was left kneeling on the ground. She rose to her feet and tried to adjust her torn dress. I was still kneeling on the ground holding Amira's lifeless body in my arms.

This can't be the end. Come back. "Come back!" I yelled. Hot tears streamed from my face. "Come back!" Her eyes were still open, staring lifelessly back at me. Death was nothing like sleep. There was nothing peaceful about this. I pulled the sword from her chest. Blood continued to spill out soaking the ground beneath us. I laid her down and pressed as hard as I could on her wounds. "Mer." I could barely sound it out.

This couldn't be it. She couldn't be gone.

All commotion ceased.

Both armies stopped to stare.

The men around us looked confused.

"Get him!" She yelled out.

I heard my name yelled out. Someone charged passed me, attacking the Queen. One of her men stepped forward and slew him.

She would pay.

I lowered Amira's head to the ground and closed her eyes. Her face was dirt-filled and smeared with blood. I didn't want to leave her. I never wanted to leave her. Oryn must have been close by. He knelt beside me and nodded. He would look after her. I grabbed my sword and slowly stood. I gaze burned through my mother. She took everything from me. I would take her down, even if it were the last thing I did.

As I ran towards her, soldiers tried to stop me. I cut through them like trees in a forest. My men raced behind me, taking on the Queen's army.

Now it was just me and her. No magic. Nothing standing in my way.

"Aryn. Everything I did, I did for you. To make you stronger." She pleaded like a beggar. She looked like a beggar now. Her dress was torn and her hair stuck tangled knots hanging behind her back.

"I am stronger." I said as I drove my sword through her heart. Her cold eyes stared back at me. I jerked my sword back and she fell to her knees. She looked down, covering her gaping wound with her hands. She looked back at me one last time before her lifeless body hit the dirt.

One-by-one they The Queen's army dropped their weapons and fell to their knees.

I stood there staring down at her.

I felt nothing.

Soon the moon and stars began to shine. Was it night already?

I awoke in a tent. Was it all a dream? Was it possible? My Amira, she was still here? Still alive? As I tried to sit up, I felt every ache and pain from the battle. It was still night. The only light was a lantern burning on a small wooden stand by the pallet that made up my bed.

I felt my heart fall from my chest. It was all real. I just knew it. She was gone.

Lorin was the first person to check on me. He was in bad shape, but he had managed to find Rachel. At least he had her. The next day or so went by like a blur. Everyone came to me for orders, but I had nothing.

They set up temporary throne room for me, but I had no desire to enter. I retreated to my old chambers. At least some of the castle had remained intact. The only thing I had to console me was my old chair and endless bottles of wine. I trusted Lorin and Oryn to armies and rebuilding… and whatever else.

Finally, Lorin stormed in and drew my curtains back. The sun stinging my eyes. I attempted to throw my half-empty bottle of wine at him, but judging by the smashing sound of glass on the ground, I missed terribly.

"Aryn. It's time. You need to get up. You need to lead your people." He said as he grabbed me by my shirt and tried lifting me up to my feet.

"They don't need me. No one does." I slurred.

"She does."

"She's gone!" I yelled.

"She is. And she deserves to be sent to the stars. It's time we let her go. She knew what she was doing. She gave her life for this kingdom. Now we need to pay her the respect she is due."

I threw myself back in my chair and fumbled around reaching for another bottle until I fell to the ground.

"Do you think this is easy for me Aryn?" Loring yelled, "She was all I had left."

"She was all I had left!" I yelled. Pulling myself back up.

"You have this kingdom. It needs you."

"I don't want it! I never have."

"Fine. Throw your royal tantrum. If you loved her, you would do this for her. You would lead these people."

"Get out!" I yelled.

"Fine. Your Majesty." He said sarcastically, "But tonight we will have her ceremony. With our without you." He turned to leave, but looked back open more time, "By the way… the finace' is here. The deal is off, obviously. He will want to negotiate some sort of alliance. Either way, he will be there tonight."

They waited for nightfall. It was the tradition. It gave me enough time to sober up. At least, try to sober up. I had stood in front of my armoire for most of the day. I dressed myself today. The people cheered when they saw my face. It felt like a knife to my empty chest.

A large bed of straw was raised on a platform overlooking the ocean. This was the same sand we had fought on days before. It was all gone. The battle, the blood, everything. Servants had dressed up her deathbed with white flowers and beautiful offerings had been placed at the base. A white dress of fine silk spilled out along the bed like milk. Her long black hair had been washed and brushed neatly. Every hair placed perfectly. She looked like a queen. It was a dazzling show, and I had the front row seat. Everything in me wanted to run to her. I wanted to throw myself on top and never leave her. I wanted the flames that would soon take her to engulf me.

Lorin was right. The pirate had finally come. There were people spread out as far as I could see. He and his armies stood by, near the front. I paid no attention to him and planned not to.

Lorin walked towards me offing the lit torch.

"You should do it."

"Together?" He asked.

Another torch was handed to me. I took it in my hands and nodded to Lorin and he lit mine. The flames ignited instantly and the heat licked my face. We walked slowly together to Amira's deathbed. I climbed inside and starred down at her. The flames from my torchlight her beautiful pale face. I bent down and kissed her lips one last time, then touched the flame to the straw. The flames quickly spread. Lorin dropped his torch and pulled me off of the ramp. The platform was pushed into the sea. The water was calm, gently rocking back and forth carrying her out.

I stood on the edge of the shore watching as the flames grew larger. I didn't move. I would stand there long after her body burned and the bed drifted out of sight.

The clear night skies grew even darker as thunder rolled through the skies. A light drizzle fell from above.

No. "No." I shouted. She belonged with the stars, not lost at sea. I tore off the top layers of my ridiculous outfit and ran out to the water. My guards tried to stop me, but I pushed them out of the way and ran as far as I could in the water before running turned into swimming.

Rain poured down harder and harder as the fire began to die down and smoke filled the air. I could hardly see what was happening as the ocean waves grew stronger, pushing me back.

Something was moving from within the now small burning fire. I could see her bright white dress emerge from the fire, completely untouched by the fire or smoke. Amira had risen and emerged from the fire. I struggled harder against the waves to get to her before the flames could take her. She was alive. For now.

No matter how hard I struggled, I could get nowhere. The salt water burned my eyes and stole the breath from my lungs. The waves began to bury me and pull me back. I had gone under. Completely capsulated in the water. I rolled and tumbled to the shore. The water washed away and I was left on the sand surrounded by guards.

It was silent at first, then I heard shouts of joy and applause.

Someone bent down beside me and their warm breath whispered in my ear. "Ryn."

I opened my burning eyes and saw Amira kneeling in the sand in her white dress staring back at me.

CHAPTER FORTY-SEVEN

I Am

Amira

It was over. The army of bones had washed away and the traitors were killed. There would be a lot to rebuild. Not just the castle, but the kingdom. We lost many. I didn't feel like celebrating. So many would never go home. We held burning ceremonies for the next couple of days.

We honored our men best we could. The whole kingdom came together to repair. Women were cooking for the people, clothes and shelter were offered up to anyone in need.

Cass had finally shown up and they had explained everything to him. He offered his men to help us rebuild. With so many people the whole city would be rebuilt before we knew it.

I can't explain what happened. I'm not sure I understood myself. It had felt like a dream. I was in a place that wasn't really a place with someone I couldn't actually see. They spoke with a voice that sounded like many speaking at the same time. Some of which I could pick out and recognize.

"Well done child." I heard in the many voices.

"You are you?" I asked.

"Why ask questions that you already know the answer to?"

"The Queen... is she gone."

"Yes." The voices responded, almost sadly.

"Why me?"

"I chose you because I knew you."

"I don't understand."

"This was your destiny."

"So I had no control over it?"

"You were always in control. The choice is always yours. You were simply brave enough to make the right choices."

"But you gave me the power."

"And you took it. It's free for anyone who needs it. I have more than enough."

"Then why didn't you take care of Beatrice."

"She is my child, just as you are."

"Then why did you give her power if she was just going to use it for evil?"

"It was her choice as to how she would use it. Everyone is given the choice of light, she just chose to remain in the shadows."

"So... it's over now?"

"No. So long as there is light, there will always be darkness and those who chose to dwell in it."

"But it's over for me."

"No child. This is only the beginning."

"I don't understand."

"You were made for such a time as this. Your time is not over, you must use your light to extinguish the darkness."

"How?"

"By sharing it with others."

"But-"

"That is enough questions, you have people are waiting to see you."

That was it. There was a blinding light, then darkness. I felt the heat from the flames and smelled the salt from the air. I should have been terrified when I woke up, but I wasn't. I had been dead for days. It didn't feel like days, it felt like seconds.

Now I was back.

"Nice beard." I giggled, caressing his face. He looked so much older than when we began this journey. It was rare to find time to spend alone, but I treasured every minute we could spare.

"Yeah… I've been… busy."

"So… King Aryn, is it?"

"Actually…" He looked nervously at me.

"I would like to appoint another leader. Queen Amira."

I slapped his chest. I didn't mean to…I couldn't help it.

"Excuse me."

"It's being approved as we speak."

"Then I refuse."

"Then Astrean's throne is left open. An easy target."

I wasn't easily convinced.

Somehow…he won.

Another week had gone by. So much had happened. Today was the day. Coronation day. My coronation day.

My brother was here, dressed in his best. On his arm was his new bride Racheal. We had found them. First Lorin, then Rachel. I begged them to have a large ceremony in the grand hall. Instead, they were married quietly as soon as possible. It was beautiful and so intimate. He went on and on about not being able to spend one more day without her.

Today I was dressed in all white as if it were my wedding. I guess it was. I was marrying the kingdom. The ring now on my finger weighed heavy. Two weddings I did not want. Astrean and Cassius. I guess being brought back to life meant the deal was still on. Aryn seemed so supportive. It broke my heart. He wanted me with Cass. He gave me away. Not only that, he had rescued Fiona. Their wedding had not been called off.

Maybe Beatrice was right…maybe queens can't have everything.

"Maybe my coin was right." I told Aryn the night before.

"What do you mean? You went from a servant to a queen."

"I served the palace, now I serve the people."

He kissed my hand. "You were meant to be Queen."

"Marry me." I blurted out.

"What?" Aryn questioned.

"Marry me. Before I marry Cassius. I can't marry Cassius if I'm married to you. You say I'm meant to be queen, but I know you're meant to be king. Don't you see? This is what is meant to be."

"Mer..." He paused.

"Do you love her?" I asked.

"What?"

"Fiona. Do you love her?"

"Mer... I meant what I said that night...in the cave." He looked defeated. "No. I won't marry Fiona. I like her, yes, but I don't love her. But I can't marry you either."

"Say yes. In secret, say yes." I got down on my knees.

He fell down with me, eye level. "Amira. I will always be yours."

He took me in his arms, both of us on our knees, he kissed me. Breathing heavily as if it were our last kiss.

I dreamt of him all night. My Aryn. My Prince. Today I married the throne. One day...maybe...I'd marry Aryn.

The room was quiet beyond the doors. It had been rebuilt exquisitely. I stood in heavy gowns and heels I could hardly walk in.

Trumpets sounded and the doors were thrown open. I was ushered in, all eyes on me. Every step I took reminded me of my journey to this point. My toes were sore and my extravagant hair itched. This wasn't me.

The Dator and other members of the court had either been killed, imprisoned, or banished. As I walked toward the altar, I locked eyes with the one who would crown me. He smiled, showing off his dimples and making my knees grow week.

I approached the altar and knelt down. Just as always, his words were lovely. Maybe it was his voice. It was like music to me. I just wish I had listened to what he said.

"Do you Amira Esmerelda Pallas promise to serve and protect you people until your dying day?"

I looked him in the eyes. "I do."

"I now pronounce you Queen of Astrean."

As I rose, cheers broke out. The crowd bowed to me. "Long live the Queen!" Echoed through the grand hall.

Most of the day had been a blur.

"Queen Amira." Came the deep throaty voice of Cassius.

"King Cassius," I replied holding out my hand. He kissed it. His warm breath sent a chill down my spine. I'd probably happily marry him…if my heart wasn't already taken.

"I first want to congratulate you and tell you how ravishingly beautiful you look today."

"Thank you," I said, trying to hide the warmth spreading in my cheeks.

"But, to be blunt there are things we must discuss."

"The wedding?" I swallowed hard.

"Not exactly, at least…not yet."

"Then what?"

"Rumors of your beauty…and power have spread. It seems I am not the only king after you now. With the throne weaker at the moment-"

"The other kingdoms?"

"There's been…a bit of talk…of war."

I wasn't sure what to say. The old man was right, darkness would still linger. Like a stain.

I saw Aryn approach. He bowed before Cass.

"An admirable man… To give up the throne to someone you see as better. Today I bow to you. And with that, I'll leave the two of you. I'm sure there is much to discuss…about the kingdom."

"Mer…Queen Amira."

"Please. No. Just. No." I laughed.

"Excuse me. May I interrupt?" I heard a voice from behind me. I felt it before I even turned around.

Standing before me, bowing actually, was a man in his late fifties. Commonly dressed, wearing a long beard. I've never seen him before, but he seemed so familiar.

"I came to give you many blessings my child. Celebrate today, for tomorrow brings its own battles. The darkness spreads, but light is available to all those who merely ask. Stay strong child. There is much to come." He said and turned to walk away.

"Wait!" I yelled after him, hiking up my dress and chasing after him. "Are you…"

He stopped. He didn't turn to face me, just paused, "I am."

About the Author

Megan D. Harding is a wife of a Marine and a stay at home mother to three children and a cat. She enjoys reading, writing, Netflix, coffee, and sleep… whenever she can manage. Megan is a college graduate with a degree in Child Development, Communications, and Cultural Studies. She has self-published two books THE FALLEN SERIES and UPRISING.

Follow Megan D. Harding

Twitter @AuthorMDHarding

Facebook Author Megan Dawn Harding

Email- Marinewife1811@gmail.com

Also, Check out her previous self- published works FALLEN and UPRISING

Printed in the United States
By Bookmasters